Finding Cassie

Finding Cassie

ANNA JACOBS

Allison & Busby Limited
11 Wardour Mews
London W1F 8AN
allisonandbusby.com

First published in Great Britain by Allison & Busby in 2020.

A CIP catalogue record for this book is available from
the British Library.

First Edition

ISBN 978-0-7490-2380-5

Typeset in 11/16 pt Sabon LT Pro by
Allison & Busby Ltd

The paper used for this Allison & Busby publication
has been produced from trees that have been legally sourced
from well-managed and credibly certified forests.

Printed and bound by
CPI Group (UK) Ltd, Croydon, CR0 4YY

Chapter One

Cassandra Bennington held out the mic so that the woman she was interviewing could give her answer. Then a deafening noise tore the world apart and everything went into slow motion as darkness swallowed her.

When she recovered consciousness, she was in an ambulance that was moving fast with its siren blaring.

A man said, 'She's coming to.' A blurry figure leant closer. 'You've been hurt but not badly, and you're on your way to hospital.'

She tried to understand how she'd got hurt but couldn't make sense of it. 'What happened? Was it – heart attack?'

When he didn't answer, she made a huge effort to bring him into focus. 'Please. Tell me.'

'Someone planted a bomb in the building you were in. It went off and wreaked havoc. You were lucky you weren't closer to it.'

She stared up at him in shock. 'Why would anyone do that? It was only a block of flats.'

'Who knows why, love? We just pick up the pieces as best we can.'

The ambulance turned sharply to the left and came to a halt.

'We're at the hospital now. Let's get you to a doctor and make sure you're all right. Worry about other things later. You're alive and in one piece. That's what matters.' He patted her hand and started to move away.

'Wait!'

He half turned.

'What about the woman I was interviewing?'

'They were getting someone else out from nearby as we left. I'm not sure who, but if you survived, she probably did too.'

The woman had been so young – and very pregnant.

As they slid her out of the ambulance and jolted her into the brightly lit building, Cassie heard the paramedic say something in a low voice, then she heard the vehicle drive away, siren blaring again. She was wheeled into a cubicle in the casualty department and someone drew flimsy curtains on a hostile world.

She felt lethargic, utterly boneless, let them do what they wanted. She tried to answer their questions, not sure she was making much sense. She didn't want to talk, wanted to hide in some deep, dark cave and lie quietly, but they kept prodding her and moving her about.

After they'd made sure no bones were broken, they tended to a gash on her shoulder that needed holding together with butterfly strips, then dealt with a few minor scratches and scrapes.

'We're going to need all our beds for the serious cases,

so you can go home in an hour's time – well, you can if someone comes to fetch you and promises to keep an eye on you tonight. Give the attendant your details when she comes round and tell her who to call.'

'Can I ask about the woman I was with?'

'Look, love—'

'She was pregnant. I can't bear to think of her being killed.' Cassie gave the woman's name and added, 'Please.'

'I'll have a quick look, see if she's been brought in.'

A couple of minutes later, the nurse returned. 'She's all right, just minor injuries. Is she a friend of yours?'

'No. I was interviewing her.'

He stared at her and said, 'Oh my goodness! You're Cassandra Benn, aren't you?'

'Yes. But please can you use my full surname on your records. I try to keep my private life out of the limelight as much as possible.'

'I won't tell anyone else here who you are, if that's what you want, but some of them will probably recognise you. I've seen you on TV. You do brilliant interviews, really incisive.'

'Thank you. Did they bring my backpack in with me? It's dark blue, only a small one. It's got a big white P painted on the back.'

'There's a pile of possessions been brought in with the injured and dumped in reception. I'll go and have a quick check.'

To her shuddering relief, someone had brought her backpack to the hospital, though she had to identify its contents before the nurse would give it to her. She sighed in relief as he stood it beside the bed because she'd have been lost without it. It was dusty but when she looked inside, the contents seemed untouched.

'Now you've got your own phone, can you call a friend to pick you up, Ms Bennington, and can you—' Yet another ambulance siren sounded outside. 'Sorry. I have to go. Please try to rest.' The nurse hurried away.

How many people had been hurt, for heaven's sake? she wondered. The ambulances seemed to be coming in one after the other.

Someone outside the entrance shouted for a crash team to come at once and she shuddered. She'd never been quite so close to being killed before, and mentally blessed whatever fate or blind chance had saved her. She should be out there reporting the incident, but couldn't summon up the strength, just couldn't do it. Not this time.

For a while, not wanting to take the nurses away from people whose injuries were worse than hers, she tried to obey orders and rest, she really did. But she couldn't manage it lying on such an uncomfortable, shelf-like bed with all that bustle and noise just the other side of a flimsy curtain.

At least she was recovering, could feel her mind slowly coming back into clearer focus. Only, that was a double-edged sword because she had nothing to do with her thoughts except worry.

She noticed her watch on a stand next to the bed and put it on. It had a big, clear dial and seemed to be working still. It ought to be. It had been expensive, not bought to be pretty but because the brand was famed for the accuracy and toughness of its watches.

A quarter of an hour crawled slowly past, only two or

three minutes gone by each time she looked. By then she felt so frustrated she swung round on the narrow bed and sat upright on the edge, swinging her feet.

That soon palled and she stood up tentatively, relieved not to feel dizzy. Staying here was silly. She was all right now, should get out of their way.

She winced as a man screamed hoarsely nearby.

A woman stumbled past her cubicle, weeping. Cassie could only see her feet, but she could hear the anguish in the tears all too clearly.

She couldn't do this any longer. Dragging off the gown, she put her outer clothes on again, grimacing at the mess they were in. It felt better to be fully covered on this chilly summer day, as if she'd taken control of herself again.

She sat down and waited, but ten more minutes crawled past and no one came to see her. 'Oh, to hell with it!' She stood up and grabbed the backpack, pushing aside the curtain at the front of her cubicle.

As she was moving through the reception area the same nurse spotted her and hurried across. 'You haven't been discharged yet, Ms Bennington. Please go and lie down again. Doctor will come back to you as soon as she can. She needs to check that you're fit to leave.'

'I feel a lot better, honestly. I'd rather go home now. I can't rest here.'

'Have you asked a friend to pick you up?'

'No. I'll catch a taxi.' It was how she mostly got about in London.

'You should—Oh, just a minute. Stay there.' He turned away to help with a woman who had walked into the busy area cradling her arm as if it hurt, followed by a man carrying a small child with a bloody leg.

Cassie took the opportunity to hurry towards the exit. She was in luck. A taxi was just dropping someone off and the driver was happy to take another fare.

She felt guilty for treating the hospital staff like that, but she had to get home, simply had to. She needed peace and quiet to recover.

She had never expected to be personally involved in a serious accident, let alone a terrorist incident even though she'd faced all sorts of risky interview situations. Did anyone expect such lunatic behaviour to touch their lives? Not unless they were in a combat zone.

As she sat in the taxi, it upset her that she hadn't known who to call for help. She had plenty of acquaintances but who could she consider a close enough friend to come to her aid? No one these days. And that upset her.

Since she and Brett had split up, she seemed to have lost contact with so many people. Or they'd lost contact with her. She'd been working hard, burying her upset about him leaving her by concentrating on other people's stories.

The taxi driver opened the rear door and it was a few moments before she realised they'd arrived.

'You all right, love?'

'Yes. Thanks.' She got out her credit card and paid him.

Once inside the house, she closed the front door and leant against it, whimpering because she hadn't realised that she wouldn't feel safe even here.

Another thing she hadn't expected.

It took her a few minutes to decide to go to bed. They'd

told her to rest, hadn't they? She'd feel better if she did that – surely she would?

It took her a while to get to sleep but she welcomed the drowsiness.

She jerked awake a few hours later as someone rang her doorbell, then hammered on the front door. It was dark outside now and the street light shining into her bedroom made everything look surreal. By the time she'd remembered why she was feeling so groggy, the front door had opened and the person had come in.

She tensed and looked for something to protect herself with, then heard Brett call her name and relaxed.

The last person she wanted to see her like this was her ex.

He came upstairs calling her name again and stopped in the doorway of her bedroom, switching on the light.

She shaded her eyes against the glare and wished he'd stop staring.

'Thank goodness you're safe, Cassie!'

She wasn't ready to forgive him. 'Who told you to come barging in?'

'It was on the news.'

'What was?'

'The bombing. They said you were amongst the injured.'

'Oh.' Her stomach lurched at the memory of how helpless and bewildered she'd felt lying in the hospital – how out of touch, too.

'I wouldn't have walked in like that, Cassie, but I was worried sick about you. The nurse at the hospital said you'd discharged yourself, so I rang round our friends but no one had heard from you. And they hadn't heard from you for a while.'

'No. I've been . . . busy.' She felt at a disadvantage sitting on the edge of the bed, so got up, wincing as her bruised and battered body protested.

He came across to steady her and she let him, which wasn't like her.

He walked down the stairs in front of her, and to make matters worse she was glad when he did that, because she felt distinctly wobbly.

'Why don't you sit in your recliner chair with your feet up while I make you some coffee?'

'Good idea. Thanks.' She should have kicked him out and got her key back from him but she felt – fragile. And she'd kill for a coffee.

The hot drink was soothing and after she'd had a few mouthfuls, she managed to pull herself together enough to ask him what they'd said on the news. 'Do they know who did this cruel, stupid thing?'

'They didn't on the one I saw. Why don't I switch on the TV now? They've got regular updates on the news channel. Half the block of flats was destroyed apparently and several people were killed. You're lucky to be alive.'

She hesitated, suddenly reluctant to see the incident, for some weird reason.

He looked at her, frowning. 'You're in shock, I think, Cassie. I've never seen you so pale.' He placed his fingers lightly on her forehead before adding, 'And your skin's clammy.'

She considered this, feeling distant from everything, as if she were looking down at herself from the ceiling, then realised he was waiting for an answer so she nodded. 'I guess I am. Bound to be, I suppose.'

'I'd better stay with you for the rest of the night.'

'You're not getting back into my bed. We're not together in any way now.'

He gave one of his wry smiles. 'No. You made that plain when you chucked my things out of the door. When was that? Just over a year ago.'

'I can't think why you came. Does your new partner know?'

'Yes. And approves. I still care about you, Cassie. We were together for four years, after all. You'd come to help me if I'd been caught up in a terrorist incident.'

She was unable to deny that so just shrugged, then winced as her shoulder hurt.

His voice was suddenly sharp. 'What's wrong?'

'Something sliced into my shoulder. It hurt me when I moved it.' She didn't know what to say, didn't want to admit that she'd welcome his presence tonight. 'Um, thanks for coming. That was – kind.'

'Look, I can sleep down here on the sofa unless you've got a spare bed.'

She shook her head. She'd been frenetically busy lately, hadn't bothered to buy spare furniture after they broke up. She only did the most essential shopping these days, ate out mostly. Lots going on in the big, wide world. *Cassandra Benn Reporting* was getting high ratings. Her career had always been important.

Oh dear, he'd said something else and was waiting for her to answer. 'Sorry. Run that past me again.'

'You really shouldn't be alone tonight, Cassie. You should see how pale and bruised your face is. In fact, whatever you say, I am *not* leaving you on your own here. Surely we can meet as friends now?'

She could have stood up and looked at herself in the mirror over the fireplace only she didn't want to move. 'All right, stay. Um, I am grateful.'

He brought a cup of coffee for himself and sat down on the nearby sofa. 'Want to talk about it?'

She considered this, her thoughts still wheeling round in slow motion. 'Nothing to talk about. Loud noise, an explosion threw me across the room and knocked me out.' She rubbed the sore spot on the back of her head. 'Next thing I knew I was in an ambulance. I've got those – what do you call 'em? – butterfly plasters on my shoulder. They think something with a sharp edge hit me, or I hit it, and I got a bit of a cut. And . . . there's a lot of bruising. Nothing serious, let alone life-threatening. End of story.'

'Shall I switch on the TV, then, see what's happening?'

'Yes.' She turned towards the screen, forcing herself to watch as the story rolled out, wincing at the images of the block of flats half destroyed, cars scattered like a careless child's toys, people clustering together, hugging one another, weeping. 'I ought to be there, reporting on it.'

'Hell no. This time you should definitely leave that to someone else.'

'Mmm. I am a bit – tired.' She looked down at her empty mug. 'Any more coffee?'

'When did you last eat? Shall I make you a sandwich or something as well?'

'OK.'

He vanished round the corner into the kitchen area. 'You've certainly let things go here. The bread's mouldy and there's nothing I'd dare eat in the fridge, not much in the freezer, either. I'll nip to the deli.'

'Don't bother. There's cereal and milk. That'll do.'

'Your favourite standby. I'm sure I can find them. It's not the biggest of kitchens.'

But when he gave her the bowl of cereal, she took one spoonful, had trouble forcing it down her throat and pushed the rest away.

'I think I'll go back to bed.'

He insisted on coming up with her to make sure she didn't fall because she was still dizzy. She hated having to depend on other people.

'I'll be downstairs if you need me.'

'Are you sure Tina won't mind?'

'I've rung her. She agrees with me that you shouldn't be left alone.'

She waved one hand. 'Make yourself at home, then, why don't you? But you're wasting your time. I don't need a nanny.'

'I'm still staying.'

She could hear the old, familiar stubborn tone in his voice, so didn't even try to answer.

She'd missed him. They'd been good friends once, until she'd become too obsessed with her job. It was no wonder he'd turned elsewhere for company. He was the sort of person who needed the company of other people.

It was a long time before she got to sleep again but she didn't leave her bedroom, didn't want Brett to see how disorientated she was. Her thoughts were still skittering to and fro, one minute back to the scenes on TV, then reliving the wild ambulance ride, and even focusing on Brett sometimes.

He was just as attractive as ever, damn him. She missed him. He'd been a better partner than she had, was still being kind to her.

Eventually everything began to go blurry and she gave in to the urge to let go.

In the morning Cassie woke with a start as something banged downstairs, setting her heart pounding. Then she realised it was only a cupboard door. Brett must have got up. She stayed in bed, hearing him go out and come back a few minutes later. Probably been to buy supplies from the nearby deli. He was a hearty breakfast eater.

Reluctantly she got out of bed. If she didn't, he might call a doctor.

Her bare feet made no sound on the stairs and he jumped when she said, 'Good morning.'

He swung round, studying her face. 'You still look pale.'

She shrugged, then wished she hadn't because that hurt her shoulder.

'Come and have some breakfast.'

She still didn't care about food, but if she didn't eat something he'd make a fuss and it seemed easier to do what he said. She accepted a pot of yoghurt, ate half a spoonful, then another and suddenly discovered she was hungry after all.

'That's better,' he said quietly. 'Piece of toast? I got your favourite black cherry jam.'

'Yes, please.'

When he was sitting opposite her, also eating toast, she asked, 'How are your kids?'

'They've both flown the nest now. Kind of you to ask,

considering they always treated you as an interloper.'

She shrugged. 'Teenagers can be like that. What about your parents? I did get on with them OK.'

He looked sad. 'They're showing their age, I'm afraid. Dad's got dementia and it's come on so quickly they've had to move him into a care home.'

'Oh no! I'm so sorry. Give your mother my best wishes next time you see her. She was always kind to me.'

They ate in silence till the toast was finished.

'Want anything else?' he asked.

She saw him looking at the clock. 'No, thanks. I'll be all right now, Brett, honest I will. You need to get to work.'

'You'll rest today?'

'Yes. And um, thanks for coming.'

'I'll pop in after work and bring you some groceries and takeaway.'

'You don't need to. I can go out and get some myself.'

'I'm doing it and Tina will agree. Surely you don't want to go out shopping and have the press following you around? There are a couple of journos hovering outside now. They tried to stop me and ask about you.'

She didn't reply, just flung her hands up in an 'I give in' gesture. 'Tell Tina thanks for lending you to me, then.'

When he'd gone the silence seemed threatening, and she found herself listening for footsteps outside the house. It was semi-detached, in an area full of commuters and the street was mostly deserted in the daytime. People could approach it without anyone noticing.

Suddenly worried that the outer doors might be unlocked, she rushed to check the front door then the back, leaning against the latter in shuddering relief when she found that it was locked and all the downstairs windows were, too.

Only, she still didn't feel safe.

She put the telly on and wished she hadn't, but couldn't bring herself to turn it off again in case she missed something important. Eleven people had been killed in that explosion – eleven! – and several more had been seriously injured, with over twenty suffering minor injuries, herself included, she supposed. The block of flats was half its former size with ragged edges and shattered windows even where the walls were still standing. The remaining occupants had been evacuated and relocated.

She'd definitely been lucky.

Why didn't she feel lucky, then?

Why didn't she feel anything much at all? Except fear.

Chapter Two

Hal Kennedy opened the letter informing him officially that his new house in the Penny Lake Leisure Village – what a mouthful for an address! – was finished and ready for his inspection. Which was no surprise because Molly Santiago had rung him yesterday to let him know unofficially. She had been very good throughout the build at keeping in touch about how the house was progressing.

He read the letter carefully then looked at his schedule for this coming week because he needed to make an appointment to go over the house with her for the snagging. He'd already researched snagging surveys online and drawn up a checklist, but didn't see the need to hire a professional surveyor. Not only did he trust his own ability to see clearly, but he trusted the Santiagos, whose development it was.

To them, this leisure village was clearly more than just a way to earn money – well, Hal had researched Euan's background before he even signed up for a house. He'd found that Euan was a multi-millionaire and that this was a semi-retirement project. The couple believed that this sort of housing development for older people filled a gap in the market, offering somewhere with a sense of community as well as a high standard of housing.

So many retirement developments featured nothing but tiny flats and he certainly didn't want to live in one of those. It'd be like living in a cupboard and he'd have to get rid of most of his possessions. But he did want, no, make that he would *need* to meet people, make friends, develop new networks.

He'd popped in to see his new house last week on the way back from Bristol, just casually, and Molly had been most welcoming, even though she needn't have let him into it yet. He'd been delighted with how his house was looking. He'd found a few minor details that needed dealing with and pointed them out to her, but mainly the interior had been nicely done and properly finished.

He was looking forward to moving out of this flat, luxurious though it was, because it was on a busy London street and he craved more peaceful surroundings. He'd have wound up his few remaining projects at work by the end of the following week. That'd be a relief, stage two of his big retirement plan completed, leading to stage three, the final one, actually moving into his new house.

He looked round and grimaced. 'Shabby' was the kindest thing you could say about his furnishings. He'd have to buy some new pieces for his house. Debbie had taken most of the good stuff with her when she moved out of here. Well, she'd brought them with her when she moved in, some lovely antiques, so fair enough for her to keep them.

How long ago was it since she'd left? Three, four years? It seemed like another life, given what had happened to him in the meantime.

He wasn't wasting his energy on vain regrets about the break-up, though he'd realised afterwards that they'd both been at fault, too focused on work. It wasn't his primary focus now. Cancer certainly put everything into perspective.

Hal paused, head on one side, surprised when he realised how long ago it had happened. He began pacing up and down again as he worked it out more exactly. Seven years ago they'd started living together and three and a half years ago they'd split up.

They'd managed the separation amicably, thank goodness, more amicably than it had been with his wife, all those years ago. Debbie was younger than him and was still an eager beaver public defence lawyer and he was . . . what? A jaded corporate lawyer of fifty-six, just recovering from a serious cancer scare and thankful these days for every breath he took.

They'd both seen the mess some couples got into when they parted company and how much it could cost both financially and emotionally to make the necessary arrangements if they quarrelled about details, so they'd agreed on the terms of their own break-up. Debbie had been fair, he had to give her that. He hoped he'd been fair too. Probably had because he'd never cared as much as she had about mere objects. He was more into books.

He passed a mirror and stopped to stare at himself in it, wincing. It wasn't the first time he'd been surprised at how old he was starting to look. Hair receding but still covering most of his skull, thank goodness, and all steel-grey now.

Distinguished, he told himself firmly. Inevitable to be starting to show your age, though fifty-six wasn't all that old. Body a little overweight, not much, but he really should get fitter.

The main trouble was he didn't feel old inside his head. Did you ever? So he had to find a new path in life, maybe volunteering with some charity or other. Once he'd stopped work and moved house, he intended to do some of the things he'd planned when he was younger, before he'd climbed aboard the legal treadmill and found out just how demanding it was.

When was the last time he'd done any sketching or painting? He might not be Michelangelo, but he'd enjoyed it. He hadn't gone for long walks in the countryside, either. As for learning to play golf, he hadn't even got as far as buying any clubs.

How quickly the years passed!

He'd had a health warning, so as far as he was concerned, he wasn't putting off anything from now on. *Carpe diem.* Seize the day. He'd seize every single moment he had left.

If he had to sum up his life since he left university and entered what people laughingly called 'the real world', what would he say? Continuously employed, one failed marriage and simultaneously failed attempt at gracious living in the suburbs, a grown-up son he hardly ever saw, one failed long-term relationship, an extremely successful career financially – and one serious health scare.

Who would miss him if he dropped dead tomorrow, though? He'd turned into rather a loner since Debbie left. Oh hell! He was getting into stupid territory. If he went on at this rate, he'd be seeing a shrink next and letting some stranger into his head to guide him into retirement as the human resources officer at work had suggested.

No way was he doing that! Self-help for coping with the coming changes was more acceptable to him, so he'd made a start by going online and researching 'mid-life crisis'. And had found that for most of the articles, he was getting a bit past the preparations stage and hadn't done any of the specified during-your-fifties planning until recently.

One sentence from his online research had stayed with him: 'Accept that you're no longer young and that no one is immortal. Get on with living.' That was a bit depressing but accurate. One of his colleagues had dropped dead last year and Hal suspected the shock of that had played a big part in his decision to retire, though not as big a part as the cancer.

But he also found 'Sixty is the new forty' repeated here and there online. Yes, that was a better motto, even if it did sound utterly corny. People generally did live longer these days. It wasn't like his parents' world. He could have another thirty years of active life left to him.

He grew impatient with himself. Why was he still worrying about that? He'd got it mostly covered, was financially secure and taking positive steps. Until he moved physically to Wiltshire and his new home he couldn't really see anything to do that he wasn't already doing.

'So just get on with it,' he muttered.

The next thing on his list was to chuck things out and pack what he wanted to take. Half the furniture was going for a start. That job was scheduled for next week.

He checked his diary and phoned Molly Santiago at the leisure village, arranging to go round his new home on the following Thursday afternoon. He was really looking forward to it.

When he switched on the news channel, he was shocked to hear of a terrorist bombing attack on a block of flats only a couple of miles away.

He changed channels after a few moments. He was sorry for the poor sods who'd been murdered, but it was nothing to do with him.

Hopefully there wouldn't be as much likelihood of an attack on a place out in the middle of the countryside.

Chapter Three

Mid-morning on the day after the explosion, the phone rang. Cassie checked who it was. Her boss. She hesitated, then answered. After all, Terry couldn't see her hand trembling, could he?

'Cassie, I heard about your narrow escape. Are you all right?'

'Um, a bit shaken up.'

'Good, good.'

What was good about that? she wondered.

'Steve's doing well with taking over your next programme. He's got it almost ready to go to air. How about you come into the studio this morning – just briefly, we don't want to stress you too much – and let him interview you about what it was like to be caught in a terrorist attack? If anyone can bring it to life for the viewers, you can.'

She couldn't speak, had begun to shake from head to toe at the mere thought of doing that.

'Cassie?'

'No. I – can't.'

'You're not all right, are you? Are you injured?' He sounded almost eager.

She fought for control of her voice. 'Only s-superficially. I need a few days' R&R to, um, put things into perspective. I'll be in touch next week.'

She put the phone down, then disconnected the whole system. Couldn't face any more calls, no matter who it was.

The trouble was, after that she couldn't think what to do with herself. She was so used to being non-stop busy. In the end she sat in front of the TV and watched it – well, she watched it now and then. The rest of the time her thoughts drifted and fluttered like falling leaves in autumn. She couldn't seem to focus on anything.

She snapped to attention, however, when her own programme came on mid-afternoon, not surprised to see that they'd found someone else for Steve to interview about the terrorist incident. He pushed too hard, he always did, and the poor woman fell to pieces on screen.

Cassie knew she'd have fallen to pieces too if she'd been stupid enough to let herself be interviewed.

She suddenly realised how she'd pushed other trauma survivors in interviews – not as hard as Steve had done but still too hard if they'd felt half as fragile as she did now. *Cassandra Benn always gets the story*. Guilt ran through her.

They turned the cameras away from the weeping woman, presumably to remove her, and brought in a psychologist to talk to Steve about the impact on survivors and what they should do to cope.

She listened carefully to the man's neat little list of the main effects. What he said made sense. She was feeling exactly as he'd said. But she could have told him a few more details about the impact on a person as well, details which mattered to an individual, not dry academic facts.

Oh damn, now he was talking about the deeper impacts on your whole life and its choices that might become evident later. Tears came into her eyes as she listened carefully.

That was never going to happen, not to her, no way. She'd always prided herself on not giving in to adversity.

Annoyed with herself for such a weakness and suddenly furious all over again at the evil sods who'd done this to her, she nonetheless watched the whole segment, then she went into the kitchen and cleared it up thoroughly. And about time too. She was getting her act together, doing something useful. Starting small.

What she needed was a few days' rest and she'd be OK. Definitely. She wasn't going to see any shrinks, thank you very much, or take more than a few days off work.

When someone knocked on her front door, she crept round to peep through the living-room window and didn't answer, because she could see that it was a complete stranger.

She had to move quickly out of sight because the person came round the house tramping right through her front garden to peer through the living-room window. The cheek of it!

When the stranger went away, she caught sight of herself in a mirror and was horrified at how haggard she looked. She'd definitely do something about her hair tomorrow, take more care with what she wore.

No one was going to see her today, though.

Wrong. Just before six o'clock a key turned in the lock

and Brett came in again. As he was closing the door she saw two people outside trying to peer past him.

She jerked quickly to one side and her voice came out more sharply than she'd intended. 'Shut that damned door! Quickly!'

He did that and studied her. 'You still don't look well, Cassie. How are you feeling? Really.'

'So-so. It's not just me being weak, mind. It takes time to recover, some expert was talking about it on the telly.'

'Of course it takes time. You're not Teflon-coated. Horrors like that don't bounce off anyone, however well they hide it. And don't worry, no person worth their salt would ever accuse you of being weak, Cassie, believe me.'

He went into the kitchen, dumped two shopping bags on the surface and began to unpack various types of food. 'There, that should hold you for a while.'

'Thanks. How much do I owe you?'

'Nothing.' He hesitated, folding the shopping bags up again and stuffing them in his pocket then fiddling with one of the packages.

'What is it?'

'Can you manage on your own for a few days? Only, it's Tina's birthday and we'd planned to go away this weekend, booked the hotel and everything.'

'You seem happy together.'

'Yes. I'm sorry about how you and I broke up, though. Very sorry. I couldn't think how to tell you about her. Actually, I reckon you and I make better friends than lovers.'

She didn't agree. He'd been a splendid lover. But she wasn't going to tell him that. 'Water under the bridge now.'

He started to leave then turned back again. 'Cassie,

love, I know you're very independent but don't push other people away if they offer to help. I tried your personal phone and it's switched off. What's with that? How will your friends get in touch?'

'I don't want them to. What I need is peace and quiet. You can contact me by my private email if it's desperate. I haven't changed that.' She hadn't looked at it today, either. Why not? She usually checked it several times a day. 'Thanks for the food. Now, go away and enjoy your weekend. Give my best to Tina.'

She showed him to the door, locked it quickly behind him and went into the kitchen. After putting away the food, she again sat in front of the TV, but didn't switch it on. She was unable to think what to do next until something the psychologist had said came back to her.

Find something important that you really want to do, something that's been left undone for a while, and focus on that.

It sounded like a good idea. In other words, find a serious distraction. What did she really want to do, though? She'd been living a very full life. Couldn't have fitted another thing into it. Well, a full working life anyway. She'd had some marvellous experiences and met some wonderful people, as well as some not so wonderful ones.

It took her until later in the evening to admit to herself that there was one rather important thing she'd tried to do a couple of years ago but had failed to make progress on. Perhaps she should try it again?

No, why bother? It had upset her greatly last time. She didn't need any more upsets at the moment.

Decision made.

Later on there was a programme on TV about finding people you'd lost touch with or never met, often members of your own family. People who really mattered to these participants.

She was picking up the remote to switch it off just as they showed an old photo of a woman holding a baby. She let the gadget fall from her hand as she covered her mouth to hold in the tears she *never* normally let herself shed.

Only this time she couldn't hold them back and they overflowed down her cheeks. It was all the fault of the damned programme.

It was the fault of her parents, too. She'd never forgiven them for what they'd done, or for blaming her for being raped. Fortunately they now lived permanently in a remote part of Northumberland and were very involved in village affairs. That made it easier to avoid them. It wasn't as if they bothered to keep in touch with her, after all, except for a card at Christmas and on her birthday.

She'd seen them last year at a family gathering, which she'd gone to at the urging of her much younger sister. She'd regretted doing that, regretted it bitterly because it had stirred up feelings she'd thought she'd put to rest. They still disapproved of her, still considered the sun rose and set over her younger brother and sister, whom Cassie didn't see much of, either.

Her younger brother had been at the gathering too, but he'd managed to avoid her completely. Deliberately. Michael was so like their father, avoiding any emotions or troublesome situations, keeping a stiff upper lip – yes, and a pillar of the local church, too.

To her surprise she'd got on quite well with her younger

sister that day, but the fifteen years between them and the fact that they'd never actually spent a lot of time together when Zoe was younger had left a gap that was hard to cross in adulthood.

Only, Zoe had got in touch and they'd started meeting for coffee whenever she was down in London. And that was – nice. Really nice.

The words from the TV psychologist came back to her abruptly: *Find something important that you really want to do.*

Cassie's stomach clenched as the image she'd just seen of the baby slipped back into her mind. Her own daughter had been born a long time ago, over forty years, and yet it still upset her that her parents had taken her baby away from her shortly after it was born and forced her to give it up for adoption.

She wouldn't even have had a photo to remember her baby by if it hadn't been for a sympathetic hospital cleaner who disagreed with the nuns' punitive policies and took a camera to work for that exact purpose. Cassie still had the photo and had made a digital copy, but she didn't need to look at it to remember every detail of the baby's appearance.

She'd had a hard birth and been ill, had felt utterly helpless and been too young at fifteen even to leave school and get a job. She hadn't seen any way out of the situation, not with no close relatives except parents who'd threatened never to see or speak to her again if she didn't do exactly as they wished.

Could she do something about that loss now? Would finding her daughter help fill the aching hole that had never gone away? It might take her mind off her present stress to try. Maybe.

It took her a few minutes to decide she would try again.

Getting slowly to her feet, she went upstairs to unearth the paperwork she'd hidden away from Brett for the whole of their relationship. It had taken a bomb to shake the information out again, she thought sadly.

Dumping the tattered folder on the bed, she pushed the box of oddments back into the wardrobe, after which she sat staring at the folder for who knew how long. She was still hesitant even to open it – because that would also reopen old wounds.

Could she face making another attempt to find her daughter? Nothing had come of her first and only attempt so far. She'd done it carefully, gone through all the right channels. And oh, it had hurt so much when there had been no response!

Someone knocked on her front door and that jerked her out of her unhappy thoughts and into the present. She peeped out of her bedroom window. Her boss. She definitely didn't want to see Terry until she'd pulled herself together.

So she didn't answer the door.

Not until she saw him drive away did she go downstairs again and switch on her laptop. When she went to the online family finder site she'd used last time, nothing much had changed, except for a bright new illustration at the top. They still only took hard copy applications – in this day and age – and they didn't answer individual questions online. You had to phone up or write in for that.

Why force grieving people to jump through all these artificial hoops? That said something about the organisation that ran the home where she'd had her daughter.

They had been distant and unsupportive the first time

and though they'd passed on her letter to the daughter she'd given up for adoption, nothing had come of it.

Even though her research suggested they might still be the best organisation to help her to contact her daughter, she didn't have good memories of them. The church they represented was one which her parents were still members of. She didn't have good memories of that, either.

She hesitated for a long time, staring blindly at the screen. Did she really want to pursue this? It would hurt, she knew it would.

In the end she knew she had to. It was unfinished business and if anyone could find a better way to do it, her public persona Cassandra Benn could. She usually enjoyed a challenge, had faced and overcome many in her working life.

Her private self, Cassie Bennington, was more hesitant.

Which side of her was in charge today?

Oh, what the hell! *Just do it*, she told herself. It was taking her mind off the attack already, wasn't it?

Sort of. Frying pan and fire came to mind.

This time she tried to think laterally and searched online for other ways of doing this. It took her until the following afternoon to find a way round the cold formalities of government and various charity organisations. Eventually she made a different sort of application to a less obvious agency.

Good thing she wasn't short of money, though. They charged like a wounded bull for their 'special confidential services'.

She still didn't want to leave the house. She knew it was cowardly, but there you were. One thing at a time.

She phoned the agency and had a discussion with a cool

but tactful woman who took her through what they could do to help her.

And she found hope creeping in. She closed her eyes. *Please let this not be a con.*

'I'd like to use your services to do that, then,' she said at last.

The woman's voice softened. 'We won't let you down, Cassie. I know we charge a lot but we give good value for it and we always act ethically, even if our methods are a little different from those of other organisations. I promise you can trust us. Now, my name's Mary and I'll be the coordinator for your case. If you need anything from now on, ask for me.'

'Oh, thank goodness.'

'Do you want me to visit you in person to discuss it? That's part of the service we offer.'

'Um, no.' She explained about the incident.

'Then we can do it via our special app, which guarantees secure communication.'

When she eventually got off the phone, Cassie did the other thing they'd asked for. She found the letter she'd written to her daughter last time, rewrote it slightly and used the app to email it directly to Mary.

She got an email back almost immediately, promising to have the letter delivered.

'But it'll have to go to her by post,' Mary said. 'And remember, I can't give you any details about her and where she is unless she gives permission.'

'You can give her any of my details she might need, though,' Cassie said. 'My address, phone number, anything.'

'You're sure you want to do that?'

'Oh yes. Very sure.'

She wasn't actually that sure, wasn't sure of anything today. But at least she was doing something. And it had kept her occupied for several hours.

Maybe the psychiatrist she'd seen on the TV had known something after all.

She wasn't consulting anyone of his tribe about her personal situation, though. Not in a million years.

On the Monday Cassie still couldn't face going to work. She booked an emergency medical appointment but it took a bit of effort for her to leave the house.

She saw a doctor at the local medical centre and asked to get signed off officially from work for a while. She didn't have a specific doctor, had hardly ever needed medical help.

She refused this man's suggestion of counselling, spurned the mere idea of tranquilisers, keeping her cool only with difficulty when he tried to persuade her to try them. 'I do not do drugs, whether legal or otherwise.' No way was she going to stuff her body full of chemicals that doped your brain, forget it. She'd seen where that could lead, knew her mother had been on them for years.

In the end she pacified the doctor by saying she was considering going away for a holiday and asking his advice about whether that was a good idea.

He approved of that but looked at her shrewdly. 'You do realise it'll take you a while to get over this? I'd like to sign you off for at least two months.'

She hadn't expected that. 'Two months away from work? Phew! I can't remember the last time I took even a week off.'

'Then perhaps your batteries have run down from more than just the recent incident.'

She stared at him as the idea sank in. She hadn't considered that possibility. But she had been feeling – well, a bit drained of energy lately. Even before the incident.

'I'm right, aren't I?'

She shrugged. 'Could be.'

'Give yourself time to recover completely, Cassie. Take a proper rest. I've only just met you yet it stands out to me. I truly believe you need it.'

She gave in, because she knew she couldn't do good work feeling as she did. 'All right. Two months it is.'

As she walked out of the surgery she wondered how she would cope with spending that long away from work. What did people who were out of work or retired do to fill their time? She had no idea. When she went back to work she might research it as a programme idea.

If she went back to work.

No, no. She wasn't retiring. She wasn't sure she ever would. And she hadn't lost her job – they wouldn't dare sack her. She was just *regrouping, pausing for breath*, so to speak.

When she got home, a journalist she knew was waiting outside her home so she slid down in her seat, telling the taxi driver to go past the front of the house and round to the rear laneway. She could get in through the garage at the end of her tiny garden.

Looking at her little-used car as she edged past it made her wonder if she really should go away for a holiday. She could slip out this way without anyone seeing her – and go where?

The idea stayed with her as she found something to eat. She put half of the cheese toastie back in the fridge uneaten, along with half the apple. She had to stop making too much. It was wrong to be wasteful. Then she told herself not to pretend: she just wasn't hungry at the moment.

As the day passed the idea of taking a holiday just wouldn't go away. Should she really take one? But where could she go that someone wouldn't recognise her?

She started pacing up and down, then caught sight of herself in a mirror and stopped dead, horrified by what she saw. Her hair was a mess, with the white roots showing all too clearly. Why did so many redheads lose their hair colour so young? It drove her mad keeping up with the colour and root treatments. Trouble was, her alter ego Cassandra Benn was famous for her bright-red locks, a 'fiery redhead' her PR blurbs sometimes claimed.

She stared into the mirror thoughtfully. She'd kept colouring her hair because she didn't feel old and wasn't giving in to anything that suggested her real age. But now, well, it'd be a brilliant disguise and would save her a load of trouble as well.

She rang her hairdresser and begged for help.

'But I'm closing shortly. It's Monday. I close early today.'

So she played the pity card and told Michelle, 'Please. I need to get away for a while. I'll pay you double if you'll take the colour out of my hair today. I know it's a big ask, but I'm being *hounded* by the press.'

'Oh, all right. You've been a good customer and it's been a quiet week, so I could use the extra money. I'll stay open if you come here straight away.'

'I can't thank you enough. I'm on my way.'

She drove herself there and had trouble finding a parking spot. Before she got out of the car she wrapped a big scarf round her head and since rain was threatening, she wasn't the only one doing that. No one seemed to recognise her, thank goodness.

When she got to the salon it was a relief to find only Michelle there. The hairdresser was about the same age as she was and chatting to her didn't feel threatening at all, even today. Indeed, she'd been going to her for so long she sometimes seemed more like a cousin or long-time friend.

'I could only face coming to you,' she admitted.

Michelle studied her and nodded.

'Tell me exactly what you want to do with your hair.'

Michelle listened without interrupting and entered into the need for disguise with enthusiasm, suggesting Cassie let her hair grow while she was at it. After all, she'd had it short for the whole time she'd been a public figure. Why not go for a complete change?

Then she snapped her fingers. 'You could even wear a hairpiece on an Alice band to make it seem longer straight away. That'd really fool people.'

She went to a cupboard and took out a box, rummaging through the packages it contained. 'We sell quite a few of these.' She flourished a silvery white hairpiece at Cassie. 'This is probably a good match for the colour of your roots. Now, let me get at that head of yours and soon you won't recognise yourself. Close your eyes and relax.'

It felt good to do something non-threatening, especially good to let Michelle take control of her body for a while – do this, move here, keep your eyes closed.

She was sure a different appearance would help her make a new life for herself. She froze as she sat there having her hair rinsed. *New life?* She was only taking sick leave . . . wasn't she?

Then she relaxed a little. Perhaps she should take a serious look at what she wanted to do in future. She'd been a voyeur into one human trauma after another for years and had seen some of the worst sides of human nature as well as the best – but all of it vicariously. Now she'd reacted so badly to terrorism she wished she'd been less ruthless about exposing other people's reactions to life crises.

To her amazement, she was indeed feeling that she'd had enough of it. A new life might be good.

How had that idea crept up on her?

Michelle continued to fiddle around in her usual quiet way and Cassie stayed tuned out.

Then suddenly it was done.

'Open your eyes, Cassie.'

She stared at a woman with a head of silvery hair. And she didn't look old, at least she thought she didn't, just . . . different.

'You're lucky,' Michelle said. 'Some people's hair turns a coarse white, but yours looks lovely, all soft and silvery. Why have you fought it for so long? Some younger people are now dyeing their hair to get that colour.'

Cassie stared at the stranger in the mirror, turning her head from side to side. 'You've done brilliantly, Michelle.'

'Close your eyes again and let's try the Alice band.'

She obeyed, letting Michelle fiddle around.

'See what you think of this.'

Cassie stared at the woman in the mirror, who looked

so much like an aunt of hers she was shocked rigid. But it was what she'd wanted, wasn't it? To look different, be unrecognisable. 'Brilliant. Show me how to put that thing on.'

She had a lesson in doing that and happily paid Michelle more than double her asking price. 'Thank you. You've helped me at a bad time. I really needed this and I can't tell you how grateful I am.'

But when Michelle broke their tradition by hugging her, she stiffened, couldn't help it, didn't want to be touched.

Michelle kept hold, shaking her gently. 'I know you don't like being hugged, love, but I'm doing it anyway. You need it. You need people, Cassie. We all do. Don't push them away. Learn to touch the rest of humanity, not just talk at it.'

That was the second person to say something similar to her.

She knew they meant well and she respected both Michelle's and Brett's opinions, but she had never been a touchy-feely sort of person. And come to think of it, her parents hadn't been, either.

What about her sister and brother? Was Zoe out of the same mould? She knew Michael didn't do 'that soppy, girly stuff'.

When things had settled down, she must catch up with Zoe. She wasn't sure Michael wanted to bother. But she and Zoe had got on quite well the last few times they'd met. She pulled a wry face – well, they'd been rather like two amiable strangers getting to know one another and liking what they found.

Could their relationship go further? Did she want it to?

She didn't know. Probably. Possibly. Oh hell, she wasn't sure of anything at the moment.

*   *   *

Cassie couldn't avoid continuing to think about it all as she drove home. If she did change her life, if that was going to be the best solution to her present – well, chaos of mind would be a good way of describing it – how would she make a living? She had some money saved but not enough to retire on completely.

There had to be a way, though. There was nearly always a way if you looked for it hard enough.

She didn't need to see a shrink, though. She'd always been independent and she was staying independent. What she needed now was to take action herself, find her own way to recovery. Surely that would make her feel normal again?

She would give the agency's search for her daughter a few days. Mary had told her they usually came up with results pretty quickly.

She hadn't asked them about the methods they used to find people – didn't care, just wanted results. After paying so much for their services, she expected a quick response, that was sure.

She needed to know one way or another.

Chapter Four

In Lancashire, Evie Milner stared at her mother in horror. 'You're going to *marry* him?'

'Yes, and then we are *both* moving into Keith's house.'

The girl's voice was flat. 'You should wait to marry him. You've only known him a few months.'

'Why? He loves me, fell in love with me at first sight. He wants us to marry so that we can be together properly.'

'He's a creep. I can't stand him, and I *won't* go to live with him.'

'How can you say that? He's always been so nice to you. Don't you dare speak about him like that!'

She couldn't tell her mother why, because she had no proof that Keith fancied her, and her mother would hit the roof and accuse her of trying to drive him away. But Evie knew the way he looked at her when they were alone together, and it made her flesh crawl. A grown man shouldn't look at a child that way, even a child of fifteen, which was nearly adult. It was illegal as well as disgusting.

All she could do was repeat, 'I will *not* live with him.'

'You don't get the choice. I'm your mother. Until you're old enough to leave home, I say where you live and what you do.'

'I'll run away first.'

'It's not happening instantly. Just let me finish explaining our future arrangements before you fire off threats. I want to try living with Keith before I make any permanent changes, so I've arranged for you to stay with Cousin Amelia for a few weeks while he and I settle in together.'

Evie couldn't see what good that would do. It'd only postpone the time her mother tried to get her to live with him as well.

'Keith doesn't want to move from where he's living, so he's going to do an attic conversion on his present house and that's where you'll be sleeping once it's finished. He's paying extra for them to do a rush job on it. That shows he does care about you and my relationship with you. You're so ungrateful.'

Evie felt helpless against her mother's blind rush into what she was sure would be another disastrous relationship, only this time she'd be tied to the guy by marriage. She dashed away a tear. She didn't know what to say or do to stop her mother or at least slow her down.

'Bear with me, Evie. It's a long time since your father left me.' After another pause, Fran added with false brightness, 'And just think of the lovely new bedroom and en suite you'll have all to yourself when the attic conversion is finished.'

And think of how I'll be kept upstairs and out of the way for most of the time, Evie thought. Children should be seen and not heard, even more so when they were fifteen years old and knew what certain noises in other people's bedrooms meant.

But when a creepy older man kept brushing against you on the stairs and staring at your chest, well, you couldn't help knowing what he was thinking. She shuddered at the memory of that, but she might have been mistaken. Or there again, she might not. Stupid she wasn't.

And her mother would be legally tied to him! It didn't bear thinking of.

Normally Evie would have protested at the thought of going to live with her mother's cousin, who was a flaky art teacher and lived way out on the other side of town. Amelia didn't know which way was up half the time when she was just starting a new painting. But anything would be better than living with Keith Burgess so Evie would put up with their cousin, with her vegan food and arty weirdos coming in and out of the house.

Though none of Amelia's weirdos had made her feel uncomfortable in the way Keith did. She'd better make sure she didn't do anything to upset their cousin and get sent home again.

Home! She didn't have a home like other kids did, never had done because they'd moved often as her mother struggled to make ends meet.

But staying with Amelia would only be a temporary fix for the latest disastrous relationship. She had to work out a way to avoid living with him long term. She didn't intend to visit for a weekend, even, simply didn't dare.

She went to stay at Amelia's for half term to see how things went, and to her surprise she found her cousin so controlling it felt like a different lifestyle from last time. Amelia made sure of what Evie was doing every minute of the day and night, and set out some rules she'd have to observe when she came to live here for longer.

She found out why, of course. She always found things out. She'd had years of practice at eavesdropping on conversations and phone calls, and at second-guessing her mother. It seemed Cousin Amelia was being paid to watch her carefully.

That sucked big time. What did they think she was going to do? Sell her body on the streets? Give it to any man who fancied her? As if.

She tackled Amelia about it one evening, choosing her time carefully, when her aunt was on her second glass of wine.

'Why do they think I need watching so carefully?'

Amelia choked on her mouthful then frowned at her.

'I don't misbehave, I do well at school, mostly get As. Why don't they trust me?'

'They haven't told you anything?'

Evie shook her head.

'Hmm. Well, you're old enough to know *all* the facts and I've told Fran that, so don't blame me. It's because your mother is adopted.'

'I know that already.'

'Did you know that *her* mother had her when she was only fifteen?'

This was news. 'Oh? Is that why she put her up for adoption?'

'Probably. But it's also why your mother wants you to be watched carefully.'

Evie was baffled. 'What's that got to do with me?'

'Your mother nearly went down the same path. She got pregnant at fifteen to someone she fell madly in love with, but luckily she miscarried before it could ruin her life. She didn't want you to know about that, so don't let on I told you. As a result, she and Keith are worried that you've inherited the family tendency to, um, start getting interested in men early.'

'That's ridiculous. I haven't even had a steady boyfriend yet.' *He* must have put that idea into her mother's head. Why?

Amelia shrugged. 'Well, me taking care of you oh-so-carefully is not only going to set their minds at rest, but help pay for a painting holiday in Greece this summer for me. And actually, kid, I enjoy your company.'

'I enjoy yours too.' That had surprised her, but Amelia had started to talk more openly to her about all sorts of things now that she was older, which was more than her mother did since she'd met *him*.

Evie lay awake for a long time trying to work out what she'd done to make her mother and Keith think she'd be so stupid and irresponsible. Or that she was man crazy. Even if she did meet a boy she fancied, she knew about birth control, for heaven's sake. This was the twenty-first not the nineteenth century.

Only she didn't fancy any of the boys she'd met at school, so it wasn't going to happen. She knew she was classified as 'gifted', for what that was worth, and she found most of the males in her year either immature, sports mad or else geeks with no interests beyond their computers.

But dull and restricted as her life was at Amelia's, she

infinitely preferred it to living with her mother in *his* house. She was dreading the move, hadn't yet worked out how to get out of it.

And openly as her cousin talked, Evie didn't dare voice her fears about Keith to her either, not without proof of what she suspected. No, more than suspected. Was sure of.

When Amelia drove her home after the trial visit, Evie found her mother in a glow of happiness and Keith beside her looking smug.

Her cousin nudged her as they got her luggage out of the car. 'It's lovely to see how happy Fran is. Don't do anything to spoil it for your mother, love.'

Evie tried to smile, but it seemed Keith was staying over, so she'd have no time alone with her mother that night.

He seemed to stay over most of the time these days, so keeping out of his way was easier said than done. Worst of all, he continued to look at her in a way that made her feel as if she had no clothes on. And when he bumped into her, as he still did occasionally, he didn't move away quickly, which made her feel literally sick.

All she could do was try to avoid him and stay in her room as much as she could, pleading homework. Which didn't please her mother.

She didn't dare talk about the problem to her friends at school in case it got back to the guidance officer. That might get her into trouble for telling malicious lies, as had happened to one girl last year.

Or worse still, get her reported to social services, who might take her away while the whole situation was investigated. One of her classmates was in care and her tales of a series of placements wouldn't encourage anyone to go down that path except in utter desperation.

About a week after she got back from her cousin's, Evie stayed home from school for an agreed study day. This was supposed to teach them to work on their own. Duh! She already did that because the homework didn't keep her fully occupied and she liked to investigate topics which interested her in more detail.

The post was delivered early and when she picked it up from the hall floor, she found a letter for her mother, who had just come back from a long dental appointment and was going into work late as a consequence. 'This is for you.'

The sight of its contents made her mother scowl and she shoved the letter into her pocket.

'Bad news?' Evie asked casually.

'Never you mind.'

It must have been really bad news because her mother slammed around the house, snapping at her daughter for nothing. It was a relief when she went back to work in the afternoon.

When it came time to clear up the kitchen after tea, her mother's phone rang and she took it in the living room, calling, 'Take that bag of rubbish out to the bin, Evie, and don't open it up again. It stinks and it's full. Hurry up. Make yourself useful, for once.'

She took it out, hesitated and crept back to see if her mother was still on the phone.

She was and it must be to *him* judging by the soppy expression on her face. If he wasn't there with them, he often rang and she had started to wonder whether he was checking on her mother.

Evie gave in to temptation, went back outside and untied the rubbish bag. She had to fumble through some yucky scraps of food but it was worth it because she found the letter that had upset her mother so greatly, torn in half and screwed up.

Still keeping an eye on the house, she wiped it as best she could on the grass and slipped it inside the top of her knickers, for lack of any other place to conceal it. It always helped to keep track of what was going on and this had upset her mother big time.

She went back into the house and up to the bathroom, where she pulled the letter out with a grimace, wiped the smears of vegetable debris off her skin, then hid the slightly soggy pieces of paper in her bedroom. No use trying to read the letter now. Her mother's latest trick was to creep in on her suddenly and check what she was doing.

Evie sighed. She was finding this very wearing and still hadn't the faintest idea what to do about it. Her mother hadn't been like this before she met *him*.

She wished, as she had many times before, that she'd been born into a normal family, with two parents, a couple of siblings and maybe a pet dog.

She had never wished it as strongly as this, though.

It wasn't till the house was quiet and her mother fast asleep that she dared take out the letter. Thank goodness *he* wasn't spending the night.

What she read shocked her rigid.

Dear Ms Milner,

Your birth mother is very eager to make contact with you and has employed our agency to facilitate this.

You may have previously received a letter from her similar to the one enclosed and if so, she begs you to reconsider your decision not to respond at that time and give her a chance.

Your mother didn't give you up for adoption willingly. She was only fifteen when you were born and was forced to do this by her parents. She has always been deeply sad about that and would very much like to get to know you.

She would be happy to meet you anywhere and at a time of your choice.

Our company can provide sympathetic professional counsellors to make the meeting and its impact easier on you both, if that would help.

We have not disclosed your address and personal information to her in case you still do not wish to have a meeting, because we do respect people's privacy. However she has asked us to give you her own details to show good faith.

These have been added to the end of this letter.

Please don't rush into doing anything you may regret later. This is important and deserves careful thought.

If you wish to ask any questions or discuss the matter with our counsellors, that can be arranged by phoning the number at the top of this page and mentioning the reference number of your case, which is beneath it. The sessions will be paid for by your birth mother, of course.

We look forward to hearing from you and helping you both.
   Yours sincerely,
   JSD Services

Evie stared at the letter in shock and read it through again, more slowly this time. She knew that her mother had been adopted because her grandparents had made no secret of doing it. Her mother, however, had always refused to discuss it, let alone speculate about her birth parents. And now this letter had turned up out of the blue.

She looked at the end of it and immediately memorised this unknown grandmother's details, just in case, then hid the torn halves of the letter amongst her art materials, hoping that a few more scruffy pieces of paper wouldn't look out of place when her mother next went through her things, another thing she'd started doing since she hooked up with *him*.

When she lay down again, she had trouble getting to sleep. She'd learnt more about her mother's past during the previous two weeks than ever before, what with Cousin Amelia's explanation and this letter. Though it was still not a lot to go on. It was as if her mother wanted to wipe away any traces of her birth mother.

But what if there was some medical emergency that needed genetic information about the family? Evie had read about such cases, because she was considering trying to become a doctor. What would they do then? She or her mother could die for lack of the correct information.

Her mother's first husband, Evie's father, had gone travelling the world to 'find himself' when she was five. He hadn't been heard of since. She didn't remember him very clearly. Her mother had got a divorce from him after a certain length of time and changed her surname to Milner, doing the same name change for Evie.

Her mother's adoptive parents, her Gran and Pop Milner, would probably have been upset if a birth mother had turned up while they were still alive. She missed them dreadfully. Drunken drivers should be stood against a wall and shot for the harm they did to innocent people and their families when they caused accidents.

Evie didn't get on with her father's parents, and was glad she hadn't had much to do with them. She had never been able to figure out why they were so cold to their daughter-in-law. Did they consider themselves so perfect they could scorn anyone who made a mistake? She felt sure if she tried to seek shelter with them, they'd bring her straight back.

But she did still have this other grandmother, it seemed, a mother who wanted desperately to meet the daughter who'd been adopted soon after birth, even if that desire wasn't reciprocated. Surely she'd want to meet her granddaughter too?

Evie didn't know whether she'd dare get in touch with this woman, though. If she did, it'd have to be done very carefully so that her mother didn't find out.

What was her grandmother like? How stupid it was that her mother wouldn't even meet her and find out.

What a tangle some so-called adults could get their lives into! Evie hoped she'd do better when she grew up. Apart from being a doctor, all she wanted was to meet a stable, normal guy who wanted to settle down, have a family and live a quiet, happy life doing something worthwhile.

Was that too much to ask?

First, however, she had to solve the problem of Keith and her own immediate future. She would not go and live with him. Didn't dare.

Thank goodness she would soon be going back to stay with Amelia again, and for a few weeks this time. It made for a long trip to and from school each day, but it was worth it. And after that, who knew?

She might even be forced to run away to escape him, but she'd only do that as a final, desperate resort.

She could only hope he'd prove to be more difficult to live with than her mother expected.

Chapter Five

On the Thursday morning, Hal set off for Wiltshire, looking forward to seeing his new home in all its finished glory. He had lunch in the hotel, something he hadn't done before. The meal was good, not haute cuisine, but who wanted that except on special occasions? He got too hungry for the prettily arranged but bird-sized portions he'd paid a fortune for when fine dining.

He'd definitely eat here regularly once he moved in.

Afterwards he strolled down to the site office and found Molly waiting for him, with a young man standing to one side, ready to take over the selling side of things.

They walked down to the detached house that Hal would soon be moving into and he paused in front to study it and nod approval. It was an elegant, classical house shape, with nice large windows and he didn't regret choosing that style. He'd never liked weird modern buildings with odd-shaped roofs and protrusions that looked as if a child had plonked the parts together.

Inside they moved slowly from room to room, going through a list of things to check that Molly had brought, after which she left him to go round again on his own.

'Come and join me when you've finished and we'll go up to the main company office in the hotel and discuss any further concerns you may have. Take your time. There's no rush.'

'Thanks. I would appreciate going round again on my own.'

He stood by the living-room window of his house for a while and realised suddenly that he was smiling. That was because from here he had a view of the lake for which the leisure village was named: Penny Lake. It was glinting in the sun, tempting him to walk round it. *Not today*, he told it mentally, *but soon.*

Then he walked round the house again, continuing to feel happy, as if he really had come home to stay. He'd tried to make other homes for himself and succeeded only temporarily. This time he was going to make sure things worked out on a permanent, long-term basis.

He needed it.

Apart from any other considerations, there was a lot of boring, fiddling detail involved in changing houses and he wanted to make this the last time he ever went through all that. He had better things to do with his life. Well, in theory, anyway.

He didn't know exactly *what* he was going to do from now on, but he'd recovered from cancer and been given the chance to live a normal life again, so he felt he should do something worthwhile. He wasn't going to waste that precious time.

First he had to learn to relax and live at a gentler pace.

No, wrong. First he had to go and see Molly, sign anything

else necessary and make the final arrangements to move here.

He chuckled softly. Which meant he'd have to buy some new furniture. He'd never done that on his own before, had always done it with a woman. Did men choose differently when it was for themselves? Who knew? He intended to take his time, moving in with his present bits and pieces and only buying more when he needed or loved something.

Home, he thought happily. Not a house to show off with, but one to snuggle into and relax. This place sure beat the stark modernist flat he was currently inhabiting in London. The sooner he got the final signing off over and done with, the happier he'd be.

Molly Santiago had been great to deal with, and her husband was just as nice.

Oh, he was so looking forward to starting his new life! He felt rejuvenated every time he thought of that.

Since her change of hair colour, Cassie found she could go to the shops or for walks without being recognised and it occurred to her that this was the first time in years she'd been able to do that.

It made her wonder whether she'd been more trapped in a celebrity bubble than she'd realised, cushioned against ordinary life, far less free than the average person in the street, for all her success.

Her boss threw a fit when she sent in a medical certificate covering two months' sick leave. Typically, Terry phoned her, was rude about her stamina and broke the call abruptly when she refused to change her plans.

After that, he sent his assistant to persuade her to come back sooner. Cassie hastily covered her hair with a towel before letting Roger in, not wanting him to see her new persona, for some reason.

She greeted him with, 'I've just washed my hair so I can only give you a few minutes.'

He talked rapidly and persuasively but she refused even to consider shortening the period of leave. 'I'm not making anything up. I really feel I need time to get over such a traumatic experience.' What the doctor had pointed out only backed up her decision.

Besides, she was suffering from PTSD, she had to admit that to herself, though she wasn't telling her boss. The mere thought of going out on interviews made her shudder and she kept jerking awake at night thinking she was in that ambulance again or could hear sirens wailing. Worst of all, the scenes from the TV footage kept replaying in her mind.

As a result of the insomnia she felt tired all day long and kept dropping off into a doze in her armchair.

What she had seen on TV made her feel sick, because she had been so close to being killed like those other poor souls. And never, not for one nano-second, did she feel safe, even though she knew logically that she was.

She jerked to attention at the realisation that Roger had said something else. 'Sorry. Run that past me again.'

'Terry won't like your refusal to honour your contract. He may even cancel the show.'

'And I don't like how the incident has affected me,' she said quietly. 'Tell him I'm doing the best I can. I'll see you out now.' She patted the makeshift turban. 'I need to attend to my hair.'

He gave her a puzzled look. She was sure he'd go back and tell Terry that she had changed, lost her edge.

She had.

And she didn't miss that sharp, almost bullying interaction with the world.

Only, as a consequence she didn't feel like she knew herself properly any longer and that was unsettling. She had to find herself again, had to – whoever she now was – but hadn't quite worked out how to do it.

Once she knew the coast was clear she went out for a walk to pick up a newspaper, relishing her anonymity. She didn't discover till she got home that it was the newspaper's day for the big display of property for sale, something she never normally looked at.

She tossed that part aside automatically, but couldn't resist picking it up again and glancing at it once she'd finished reading the main section of the newspaper. Maybe 'reading' was the wrong word. 'Skimming through' was a better description. She couldn't seem to concentrate on anything for long.

Her eyes were caught by an advert in the supplement showing houses for sale in her suburb. When she followed the online link it gave and looked through the various photos, she saw a house nearby that was very like her own and couldn't resist studying the details.

She was astounded at how much hers was now worth. She'd known it had increased in value, of course she had, but hadn't realised by how much. Well, she'd certainly taken her eye off the ball there. She'd been too busy watching over her 'brilliant career' – which didn't seem important any longer, or even all that brilliant when viewed from the inside.

In the middle of the night, as she was tossing and turning yet again, she had a sudden idea. She got up, padding downstairs to switch on her computer and check out property prices outside London and the big cities, trying Lancashire and Wiltshire as examples of places she knew a little after doing projects there fairly recently.

She sat for a long time staring at the screen, amazed at how much lower the prices were in both places. Was this her key to freedom, taking money out of her house?

It could be. It really could.

But did she want to quit London and her public life completely and become simply Cassie?

What would she do with herself all day?

No, she couldn't possibly retire . . . Could she? . . . Should she?

She rubbed her aching forehead which seemed full of tangled thoughts, then switched off the computer and walked slowly back upstairs to bed, yawning. Lots to think about tomorrow. Lots to research.

Who'd have thought she'd suffer from PTSD? She would never in a million years have expected that to happen, had thought herself an exceptionally strong person. But no one was made of steel. She was flesh and blood, just like the rest of humanity and just as fallible.

She'd never have believed, either, that she'd recoil from the mere idea of grilling the poor innocent victims of similar crimes. She couldn't do it any longer. Just – could – not.

So, she had to find her way towards a new style of living, tread a gentler path through life. It was more than time to stop this breakneck rush from tragedy to comedy, violence and other extremes of human experience.

* * *

The following day Cassie decided to go for a drive in the country to take her mind off her problems. She'd not heard from the agency she'd contracted to help her and in her gloomier moments, felt as if she'd never find her daughter. But she was totally fed up of sitting around the house and could at least do something about that.

When the phone rang early that morning, she checked the caller ID and saw that it was her sister. 'Zoe. How nice to hear from you.'

'How are you?'

'Fine, thank you.'

'I doubt that. I worked with someone who was involved in a violent incident and it upset him big time. Took him ages to get over it.'

'Oh. Well, I don't think I'm that bad.'

'Don't lie to me, Cassie.'

She didn't know what to say to that, so said nothing and waited to find out what Zoe wanted.

'Look, I'm in London and about to go down to Wiltshire to drop off a piece of furniture for a friend. She'd intended to come with me and we were going to visit an antiques centre we'd heard of afterwards, make a day of it. Unfortunately, she fractured her arm yesterday in a fall, so she doesn't feel like jolting about in a car. It suddenly occurred to me that you might like to come with me instead. It'd make a nice outing.'

'Thanks, but—' She broke off. Why was she refusing? 'Are you sure?'

'Very. I'd welcome the company and—' There was a distinct pause, then, 'Well, I don't think you and I see each other often enough, considering we're sisters. How about

I pick you up at nine, and hopefully we can avoid the rush hour on the M4?'

'All right. Lunch is on me, though.'

'OK. And Cassie, I'm really looking forward to our outing.'

So was she, Cassie found to her surprise.

Zoe greeted her with a 'Wow!' and touched her hair.

'The long part at the back is a hairpiece till my own hair grows. I felt like a change.'

'It suits you much better than the bright red did. Older faces don't show to their best advantage against harsh colours. And I like the jaw-level look too. It's more flattering than the short style was because your chin's starting to sag a bit.'

Cassie had forgotten how frank her sister could be. Such utter honesty came as a bit of a shock each time they met, though Zoe never said anything malicious so you couldn't exactly take offence.

She shrugged. 'I must admit it's nice not to be recognised when I go out and about, and it's going to be a lot easier to maintain this hairstyle.'

'Have you had much trouble with the press since the incident? I found out about it in a newspaper article so they must have tried to poke their noses in further.'

'Yes, they did. But the fuss seems to be dying down now. At least there wasn't someone parked outside this morning, waiting for me to come out.'

'I'm glad to hear that. Must have been hard to be at the other side of the camera.'

'Mmm. It was.'

Zoe patted her arm. 'Buckle up your seat belt. You can relax today and I'll play chauffeur. No one will be looking for you in Wiltshire.'

As they headed west, Cassie tried to think of something safe to chat about, but Zoe stopped her. 'You don't have to force conversation. You're not the only one who wants a restful outing.'

'Something wrong?'

'Not wrong, exactly, but I'm feeling a bit wobbly about committing to one man for ever.'

'I thought you loved him.'

'So did I. But I didn't realise how keen he is to settle down and have children – the whole shebang. And he's the one who wants a white wedding. I'm not nearly as certain about that part of it. It's all happened so quickly, I feel like a spinning top.'

After a slight pause, she added, 'And he's got an offer of a job in the Midlands, the sort of offer you don't refuse. I'll have to give up my job and find something else. No use getting married and living apart. So lots to think about.'

'Are you going off him?'

A sigh, then, 'I may be. I don't want children yet and as for parading around in a big meringue of a dress, he can forget it. I'm definitely not into white weddings.'

'I thought it was usually women who wanted all that fuss.'

'George is an old-fashioned guy in some ways. I thought I liked that. Mum and Dad still think he's perfect, but he isn't. No one is. But he comes pretty close to it, compared to other men I've gone out with. I think he must have been born amiable. And kind. And he's interesting to talk to. But . . . oh, who knows?'

'I wish you well, whatever you decide.'

'Thank you. Will you come to the wedding if we do get married? And be my matron of honour? It'd not be for a few months, but I'd like to have you there.'

'Oh. Well, I'll definitely try. But I'm not so sure about being a matron of honour.'

'I'd really like you to do it. I know you'd need to grit your teeth about Mum and Dad – and yes, I have noticed and been saddened by how they treat you, and it's got worse since you and I started seeing more of one another. But maybe it won't happen anyway. I am so confused.'

She reached her left hand across from the driving seat to pat her sister's arm quickly.

That simple touch felt good. Perhaps Brett and Michelle were right about not keeping people at arm's length.

A short time later Cassie found herself telling Zoe about her idea of selling her house in London and moving somewhere cheaper. 'Like Wiltshire, actually,' she admitted. 'I've been researching house prices online, so it's a nice coincidence that you wanted to go there today.'

'Are you really giving up work?'

'Probably.'

'Because of the incident?'

'Partly. It's made me think. The past few years have been great but stressful and – well, it's not just the incident. I think I may have run out of steam.' She didn't tell Zoe about searching for her daughter. Nothing might come of this second attempt.

They drove in silence for a few miles, then as they turned off the M4 motorway, Zoe suggested, 'Why don't we look at some houses while we're there, then? I love having a poke round. Shall you buy one with a garden and then get a dog? I've never had a pet.'

'I asked for a puppy once but Mum and Dad wouldn't allow it.'

'No. You've got to keep your house immaculate all the time, haven't you, or the world will come to an end. Perhaps that's why I'm so untidy, in reaction.'

'Do you think George will accept the job?'

'Oh yes. I wouldn't try to stop him. But I'm not having the wedding till that's all settled and I'm sure of myself.'

'I thought you'd fixed a date.'

'Mum pushed us into doing that.'

'What did she say to postponing it?'

'Told me to stop being precious and snap him up or someone else will. If I read her correctly, she wants to rush me into marriage in case I change my mind and wind up single or divorced like you. It's the only future she sees for a woman, marriage, and she doesn't believe in divorce for any reason whatsoever. Let's face it, Cassie, her and Dad's views come right out of the Ark.'

Cassie envied the way Zoe could chuckle at that. She'd never learnt to be light-hearted about her parents' old-fashioned views or the way they seemed to see only her previous faults and had never stopped criticising her for any other mistakes she'd made. No wonder she'd taken refuge in studying hard as a key to the longed-for independence from them.

And no wonder her recent relationship had broken up. Brett had once told her she didn't know how to be part of a loving couple.

Chapter Six

When the sisters arrived at Marlbury, it proved to be a small town, not the village they'd expected from what Zoe's friend had told her.

They dropped the little table off first, but Zoe refused an invitation from her friend's aunt to have a cup of tea and came straight back to the car. 'Let's grab a quick coffee in town then go and look in estate agency windows. I saw one as we drove through. I'd much rather look at houses than antiques.'

The window display of the first estate agent's gave them a very helpful start, as it was full of photos of houses of all shapes and sizes, and all prices too.

'Wow, the prices are wonderfully low compared to my part of London.' Cassie pointed. 'Look at that one.'

After a while Zoe said, 'Let's check that other agency over there on the other side of the road, see if this really is the correct price level.'

It was she who wandered round to the small side window and called, 'Come and look at this display.'

'Penny Lake Leisure Village! I don't want to live in an old folks' home,' Cassie said indignantly.

'It's not, you idiot. It's a leisure village. Haven't you heard of them?'

'Sort of. Not the details.' She was starting to find a lot of gaps in her knowledge of everyday matters, Cassie decided. Small picture stuff for living in the real world.

Zoe clicked her tongue in disapproval and explained. 'Listen and learn, oh sister mine. They're places adults move to when they want to lead a more chilled-out life. And yes, some people do retire to them, but they aren't usually based on a retirement ethos.'

'Good. I did an interview in a retirement complex once and it left me shuddering, the flats were so small. It felt as if they were storing old people in cupboards. And there was hardly anyone to be seen, as if they were all cowering inside their death nests.'

Zoe threw her a puzzled look. 'That's a strange way to look at them and a horrid way to describe them. George's aunt lives in a retirement village and she loves it. Lots of people to chat to if you want company, privacy in your own flat if you don't. No garden to maintain, but places to sit outside if you feel like it.'

Cassie shrugged. She wasn't old enough to need either type of place. How decrepit did her sister think she was, for heaven's sake? Fifty-six wasn't old.

'Anyway, let's go and look at this place, Cassie. It says it's attached to a golf course and there's a hotel on-site which serves meals. We can grab a late lunch there.'

'If we're going to be practical during this short visit, I'd rather grab a quick sandwich in town and look at proper houses than spend all our time in some little enclave. Might save me a trip in future to Wiltshire, if I don't like this area or the sort of homes you can buy round here.'

Zoe stopped dead. 'You know, for someone who makes her living interviewing people, you display some very fixed and limiting views at times. You've never even seen a leisure village so how do you know what one is like? I've noticed you making that sort of snap judgement before. Black or white, no shades in between. Surely if you do retire, you'll want to meet people and make new friends? Surely it's worth looking at *every* option?'

Cassie shrugged. 'I haven't thought that out properly yet and to tell you the truth, since the incident I'm still having trouble thinking clearly. And speaking the word "retire" out loud freaks me out big time. I hadn't planned to do that so soon – if ever.'

She stared into the distance. 'That explosion has turned my whole life upside down.'

Zoe gave her arm a little squeeze. 'Sorry. I shouldn't scold you when you're still upset. But since we have to eat and I don't fancy a high street café full of shoppers, let's go to this hotel and give ourselves a leisurely meal. I doubt it'll be crowded midweek.'

So Cassie let herself be taken to this Penny Lake place. What did it matter? Her sister wasn't trying to force her to buy a property there, after all.

Well, she wasn't buying anything anywhere till she'd had a good look round some of the nicer rural areas with easy access to London. She was determined to be sensible about this move, research everything carefully.

* * *

After delicious and innovative salads followed by a not so healthy shared piece of chocolate gateau at the hotel, the two women strolled across from its car park to the sales office to get some information about the type of houses being built here.

As they walked Cassie glanced to the right, where a smallish lake was glinting in the sun a short distance away. That was at least one thing in favour of this place, she had to admit, and what she'd seen of the Wiltshire countryside so far was lovely.

They picked up a brochure each and studied the site map on the wall. The woman sitting behind a desk didn't attempt a sales pitch beyond suggesting they might like to look round the two houses that were on show and open today.

'Both houses are for sale, of course,' she added as they started walking out of the display centre.

Cassie turned round. Might as well do the research properly. 'How much are they?'

'Here's a price list and details of other types of house that can be built as well.'

The woman held out a leaflet and she took it, amazed all over again at how cheap the houses were compared to London property prices in decent areas. Why, they were only about a third of the cost of her home, even for the larger of the current two show homes.

As she followed Zoe down the road and turned to the right past some occupied houses on their left, a woman came out, gave them a friendly smile and began to water the big pots of flowers that stood on either side of her door.

It was such a peaceful scene, Cassie thought wistfully. No crowds or sounds of nearby traffic, clear sparkling air, birds fluttering amongst the trees. She stopped to watch a wagtail bobbing up and down as it pecked up who knew what from the lawn. How long was it since she'd seen one of those? Years. They were her favourite birds, so tiny and always seeming happily busy.

Zoe waited for her. 'I'm enjoying this place. There's something about looking at water that soothes the soul, don't you think?'

'It's nice, yes.'

Her sister gave her a disbelieving look at this lukewarm response but didn't comment, thank goodness.

The first house that was open was the end one in a row of three. It was a neat little place, about the same size as Cassie's present home, and even less than a third of the price. It was well designed, but going round it and mentally planning how she'd live there made her realise that if she were spending most of her time at home, writing articles to bring in a little extra money, she'd need more space than this so that she could have a proper office.

The other house open for viewing was detached, much larger, with a spacious entrance and larger rooms.

'Nice family home,' Zoe said.

Cassie didn't respond but moved ahead to explore the interior, which had several linked living areas, one of which could easily be used as a home office. This house wouldn't make her feel as if she were shut up inside a rabbit hutch as some so-called office spaces had done at work, and her present house was doing since she'd been mostly confined to it.

Outside at the rear there was a sunny patio where you could have a table and chairs. All it needed were a few pots of flowers and it'd be perfect.

She went back inside, shooting a quick glance at Zoe, but her sister was opening and shutting cupboard doors. 'I'll just nip upstairs.'

'I'll follow you in a minute. I love looking at kitchens. I'm going to have a big one someday.'

The rooms upstairs were just as light and airy, with a big master bedroom with en suite.

Cassie fought a battle with herself and lost. She could imagine so clearly what it'd be like to wake up here.

And then a daring thought crept into her mind: why not buy it?

No! The idea was utterly ridiculous. Had she lost all common sense? She mustn't allow herself to go too far with her visualisations about the houses they went round. Doing that might lead to stupidly impulsive acts.

Zoe came up to join her and after they went down, she slipped her arm into her sister's. 'You like this house, don't you?'

Cassie debated whether to admit that, then sighed and gave her sister's arm a return squeeze. 'I do. Very much. I didn't expect that. I'd definitely want to buy something similar.'

Zoe stared round. 'I like the situation and the interior layout, but surely you'd be more interested in the smaller house with only yourself to bother about?'

'No, no. That one's too small. What I like best about this one is the sense of space.'

She surprised herself with her next words. 'I'm tired of being shut up in small places: aeroplanes, radio station interview booths, cars, trains, tents, people's front rooms. I hadn't realised how much I'd like the feeling of freedom that a big house and having open countryside nearby gives you. Anyway, if I do retire, I'll need a decent home office, because I'll still be doing some writing, you know, articles and opinion pieces. They pay quite well.'

She grinned and added in a mocking tone, 'I might even write a great English novel.'

'You can do what you want.'

Those words were fatal. They seemed to breach the wall of reason Cassie was trying to build round the temptation to buy this beautiful, near-perfect house. She stood stock-still, the words seeming to echo in her brain.

Yes, I really can do what I want from now on.

Eventually, after what seemed a very long time, she turned to Zoe and said, 'You'll probably think I'm mad, but I'm seriously considering buying it.'

'Wow, that's quick.'

'It's perfect for what I'd need, you see. Even the setting, with that lake, is gorgeous.'

Zoe gave her a nudge. 'Well, snatch it up then. I could recognise love at first sight when I saw how you looked as you walked round, which is why I stayed downstairs and let you continue exploring on your own. But I didn't think you'd let yourself buy it.'

Let herself?

Zoe studied her sister for a minute or two, then said, 'I'm looking for the same reaction in myself when George talks about weddings and searching for a house. The only trouble is – I'm not getting it.'

'Ah.'

'I'd intended to do some travelling before I got married. Or even try living in London for a while.'

'You should have told me. You could have stayed with me for a while and had a taste of life at the hub.'

'I wasn't sure what you'd say if I invited myself to stay for a weekend, even.'

'I'd have been delighted.' Then Cassie added something as blunt as her sister's remarks often were, 'You and I are like two distant relatives, not sisters, aren't we? There aren't only fifteen years between us, but there's the way our parents feel about me letting them down and how they've tried to keep us apart.'

'Well, I found out you were raped and how could that have been your fault?'

Cassie sighed. 'Apparently I must have been encouraging it with my wanton behaviour.'

There was dead silence, then Zoe added, 'Did they really tell you that?'

'Yes.'

'Damn them! They're worse than I thought. Have you tried to find it? Sorry to say "it". I don't know whether it was a boy or girl.'

'I had a daughter. And yes, I have tried to find her but nothing came of it. I'm, um, trying again at the moment.'

'Oh, Cassie! I do hope you succeed.'

Zoe suddenly gave her a rib-cracking hug and they stood together for a few moments, rocking slightly. It was comforting. When they pulled apart, Cassie had to wipe her eyes and she didn't mind her sister seeing that, even.

'I'd really like us to get together more often from now on.' Zoe looked at her, head on one side as if asking whether that was acceptable.

Cassie felt her throat fill with more tears and said huskily, 'I'd like that too. I really would.' She fought for self-control but more tears escaped her. 'Sorry.'

'What for? Being human?'

After she'd pulled herself together, Cassie said, 'Let's go and talk money to the sales lady. It's about time I learnt to follow my instincts.'

'Don't you have to sell your present house first?'

'No. Not to buy one at this price, anyway. I've never been extravagant with what I've earned, and I've earned rather good money in the past few years. You wouldn't catch me wasting hundreds of pounds on a pair of shoes as some women do. But I will have to sell my current house to give me enough to invest and live on long term.'

'You could rent it out.'

'I don't want the bother of doing that. I want to shed my worries, not add to them.'

'So you *are* going to retire?'

She tried saying it aloud to make it seem more real, and all of a sudden, it did, it really did. 'Semi-retire, yes. Definitely. I'm quitting the public eye and giving myself time to recover.'

'Was the bombing very bad?'

'I missed the worst because I was knocked unconscious and yet it's still hit me hard, made me feel off balance, afraid. I was so close to being killed, you see, so very close. And there were a lot of photos on the TV so I felt as if I'd been there, even though I'd been knocked unconscious.'

After a pause she asked hesitantly, 'Am I mad to consider buying it, Zoe?'

'Yes. Beautifully mad. And you know what? I'm going to be a bit mad, too. I'm not going to get married to George. I'm not ready to settle down yet and I want to see a bit more of the world. If you buy the house, I warn you, I'll visit you here often.'

'Good.' She took the initiative, linking her arm in Zoe's. 'Let's go and do it.'

What a strange day this was! She couldn't remember being quite so frank with anyone, ever. She really did feel like she had a sister now.

How wonderful was that!

She tried to tell herself to wait before buying a house, but it felt wrong. And why should she?

That was wonderful too. Well, it was worth a try. She really did need a change of scene.

In the sales office the woman looked up with a smile as if ready to talk but she waited for them to speak first.

'I'm interested in the larger of the two show houses,' Cassie said.

'Buying it, you mean?'

'Yes. Buying it.' There. She'd said it aloud.

Zoe grinned and dug an elbow in her side.

'Then do take seats and we'll go through what that involves. I'm Molly Santiago, by the way. My husband and I own this development.'

After that, it all seemed easy, as if it had been meant to happen. Molly was certainly highly efficient, which boded well for the quality of the house, Cassie thought.

When they got back to her home, Cassie turned to her sister and said, 'Thank you.'

'What for?'

'Pushing me out into the real world. I think I've been a bit stuck in the London bubble.'

'Would you say I *pushed* you?'

'Not exactly, perhaps "led me gently outwards" would be more accurate.'

Zoe gave her a wry smile. 'Well, perhaps a bit. I'm rather concerned about you buying a house at the first place you looked, though. It's a really rash move. Still, you've time to get out of it if you change your mind.'

'I'm not worried and I feel sure I won't change my mind.' It was surprising how certain she felt about that. 'It felt good in that house and I can't bear to stay in this one if I give up work.' She gestured behind her to her house, frowning at how cramped it looked after the other one. 'Do you want to come in for a coffee or something?'

'Not this time, but on another occasion I'd love to spend more time with you. I've arranged to meet a friend tonight for dinner. I wasn't planning to catch up with you today, you see, but I'm so glad I did.'

When she'd waved her sister goodbye, Cassie went into her present home and waited for reality to hit her over the head and that inner voice to tell her how stupidly she'd acted today. Only it didn't. Instead she got out the brochures and smiled at the mere sight of the photos of the house like hers. She went through the details again, just in case she'd missed something. But actually, she could remember the layout of the house exactly and mentally walk round it.

It made her feel excited, with something to look forward to.

That night she slept better than she had for ages, only waking up a couple of times, once with a start because a vehicle misfired nearby. It took a while for her heart to stop pounding but she fell asleep again quite quickly.

The second time she had to use the bathroom and then lay smiling into space at the thought of how much more peaceful it would be at her new home.

*   *   *

In the morning she tried to go through reasons why she shouldn't rush into buying the house. She had to be sensible. This would change her whole life.

But she stared at the pictures in the brochure and all she felt was a longing to be there again. Some would say it was sensible to live where you'd be happy, that buying a house was as much an emotional act as a financial one.

Ah, she was making too much of this. If she wanted the house, she could afford to buy it. There was only herself to consider. Simple. No, there was no reason for not carrying through the purchase. She could always sell the house again later if she didn't like living there and wanted to come back to London.

Her many years' lack of interest in spending money extravagantly and her ability to invest it carefully was paying off big time now, though she'd still be careful not to waste money.

What's more, doing this seemed to be helping overcome the impact of the incident. Once she moved, she felt sure she'd settle down again quickly and completely.

And the prospect of not going back to work with Terry made her feel good. She hadn't expected to feel quite as happy about that. He was such a twerp about people, so irritating to deal with, even though he had excellent ideas for features. It was amazing he'd been so successful, given how frequently he rubbed people up the wrong way.

So that was that. She was buying the house. Starting a new life. Moving on.

Once she'd set in motion the rearrangement of her finances to provide the money for the house purchase and hired a firm to oversee the settlement process, Cassie started going through her cupboards. If she was going to move in as soon as feasible, she had a lot to do.

She'd neglected this home recently and allowed clutter from all sorts of work-related travel to pile up. This place would have to be in a much better state to sell quickly. And there wasn't a lot she wanted to keep.

Good. She needed something like this mini-project to occupy her time.

To set the crown on her improved mood, Cassie had a phone call from the agency to say they'd located her daughter and sent her the prepared letter.

They hoped to hear something within a day or two, but sometimes it could take longer for a person to respond, so she wasn't to worry.

She did worry, of course she did. They'd located her daughter as quickly as they'd said they might, but would that daughter refuse to see her again?

No, she had to hold on to the hope that this time there would be a good outcome.

And if there was still no reply, well, it'd end the suspense she'd lived with for so long and she would just have to find a way to get past it.

She so regretted not having had any other children. Too late for that now.

Did all people feel like this as they grew older? Was it normal to have a hunger for family and passing on one's genes? She'd have to research it.

In the meantime she'd got plenty to keep her busy, preparing to move house.

* * *

Hal was packed and expecting to move to Wiltshire in a couple of days when he was asked to follow up a rather important but unexpected outcome to the last project he'd undertaken. It was something he'd be able to fix in a few days but others might take several weeks to get up to date on all the legal details before they could be sure of everything.

He didn't really want to delay his move but agreed to this small project on condition they not only paid him the juicy sum offered, but covered any extra expenses which cancelling his move would cause. He wasn't happy about it, but there you were. He'd always prided himself on doing a good and thorough job, in whatever he undertook. It was called professionalism.

But this was the last time anyone did this to him, however urgent their need, and he made that absolutely clear, too.

He camped out in his flat, which he'd not yet sold fortunately, leaving most of his goods and chattels in the boxes in which they'd already been packed ready to go.

Then he set to work to get the project finished as quickly as possible.

Never had the work seemed so fiddly and boring. He realised how much he'd changed his attitude already, something which had started with the cancer diagnosis. He was still changing, wasn't sure where it would lead, but he hoped to enjoy every precious minute of the new stage of his journey through life.

Chapter Seven

Fran moved in with Keith as soon as Evie had settled down with Cousin Amelia. They were going to get married while her daughter was away, so that they could stop her protesting and make her realise this was for keeps.

She was more nervous than she'd told anyone about this and living permanently with a man again after all the years of managing on her own, and nearly backed out of it at the last minute.

Only, Keith was being so kind and helpful, she couldn't do that to him. And when they turned up at the register office to get married, he had friends waiting to act as witnesses – not his friend Ryan, thank goodness; he knew she didn't get on well with him. And Keith had a lovely meal booked after the ceremony.

It would all work out, she was sure it would. He was so kind to her, loved her so much. *He* wouldn't let her down as James had.

They went back to her house the next day to move the

rest of her personal possessions. He'd insisted she didn't need to take any of her furniture with her but she hadn't sold it as he'd suggested, had put it in storage instead. She'd worked so hard to buy it, had restored old pieces bought cheaply at charity shops. *He* might want all new stuff, but she intended to persuade him to let her bring a few of her own near-antique pieces once they'd settled into marriage.

He had flowers waiting, a meal simmering in the crockpot and candles ready to be lit when she got back from cleaning her house ready to hand it back to the agent to rent out again.

When they went to bed, he was a tender and caring lover.

Things were going to be all right, she thought as she slid happily into sleep. Well, they would be once Evie got used to the new situation. The only thing marring her happiness was being at odds with her daughter.

When she got home from work the following day, she phoned Evie to check that things were going all right at Amelia's and they got chatting. That made her late starting the preparations for the evening meal.

To her surprise, Keith went suddenly grim-faced about that.

'We did agree to eat at six each evening,' he said.

'So we'll eat at seven instead tonight.'

He opened his mouth to say something, then snapped it shut, but he remained rather distant and disapproving all evening, especially as she'd burnt the steaks in her hurry to get them finished.

The following evening he came home earlier than usual and caught her chatting to Evie on the phone again.

'Dammit, does that girl still rule your life? You're married to me now.'

She ended the call and put her phone into her bag, then turned to go into the kitchen.

To her astonishment, he grabbed her by the shoulder and swung her round, throwing her against the wall. For a moment or two she thought he was going to hit her, then he let go, took a deep breath and stepped back.

'I thought you might put us first for a while, Fran. This is supposed to be a honeymoon period, after all.'

She rubbed her shoulder. 'That doesn't give you the right to manhandle me.'

He smiled and grabbed her again, still using his strength against her but this time taking care not to hurt her as he persuaded her to take her clothes off.

She wasn't sure she liked that way of starting to make love, but it seemed to put him in a good mood.

She woke in the middle of the night and found him gone from their bed, heard a low voice from downstairs and realised he was talking on the phone.

It soon became obvious who to – his friend Ryan. The two were as thick as thieves.

She was about to go back to bed when she heard him say, 'I soon persuaded her to pay more attention to me.'

Then a minute later, 'No, of course I didn't hit her. That's no way to make a woman want to be with you. You and I will never agree about that. Anyway, I have to go back to bed now. I need my sleep, got to keep my strength up.'

She crept back into bed and pretended to be asleep.

He didn't try to snuggle up to her, just settled down and

was soon snoring slightly, something that had annoyed her both nights.

It wasn't so much what Keith had said to his best friend, but his tone of voice when he'd spoken about her that had annoyed her.

She yawned and told herself she was imagining things. It had been a rush into marriage, so it was bound to take time for them to settle down together.

But it was a long time before she got to sleep.

A couple of days went past smoothly. She kept her calls to her daughter short and got dinner ready by six, but wasn't feeling comfortable about pandering to him about that. In his own home, he seemed . . . well, different, somehow. More bossy, needing to show his dominance. Which wasn't something she'd expected after the way he'd been before.

'I shall be glad to hand this over to you at the weekend,' she said as she waited for him to offer to help her clear up. He hadn't done that on the previous few evenings.

'What?'

'The cooking. Since I'm cooking during the week, I think you should clear up afterwards. I'll do the same at weekends: you cook and I'll clear up.'

'I have work to do sometimes in the evenings. I've had to put things on hold as we were getting to know one another, but I must start catching up now. And really, Fran, you can take this women's lib business too far. I doubt you'll be volunteering to do the heavy work about the house.'

She stared at him open-mouthed.

He gave her a hard stare back. 'I asked the guys at work before we married and none of them do that sort of thing, whatever they claim in the media. There are still women's roles and men's. It's always been like that and it always will be. This women's lib stuff is just a phase.'

He started to walk out on her as if he'd won the argument, and she felt suddenly furious. She rushed after him and grabbed his shoulder. 'Just a minute.'

He gave her a back swipe with one hand, sending her sprawling.

She lay there in sheer disbelief for a moment or two, then started to get up.

He rushed across to help her. 'I'm sorry, love. So very, very sorry. It's been a hell of a day at work and I let my temper take over. I won't do it again.'

She let him hold her and then watched stony-faced as he did the washing-up.

If he ever laid one finger on her again, she'd walk out. Only, she'd rented out her house, so where would she go?

Had she walked into another abusive relationship?

Surely not?

He continued to be so apologetic that she decided to give him a second chance.

But there would be no third chance if it happened again. She didn't say that, though.

How could things have turned chancy so quickly?

Why had she let him persuade her into such a hasty marriage?

What was her daughter going to say when she found out?

Evie had been settled in at Amelia's for a few days when without warning she received a visit from her mother and Keith one evening.

After a few minutes' chat, she tried to claim homework to do, but they insisted on taking her out for a meal at a local pub. And it was no use trying to pretend she'd eaten because Amelia had left the bag of groceries lying on the kitchen table while she 'just had to' add a few touches to her latest painting.

Amelia refused to come with them, saying she'd grab a sandwich and go on with the painting.

At the pub, they ordered and sat waiting for the food to be served. Evie's mother looked at her uncertainly. 'I've been worrying that you feel pushed away by us sending you to stay with Amelia. We've never been separated for more than a weekend before. Wouldn't you rather come home now, even though there's still a mess on the top floor at Keith's house? There's another bedroom you can use temporarily.'

Panic ran through Evie. Was this the start of him manoeuvring to get her under his roof? She knew her mother cared about her, but she could be so credulous when she was in love, she seemed to stop thinking for herself. Evie had seen this a couple of times before.

She wasn't quite sure how the two of them were getting on. Was it her imagination or was there a little less lovey-dovey between them tonight? Perhaps they'd had a quarrel about her.

She realised her mother was waiting for an answer and shook her head. 'No, thank you, Mum. Though it's, um, kind of you to think of me. I'm finding it easier to study at Amelia's than I would somewhere with builders coming and going.'

'But what about the longer time you have to spend travelling to and from school?'

'I'm using that to keep up with my reading. It's very helpful, actually. No one to interrupt me. And school's nearly over now anyway.'

Keith leant forward and took her hand.

Evie jerked hers away and watched him exchange rueful glances with her mother.

He said in a soppier voice than usual, 'I really do want you to live with us, dear, to make us into a proper family. Though of course, Fran and I are hoping to have children of our own after we're married, as I'm sure you must realise. We don't want to leave that too late.'

Fran relaxed a little at those words. It was so important to her to have another child before it was too late. She smiled at him and he smiled back, but she had to ask her daughter again, 'Are you sure you want to wait till school ends, love?'

Evie nodded vigorously. 'Very sure. I have important exams coming up at the end of next school year and I'd really like to get through them without hassle, so I've started laying the foundations already. Having nowhere quiet to study wouldn't be a good thing at the moment. You know I want to become a doctor, Mum. I always have done. I need to get top results for that.'

Fran sighed, wishing her daughter wasn't so set on this. 'And *you* know I'm worried about how we can afford that.'

'There are student loans and I can get a part-time job. I'll find a way to keep the burden off you, I promise. There are scholarships I can go in for next year as well, which is even more reason to study hard. And of course I'll get jobs in the holidays while I'm at uni.'

Keith turned to Fran and shrugged, as if to say that he'd tried.

Evie repeated, 'I do need my quiet study time at the moment. I'm working on a couple of special projects.'

'I'm really missing you, love.'

'I'm missing you too, Mum. But you and Keith need time on your own to settle into your relationship.'

'I suppose if you're sure you'll be all right with Amelia, we'll leave it at that for now, then. I'll, um, be at Keith's all the time now.'

It was Keith who'd pressed her to make this offer before the date they'd agreed on and convinced her it was the right thing to do. Now she wasn't so sure and was glad her daughter had turned it down. She wanted to be more sure of Keith, didn't want Evie watching them in that sharp, disapproving way she had. Her daughter could be all too perceptive.

Besides, she had to learn to stand up to him. When she was with him, he convinced her of things she didn't agree with when she had time to think them through on her own.

She saw Evie push her plate away, with half the food uneaten and that reminded her of another worry Keith had raised about girls that age. 'Are you trying to lose weight, Evie Milner?'

'No. I don't need to lose weight. I like the size I am. You gave me good genes for weight control, and I'm not stupid enough to want to look like a human stick insect. I'm simply not hungry tonight. And I have an essay to finish so I don't want to be late back.'

Fran gave her a searching look and glanced at Keith, who frowned and shook his head as if not convinced by this.

*　*　*

When they got back to Amelia's, Evie again claimed she had an essay to write and gave her mother a farewell kiss.

'How about giving Keith a hug?'

Evie backed away. 'No. He's your boyfriend not mine.'

'Apologise for that at once. It's very rude.'

'It's all right, darling,' Keith said. 'I know better than to take offence at a teenager's moods.'

Evie backed towards the door, leaving the three of them chatting. But she started to worry because they did this in hushed voices and when even these faded, she looked over the bannister next to her bedroom and saw that they'd closed the door of the front room, closed it without making any noise, something Amelia never did normally.

So they must be plotting something. What?

She went to sit on the bed, really upset by this visit, especially the smug way Keith looked at her before they left, as if he'd won some point or other.

In fact, she was so upset and so worried about what he might do that she lay awake fretting. First thing in the morning she decided to pack an emergency bag in case she had to run away. She'd meant it when she said she'd do that rather than live with him, and each time she saw him only made her more certain it was the safest thing to do.

Was she over-reacting? She shook her head. No. Already it seemed as if he'd brainwashed her mother into being an obedient slave. She was so much quieter since Evie had come to stay with Amelia.

What on earth was going on?

The trouble was, if he and her mother came here with an ultimatum before she'd worked out what to do, he was stronger than her. Would he go as far as forcing her into his car? She wouldn't put it past him.

But he wouldn't be able to keep an eye on her every minute of the day.

Her eyes were accustomed to the semi-darkness now and she stared round. She usually enjoyed thinking 'What if?' and working out how to deal with situations but this time she felt it was a genuine necessity.

There was only one way out from her bedroom once he was downstairs and he could easily block the stairs. She looked across at the window, then got out of bed to go and open it as far as she could and stare down. This was the only other way out.

Oh, she was being stupid and melodramatic.

Then she remembered the smug look on his face as he stared at her, and her mother's unusual quietness. No, she wasn't being stupid.

She had to work out a way to escape from Amelia's house in case he was waiting for her downstairs. It had to happen without them realising what she was doing, too. She was *not* going to move in to his place, not under any circumstances.

Think! she told herself. If they came with an ultimatum about moving in to his place, they'd have to send her upstairs to pack her things. She looked at the door, which already had a bolt on it. Good. Then she went back to look out of the window. Could she climb out and escape across the back fence before he broke the door down?

All this made her feel as if she had suddenly been transported into a children's adventure story, the sort she'd read when much younger. It felt surreal but her instincts said to have an escape route planned, just in case. And her instincts weren't usually wrong. She hadn't been brought up with a protective father, only a rather weak mother.

She'd need a rope, could buy one the very next day from the sports goods shop. She'd tie knots in it and hide it in her wardrobe. Looking round it was easy to work out exactly where she could anchor a loop of rope if she created one at the end of the line, round the foot of the old-fashioned, iron-framed single bed. The rope would have to be long enough to dangle out of the window with knots tied in it at intervals, right down to the ground.

Good thing Amelia didn't go through her things like her mother now did!

The next morning Evie got up early and took her old backpack out from the back of the old-fashioned wardrobe. Thank goodness their cousin had inherited all her grandmother's furniture with this house and never bothered to change most of it!

She put a few sensible changes of underclothing in the backpack, as well as an extra sweater and pair of jeans. As an afterthought, she stuffed in the scruffy dark wig she'd once worn in a school play, then fastened an old anorak, one her mother had told her to throw away, to the backpack strap.

The anorak was a faded red and frayed at one part of the bottom edge. But if anyone were searching for her, it would look very different from her usual outer clothes, especially if she wore the wig.

She sighed as she set the things ready. She really, really hoped this would be unnecessary. The last thing she wanted was an adventure.

Finally, she wrote a note and put it in an envelope addressed to Amelia. She'd post it if she had to flee, to make sure *he* couldn't find it if he went through her things.

She shoved the old backpack and anorak into the wardrobe then tested out grabbing it in a hurry. If she moved her winter shoes, it was the work of seconds to pull it out.

She turned to look at the bedroom door, an old-fashioned one, quite sturdy. She thought it might be best to find an additional way to secure it. That bolt was rather flimsy. When she bought the rope she'd need to find something to wedge the door shut.

Could she persuade Amelia to let her live here permanently? Would her mother even consider that? It might be worth trying because even if nothing ever happened and she didn't need to escape, she'd still have to find some way of refusing to move in with him once the attic conversion was finished. But that wouldn't be for some weeks yet, thank goodness.

She was worried sick about her next year's schooling and the all-important final exams, so she had to sort her life out before then, had to.

She dreamt that night she was struggling against a fast-running river that was trying to wash her away.

Things had started going wrong when her mother got together with Keith. How had he managed to make her mother like him so much she didn't seem like the same person? It was as if he knew exactly what to do to manipulate her.

Well, he isn't going to manipulate me! Evie thought. *Not a chance, you horrible, slimy creature.*

The next day Evie managed to slip out of school during a study period on the excuse of having an upset stomach. She nipped across the playing field to the local shopping centre without being seen. At the post office she withdrew a large amount of money from her savings account, just in case she had to run away.

On her way home from school, she stopped off at the sports store and bought the correct length of rope and then at a hardware store where she found a wooden wedge for holding doors open. Only, she'd be using it to help keep the door shut if someone was trying to break in from outside.

Back at the house, she ran upstairs to put her schoolbag away and hid the things she'd bought at the back of the wardrobe next to the backpack. Summoning up a calm smile and checking it out in the mirror, she then went back down to make herself a cup of tea.

Amelia joined her in the kitchen and began fiddling with a teaspoon before saying thoughtfully, 'You know, I don't really like your stepfather-to-be, even though he says all the right things.'

Evie shrugged.

'And you don't seem to like him, either. You actually shied away when he touched you.'

'Well, all right. I admit I don't like him, but I'm not the one who's going to marry him, am I?'

Amelia seemed to be struggling with herself as if she wanted to say something, then she shook her head and a minute later said, 'Is there something you haven't told me about him? There must be some reason for you to feel such strong antipathy towards him.'

Evie shook her head. She was quite sure if she told Amelia it'd go straight to her mother, who wouldn't hear a word spoken against her darling Keith.

Their cousin gave her a strange look and said only, 'Well, if you ever need to tell me anything, don't hesitate. I'm on your side, not his, believe me. Just because your mother loves him, doesn't mean you have to.'

Evie opened her mouth then closed it again. No, she'd thought and thought about telling someone, but simply didn't dare say anything without proof. 'I won't hesitate. Thanks.'

When she went up to study she used the time to tie the knots in the rope and since Amelia was busy in her studio, she tested out the length. Good. It would work.

To Evie's shock and dismay, the need for her to act happened sooner than she'd expected.

Keith turned up the very next day soon after she got home from school. She was grateful that Amelia was around and though she saw him arrive from her bedroom window, she didn't try to join them.

Eventually Amelia called up the stairs, 'Have you got a minute, love?' and she couldn't delay going down any longer.

She stayed next to Amelia and only nodded at him when he said hello.

'I've got to nip to the shops,' Amelia said. 'Don't go before I get back, Keith. I want to say goodbye to Evie properly.'

Alarm bells rang in Evie's brain. *Don't go. Say goodbye to Evie properly.* What did that mean? He must be planning to take her away.

'Aren't you going to sit down?' He patted the couch beside him.

'I've been sitting all day. I'd prefer to stand.' She made sure there was a stool between them.

'I'll get straight to the point. Your mother is fretting about having sent you away, thinks it's putting a barrier between you and her, so I've come to take you to my house, to stop her fretting. There is a spare bedroom, even if it's small. We'll manage, I'm sure.'

'I don't want to go there. I've got studying to do and that's far easier here.'

'I'm not taking no for an answer, Evie. I intend to keep your mother happy in every way I can. And you, if you'll let me.'

He glanced at her figure as he spoke. Whenever they were alone, he did that without attempting to hide his focus, though he never made the mistake of doing it in front of people. She didn't try to hide her shudder and watched him smile in response to that, as if it pleased him. Ugh! What a total and utter creep he was!

'Go up and pack your things.' He glanced at his wristwatch. 'I'll come up in a few minutes and see if you need any help.'

No way was he coming into her bedroom when they were alone in the house!

How did he think he'd get away with all this? If he laid one fingertip on her, she'd scream the place down. Or was he planning to drug her? She'd read about date-rape drugs and how you didn't remember what had happened to you under their influence.

She couldn't see any other choice now about what to do.

She locked the bedroom door and put the wooden wedge she'd bought under the bottom of it, kicking it tightly into place. Then she got the backpack out of the wardrobe and opened the window fully. It was the work of a minute to put the rope in place and climb up on the bed. She tossed the backpack down onto a soft patch of soil and squeezed out of the window.

Thank goodness she'd always been good at gymnastics and could shin up and down ropes 'like a monkey' as her PE teacher had once said. And thank goodness the sitting room was at the front of the house so *he* wouldn't see her leave.

She was so thankful she'd not waited to work out this escape plan, even though she'd only thought there was an outside chance of it being necessary. It was lucky the weather was fine today, too. That would help.

Chapter Eight

Keith ran lightly up the stairs, smiling. It was all coming together. He knocked on the door of Evie's bedroom, but there was no answer. After knocking a second time in vain, he tried the door. Locked, of course.

'Evie! Open up. This won't solve anything. Think about your mother. She needs you at home. She's worried.'

Again there was no answer.

He tried to bump against the door, but it didn't give and he didn't want to damage anything.

It was a further quarter of an hour before Amelia came back and when he told her what was going on, she rolled her eyes. 'I have a ladder in the shed. I'll go up it and see what she's doing.'

But when they went round the back, they saw the rope before they even got as far as the shed. Cursing, he went to tug on it as it lay flapping against the wall in the light breeze that was blowing.

'Can you climb up the rope?' Amelia asked.

'No, of course I can't. What do you think I am, a monkey? Where's that ladder?'

He pushed her out of the way and climbed it. 'The room's empty.' He tried to open the window wider, but gave up when it stuck. 'I'm not trying to climb through that because I'm no good with heights. I'll have to break the door down, see if she's left a note.'

'You're not breaking my doors down. Let me come up. I'm pretty agile. I bet I can get into the room.'

He watched Amelia carefully manoeuvre her way into the bedroom and disappear from sight. A couple of minutes later she stuck her head back out of the window and gave him a cheerful wave.

'Come back into the house. I've got the bedroom door open.'

Muttering under his breath, he went into the house and walked up the stairs. But though he searched the drawers, there was nothing to tell them where she had gone, let alone a note.

'Damn her!' he exclaimed.

Amelia scowled at him. 'I don't know what you've done to her, but when we get her back, she can come and live with me if she can't stomach living with you.'

'That will be up to her mother.'

'We'll see. You'd better phone Fran and tell her what's happened.'

He did that and then rushed home.

As soon as he left the house, Amelia phoned Fran and again offered to have Evie to live with her till she went to university.

'Keith won't want that. He wants us to be a real family.'

'It isn't just up to him. Evie can't stand him and frankly, I haven't really taken to him, either. He must be very good in bed to have won you over so quickly.'

There was silence at the other end.

'If she doesn't come back, you'll have to call the police.'

'She'll be back.'

Amelia wasn't so sure. 'Well, if you're not going to let her come to me when you get her back, I'm not going to delay my trip to Italy. I don't want to be caught in the middle of a family row. But I think you're wrong, very wrong, to let Keith dictate what you do.'

'He doesn't dictate anything.'

It was no use arguing. Fran was besotted with the fellow. But Amelia couldn't help worrying about Evie. She tried phoning the girl, but there was no answer. She left a message on Evie's phone but wasn't at all sure she would get a response.

Oh hell, she was fed up of being piggy in the middle.

There was only one more day of the school term for her to work. She was going to pack her things and go to Italy as soon as she could arrange it. She planned to drive to the villa she and her friends were going to stay in. It'd be wonderful.

Evie walked quickly down the road, wanting to get as far away as possible before they found she was missing.

When she'd got out of her bedroom, she'd crept across the garden, not sure where she was going to sleep that night only that it wouldn't be in *his* house. What did homeless people do at night?

As she walked, she reviewed her options again, worried at this drastic step. Her friends' parents would just send her back to her mother if she tried to stay with any of them. No, her only chance was the unknown grandmother, who sounded so anxious to catch up with her daughter. Oh dear! She hadn't brought the torn letter with her. Thank goodness she'd memorised the address.

If the stranger didn't want her and tried to send her back to her mother, she'd have to become a street kid till she was a legal adult. That wouldn't be anything but the last choice of utter desperation.

Maybe there was a late bus that would take her closer to the London suburb where this grandmother lived. It was too far to take a taxi, even if one would accept her as a passenger at this late hour. And anyway, she didn't want to use her phone, wasn't sure whether they'd put an app on it to trace where she was. She'd checked, didn't think they had.

She had to believe this Cassie Bennington, who was so eager to contact her daughter that she'd paid a private agency to find her, would also want to meet – and help – her granddaughter.

This stranger was still the only person Evie could think of who might, if she was really lucky, help provide a long-term solution to her problem.

She found a bus that took her to the outskirts of their small town and the only other passengers didn't even glance in her direction. When she got off at the terminal, she saw a post box and hesitated, but decided not to send the letter yet. Give them a day or two to hunt for her, then maybe she'd send the letter to Amelia, who wouldn't give it to him, but to her mother, as she'd asked their cousin to do on the back of the envelope.

She began making her way along the road that led to a village on the outskirts that she'd found on an online map. She hadn't visited it before but knew if she went straight through it, she'd be going in the right direction.

Strange how little she knew even about the area where she'd always lived. If there were any teenage girl who'd had less chance to travel and see other places, it was her, thanks to her neurotic homebody of a mother. The only exceptions had been school camps.

She stuck to the verges, hiding whenever she heard a vehicle approaching. There was hardly any traffic. Anger at being forced to do this fuelled a fast pace of walking at first, then she gradually slowed down.

But the anger wouldn't go away.

Her mother had made another bad choice and must have done the same thing all those years ago as well, because Evie's father had left them, hadn't he, and no one on his side of the family had seemed to know where he could have gone. Or if they did, they weren't telling.

At least her mother hadn't given her up for adoption and she knew that she did love her. In her own way. She was more like a rather dopey older sister than a parent.

Maybe being adopted was what made her mother so clingy to anyone who seemed to offer her love and security. Evie would have to research that properly once she started her medical studies and had access to better libraries as well as better online access to medical sites.

Her grandmother's recent letter had explained why she'd given her baby up, and Evie had felt there was a warmth behind the words. Surely the person who'd written like that could be trusted?

She hoped she wasn't wrong. She was staking her whole future on it.

After just over an hour's walking, she came to a transport café and couldn't resist going inside to buy a hot drink because she'd missed her evening meal. Only, it was full of people, mainly men, who stared at her as if they'd guessed she was running away from home. A horrible old man even came over and asked her if she needed a lift anywhere.

She answered as cheerfully as she could manage. 'No, thanks. I'm being picked up by my dad soon.' She glanced at her watch and forced a smile. 'In a couple of minutes, actually.' She picked up her takeaway coffee and left the warm interior of the café reluctantly.

After waiting behind a clump of bushes to make sure no one had come out to follow her, she finished drinking the coffee and continued along the road.

A little further on she found a country bus shelter near a junction between two roads and put the empty container into the rubbish bin there. A quick glance at the timetable with the tiny torch on her phone showed her that there would be no more buses tonight, so she decided to spend the night there.

She put on her extra sweater under her anorak, jammed her beanie down over her ears, then sat on the ground, leaning into the corner of the bus shelter. As there was glass only in the top half and the bottom panels were solid metal, she was out of sight of passing traffic, and surely no one would be wandering along such a minor country road at this late hour?

She huddled down with the backpack on her lap, trying in vain to keep warm.

What was her mother doing? Were she and Keith making a fuss? Had they reported her going missing to the police?

The night seemed to go on for ever and she felt far colder than she'd expected. She didn't sleep much, just a few uneasy dozes, because she had to get up from time to time. She jogged up and down the road near the shelter to warm herself up, but hated the feeling of being alone in the windy darkness which was full of night noises. She went back to the bus shelter as soon as she was warm because it was slightly less frightening there.

It was a relief when the sky started to lighten. But that also meant the occasional car coming past. According to the timetable the first bus would arrive soon, not going in her direction unfortunately. She needed to get to a railway station and into London.

She couldn't sit here any longer, was shivering with cold, so decided to walk openly along the side of the road again, wearing the dark wig and ratty old red jacket.

Even if they were looking for her, they wouldn't be looking for a scruffy brunette, surely? She was banking on that.

And on the help of a complete stranger.

Chapter Nine

Cassie had done everything she could think of to get ready for her move to Wiltshire and was feeling a bit at a loss as to how to fill her time on the last day. Why did house settlements always take so long, even on a new build? She hadn't liked to put her present house on the market till the final settlement was complete in case something went wrong with her purchase and she had to stay here. It always paid to keep an eye on the worst-case scenario.

She'd been more than ready to go last week, and it was a new home so there was no chain of buyers and sellers to slow things down, so she was probably worrying needlessly. She'd done a lot of worrying since that damned incident. And a lot of nearly jumping out of her skin at sudden loud noises.

Last night she'd again slept badly and this morning she felt weary, unable to settle to anything.

Towards lunchtime she was standing at the bedroom window looking down the street for the postman when her eye was caught by a shabby woman in a red jacket walking along towards her end of the street.

As the figure trudged closer she realised it wasn't a woman but a teenage girl. What's more, the poor thing looked as if she were homeless and had slept rough the night before. Cassie had interviewed a few similar people for one of her TV reports the previous year and recognised the signs.

What was someone like that doing round here at a time of day when the street was usually like the land of the dead? This was a quiet, middle-class suburb and most people were at work or school now.

The girl was looking at house numbers and as she got closer, Cassie could see how utterly exhausted she was by the droop of her body. *Join the club!* she thought, easing the tension from her own shoulders.

A police car came cruising along the street. It passed the girl and stopped. The poor creature glanced back at it then speeded up, looking terrified now, giving out all the wrong signals to the officers inside it.

Cassie's heart went out to her. She wasn't doing any harm, after all. On a sudden impulse she ran down the stairs and opened the front door just as someone opened the passenger door of the police car and started to get out. She called at the top of her voice, 'There you are, Mary! Where on earth have you been? You're late.'

She beckoned vigorously and after an initial surprised look, the girl hurried across to her, hesitating at the door, then glancing back at the police car and going inside.

Cassie closed the door, saying, 'You looked as if you needed rescuing.'

'I did. Thank you.'

They stood staring at one another in the hall for a moment.

'I'm not going to hurt you. Are you in trouble?' she asked gently, not moving, afraid of sending the girl fleeing.

'Are you Cassie Bennington?'

'Yes. How do you know my name?' And it was her real name too, not her working name.

'You wrote to my mother about getting in touch.' The girl took a deep breath and added, 'I think you're my grandmother.'

The phrase seemed to echo round the stairwell. *Grandmother!* Cassie gaped at the stranger. Was this for real?

The girl sagged suddenly against the wall just inside the door. 'Sorry. I'm feeling dizzy. I'll be all right in a minute. *Please* don't call the police.'

But she was far from being all right. Her eyes rolled upwards and she fainted, letting go of the backpack dangling from one hand and crumpling slowly to the floor like a graceful rag doll. Luckily her head came to rest on the backpack, because Cassie had been too frozen with shock for a few seconds to catch her.

She knelt by the girl who was already coming to. The tatty dark wig had slipped, so she pulled it off to reveal red hair exactly the same colour as hers had once been. That shook her.

Is it possible? she thought. *Is it really possible she's telling the truth?*

Then she realised this wasn't the time to worry about anything except that the girl needed help, whoever she was. She seemed to have regained consciousness, thank goodness, so Cassie slipped one arm round her. 'Can you stand up? I want to take you into the front room so that you can sit comfortably.'

The girl jerked, half sat up and looked round with fear written all over her face as if she couldn't at first remember where she was. She sagged in visible relief at the sight of Cassie and clutched her arm. 'Don't let him catch me.'

'No one's going to catch you but we do need to get you off the floor.'

When she had her visitor sitting on the couch with the backpack by her side, she decided the first priority was probably food. 'Haven't you eaten today? Is that why you fainted?'

'I've had nothing since yesterday lunchtime.'

'Mug of tea and a piece of cake suit you – for starters?'

'Yes, please.'

As Cassie turned to go into the kitchen, the girl said, 'Can I come with you? I – I don't feel safe anywhere on my own at the moment, but I do feel safe with you.'

Cassie could relate to that feeling of constant danger looming after her recent clash with terrorists. Oh boy, could she!

'Of course you can.' She walked along the hall into the kitchen, gesturing to one of the two wooden chairs at the tiny table where she ate most of her meals. After putting the kettle on, she took out the cake she'd made yesterday to use up an ageing packet mix, for lack of anything better to occupy her time. How lucky! Cutting a piece, she put it on a plate and shoved it across the table.

'Thank you.' The girl waited, looking at her as if out of politeness.

'Do start. I'm not hungry.'

'Could I have a drink of water first, please? My mouth's a bit dry.'

'Yes, of course.'

Her guest drank the whole glassful, so Cassie refilled it, then made them both mugs of tea.

By that time the piece of cake had vanished. The girl cradled the warm cup in her hands, sipping it slowly and with obvious relish.

'Do you want to tell me why you think I'm your grandmother?' Even to say that aloud made Cassie feel strange.

'You wrote to my mother, Frances Milner.'

'I don't know your mother's name. I hired an agency to trace my birth daughter and they forwarded a letter from me to her. Did she show it to you?'

'Not exactly. I'm sorry but she threw it into the rubbish bin. I fished it out and read it. I saw the bit about you being forced to have her adopted because you were very young, so I could see why you'd done it. Mum's always been angry at you for giving her away, you see.'

She frowned as if thinking back, then nodded. 'That's right. You didn't address her by name in your letter, it was just typed on the envelope.'

Cassie stared at the girl hungrily. This really was her granddaughter. Must be. Her voice came out choked. 'How wonderful!' She wiped away a tear then reached out to clasp the girl's nearest hand. 'I'm so glad you came to me.'

The girl nodded, holding that warm hand tightly. Her eyes were also brimming with unshed tears.

'I'm sorry your mother threw my letter away, though, more sorry than I can say. I tried two years ago to contact her and heard nothing back from her then, either.'

'Well, *I* want to get to know you and . . . I really need help. In fact, I'm desperate.'

Cassie saw more tears gather in the girl's eyes and roll down her cheeks, so sat down next to her and reached out to take her other hand as well. 'Anything I can do to help you, I will, I promise. Let's start with your name. I don't even know that.'

'Evie, short for Evelyn, Milner like my mother's maiden name.'

The girl struggled against tears then started sobbing. 'Sorry. I didn't know where else to turn for help. I've been so frightened.'

Cassie moved her chair so that she could take her granddaughter in her arms. She cuddled her close till the tears slowed down, not speaking, letting her cry her anguish out.

When the girl pulled away, she let her go reluctantly. 'Finish your tea now then we'll go back into the living room and sit more comfortably while you tell me all about it. Most of all I need to know why you need help so desperately. I'll do anything I can to help, I promise. Will that be OK?'

'Very OK.'

When they were comfortably settled, the story came out, with extra details prompted by a question here and there.

Every word Evie spoke rang true. Cassie felt quite sure of that and she'd interviewed enough people over the years to be able to judge it with a fair degree of accuracy. For one thing, the story was awkwardly put together, coming out in short spurts. She didn't expect what she heard about recent events, though, and felt furious that someone like that sleazy fellow could treat a young girl in such a disgusting way and expect to get away with it.

Some men did get away with it, though. She'd done a story on paedophilia and it had upset her big time. It felt even worse when it happened so close to home, to her own newly found granddaughter. She'd felt a sense of anger in the past; now, she felt absolutely sizzling with fury.

The girl finished her tale and fell silent, looking at her. 'You really believe me when I say I'm your granddaughter, don't you? Can I ask why?'

'Give me a minute.' Cassie went to the corner and took out the cardboard box of photo albums she'd packed away so carefully a few days ago, slitting the sealing tape on it without hesitation. She flicked through one particular album till she came to a page with photos of herself as a teenager then handed it to Evie.

The girl stared at it then gaped at her. 'Oh! This could be me! Or a photo of Mum at the same age.' She touched her hair.

Cassie glanced ruefully towards a mirror. 'Red hair is lovely when you're young but unfortunately it seems to go white earlier than other colours of hair. I've recently stopped dyeing mine.'

She saw the moment Evie figured out who she was, or rather who she had been.

'Oooh! You're Cassandra Benn, aren't you? I've seen you on TV.'

'I used to be on TV. Not any longer.'

'I watch your programmes whenever I can. Mum's not much into serious stuff. You've investigated some very interesting topics. Oh!' She snapped her fingers as something else occurred to her. 'Weren't you caught up in that terrorist incident not long ago? At the block of flats?'

'Yes.' Cassie couldn't hold back an involuntary shudder, fighting to keep calm, which took an embarrassingly long time.

Evie watched her knowingly, then asked quietly, 'PTSD?'

'Sort of. And it's also given me a nudge to review what I'm doing with my life. How did you guess? They didn't put how I've been affected on the news, surely? I've tried to stay out of the limelight.'

'I did a project about it once. I want to train as a doctor if possible, you see.'

'Wow. My grandfather was a doctor, your great-great-grandfather, that is.'

'So it runs in the family?'

'Yes, definitely. His father was a doctor, too.'

Evie's face lit up. 'That's cool. And it's the sort of thing I've always wanted to know – what sort of ancestors I come from.'

'Intelligent ones.' Even her parents with their very limited view of the way the world should function ran a small business very successfully. Cassie waited a moment, then heard the girl's stomach rumble. 'Would you like a proper meal now?'

'If you don't mind. I am a bit hungry still.'

'Mind? I'm over the moon that you've come to me.'

'Good. I'm not going back to my mother and *him*, not for anything.'

'I wouldn't ask you to. Not without . . . an intervention of some sort, anyway, one you'd have to agree about. I'm happy to have you stay with me for a while till we've worked out what's the right thing to do.' She'd have to wait till she knew Evie better to organise something permanent, though. She didn't intend to rush into anything. If she got into trouble with the law about that later, so be it. Her granddaughter's safety came first.

'Thank you. I doubt Mum will remember your address from that contact letter. She hardly even glanced at it. I forgot to bring it with me, but I hid it, so I should be safe here.'

'Won't matter if she does remember. I'm moving house tomorrow and I don't know the neighbours except to smile at because I've been away so often. They won't have any idea where I've gone. You can come with me and if it's all right with you, I suggest we take a few days together in my new place to work out what to do before we get back to your mother.'

Evie let out a huge, heartfelt sigh. 'That'd be great. I don't want to upset Mum, but she's too besotted to see any harm in him.'

Cassie was already trying to work out how to find a good lawyer who specialised in this sort of thing because they'd undoubtedly need legal help, but she didn't tell Evie that. She didn't intend to do anything immediately. She was sure a peaceful country setting would help them both work out some reasonable steps to take that would still keep Evie safe.

In the meantime, there was food to be thought of and catering wasn't her strong point. 'I'm sorry, Evie, but apart from the cake, I only have bread, frozen ready meals, tinned stuff or packaged goods. And a few elderly pieces of fruit. I'm not a mad keen cook at the best of times, and I've let supplies run down lately because of being about to move house.'

'Where are you moving to? You didn't say.'

'A leisure village in Wiltshire. Near a lake. It's very peaceful there.'

'Sounds lovely. I enjoy cooking, so I can do some of it, if you like. Mum sometimes lets me into her kitchen. She's a great cook but she always follows recipes to the letter. I like to add new touches sometimes.'

Already her granddaughter's colour had returned and she was looking less stressed, thank goodness. 'Let's go and see what there is to eat.' Cassie opened the freezer and they inspected its meagre contents.

After they'd eaten, she suggested Evie take a shower and have a nap, and her granddaughter hesitated.

'You won't . . . contact the police or anything?'

'I promise I won't contact anyone at all. And as you'll find out, I always keep my word.' She made the crossing the heart sign, then gave her granddaughter another tentative hug.

It was returned, just as quickly and shyly. Cassie had to swallow hard to rid her throat of the lump emotion had dumped there.

'I'd love a shower. I did bring clean underwear.'

Cassie unpacked some sheets for the spare bed she'd bought and gave Evie a nightdress to wear. That brought a smile to her granddaughter's face.

'I can't remember ever wearing a nightie before.'

'I find them comfier and freer than pyjamas.'

Cassie peeped into the bedroom a few minutes later, worried by the silence, and found Evie fast asleep, her face smooth and unlined, her hair so bright red, it was like looking at a younger self.

She tiptoed downstairs and sat for a while staring into space, trying to come to terms with the ramifications of this. She had no doubt now about their being related, none whatsoever, given their close resemblance to one another, not just their hair but the shape of their faces and even the fact that they were neither of them tall.

And oh, to have found a granddaughter was like a dream come true. Would her daughter still refuse to meet her? She was hoping desperately that she wouldn't refuse again. Fran. That was her daughter's name, short for Frances. Nice name, one she might have chosen herself.

Was she doing the right thing in not contacting the mother immediately, though?

Legally, probably not.

Emotionally, she hoped she was, for the girl's sake. It was her best guess and anyway, she'd given her word.

She bounced to her feet and went to stare at herself in the long mirror that was now leaning against the wall, ready to be taken away.

I'm a grandmother! She felt she ought to look different. No, that was silly.

Her phone rang and she rushed into the kitchen to snatch it up before it woke Evie. 'Yes?'

'Zoe here. Just wanted to wish you happy moving day tomorrow.'

Cassie relaxed. 'Thanks. You must come and visit me soon.'

'I'll do that. Stay in touch.'

She almost told her sister about Evie, but something held her back. If their parents found out, she had no doubt they'd report the matter to the police. To them, parents' rights to control their children were immutable. They had few nuances in their view of life.

Another thing occurred to her and she frowned. It'd be better not to use Evie's real name when they got there, in case the police put out a missing person call.

Could they maintain their secrecy? Keep Evie's identity hidden? For a time, surely?

Unable to settle, she fiddled around as the girl continued to sleep. When they said truth could be stranger than fiction, they were right.

Evie didn't wake up till late afternoon. Cassie heard her stirring and put the kettle on, but waited for her to come down in her own time instead of going up to check she was all right.

She turned round when she heard footsteps on the stairs. 'Hello, sleepyhead.'

'Sorry. I didn't sleep well last night. I was cold – and frightened of someone attacking me.'

Cassie ventured another quick hug. 'I'm very glad no one did. Are you hungry again?'

'I am rather. I'm sorry to be such a nuisance.'

'You could never be a nuisance to me. You're more like a dream come true.'

She saw the girl's mouth shape an O of surprise and then a smile creep across her face, making her look suddenly younger and more vulnerable.

'Let's get you some food. I took a few things out of the freezer. I hope you don't have any problem foods. I forgot to ask.'

'No. I can eat anything, and without putting weight on luckily.' She assessed Cassie. 'You're quite slim.'

'I'm lucky, like you. I have a friend who has an underactive thyroid and she puts weight on if she so much as looks at a piece of cake. This stuff about calories in, calories out and how much to eat to lose weight is rubbish. One size doesn't fit all in any aspect of human life, I've found. I was meaning to do an investigation into it when—' She shrugged and finished, 'When the bomb went off.'

'It tore your life apart, didn't it? Just as Keith has torn mine.'

'Yes. Since then I've been regrouping but I may get to do that article one day. I've come to believe that people are being conned about many aspects of life, and made to feel guilty for things that aren't their fault.'

After clearing her plate and topping up with some cheese and biscuits, Evie sat back, prepared once again to chat. 'What time do we leave in the morning?'

'The movers are coming at seven. I think it'd be better if they didn't see your hair. Could you wear that wig, do you think, and maybe sit outside on the back patio while they take everything out to the removal van?'

'Yes, of course. I'll do whatever you think best.'

'When we get to Wiltshire, you won't be able to keep wearing the wig, but I wonder if we should use another name for you, just for the time being? What do you think?'

'Good idea. It felt like being in an adventure story running away from home yesterday and it still feels like one. They're not as much fun as they sound in books, though! I didn't mind climbing out of the window and shinning down a rope but I got very cold at night. And afraid.'

'What made you prepare like that?'

'I don't know. Everything just felt wrong about him and I grew frightened. It felt as if he were a predator moving in for the kill. I just wish I'd thought of food, though.' After a pause, she added, 'Everything still feels a bit unreal, even now I'm with you.'

She stopped talking, frowning, reliving her memories of escaping, if Cassie guessed right.

She gave her a little time then changed the subject. 'Shall I think of a new name or will you?'

'We-ell, I rather like the name Lacey. How about we use that?'

'Fine by me. I like it too. Don't forget to answer to it when other people are around.'

'I won't.'

No, anyone who prepared a successful escape rope in advance could be trusted to remember details, Cassie was sure. She saw Evie studying her, head on one side, and smiled at her. 'Something wrong?'

'No. It's just, you don't seem as old as I'd expected. My mum's adoptive parents used to be a bit old-fashioned in their ways. Mind you, now I come to think of it, they were older than you by about twenty years if you were only fifteen when you had my mother.'

'Were older?'

'They were killed in a car crash.'

'Oh. I'm sorry.'

'Yes, I was too. They were really nice.'

'Well, thank you for the compliment. I don't feel old in my head and it's nice to know I'm wearing well on the outside too.' *Bless!* she thought. Her granddaughter was still a child in some ways and anyone past forty no doubt seemed old to a teenager.

Within a couple of hours, Evie-Lacey was yawning again.

'Why don't you go to bed?' Cassie suggested. 'We'll have to be up very early tomorrow.'

'Would you mind?'

'Of course not.'

Evie stopped at the door to say, 'Thank you, Grandma.'

'You're welcome, darling.'

'Or should I call you Gran?'

'Mmm. Yes. I think I'd prefer that.'

'I do too. Gran it is.'

That brought happy tears to Cassie's eyes as she checked that everything was ready for the move, before following her granddaughter's example and going to bed early.

What an eventful day it had been! Who'd have thought life could change so drastically in such a short time? Surely this relationship would now form part of her new life? Or was she being too optimistic? Would her daughter be cruel enough to keep them apart?

Perhaps one day she'd even get to meet Fran. Or would she continue refusing to see her birth mother, even after they'd sorted out Evie's problems?

It hurt to be rejected. Twice it had happened now, so it wasn't just a whim on her daughter's part.

Please let that change now! she prayed desperately as she slid into sleep. *Oh, please!*

Chapter Ten

Hal was relieved when he finished the extra project, which had taken longer than he'd expected. He was lucky enough to catch the removal company with a day when they had a crew and vehicle free, so within twenty-four hours he had everything ready once again for the move. Well, he'd never unpacked most of his stuff.

He went to bed on the final night in his flat feeling happier and more relaxed than he had for a good long while. It was over. He was free to choose his own path from now on.

The following morning, the movers were on time and packed everything into their truck with speed and efficiency. He watched them drive away, did a final check that everything was clean and tidy and locked up the flat one final time.

He set off at once for Wiltshire, not looking back. He wouldn't miss the isolation of living in a block of flats where no one did more than nod at a neighbour in passing and silence was more common than the faint daily noise of fellow humans nearby.

He soon overtook the movers' vehicle. Good. He'd be able to open up the house and have everything ready to let them in. To crown it all, a lovely day was forecast, sunny but not too warm, the weather report had said.

'Perfect!' he said aloud, not switching on the radio because he was enjoying the feeling of driving quietly into the future. He absolutely craved peace and quiet these days.

An hour and a half later, as he was leaving the M4, the car engine misfired.

'No! Don't do that!' he begged it aloud. To his relief the engine picked up and he continued.

But the car misfired again just after he'd passed through Marlbury and was on a narrow stretch of country road with no places to stop. This time it continued to misfire and when the car began to lose speed and move jerkily, he looked ahead for somewhere to pull off the road. To his dismay, before he could find a suitable place, the engine cut out altogether.

The best he could do was pull over to the very edge of the road before he totally lost momentum. Unfortunately his car was still blocking most of one lane and to make matters worse, he'd been forced to stop just after a bend. He sat there for a moment or two, feeling a strong sense of aggrieved disbelief. It wasn't an old car, it had low mileage and he had it serviced regularly. What the hell could have gone wrong?

He had no idea, of course. He'd never been into cars and because he lived in a fairly central part of London, he'd used public transport much of the time.

He phoned his breakdown service but they said it'd be about an hour before they could get someone out to him.

Sighing, he put his phone away and decided to get out and stretch his legs by moving up and down by the roadside. There was just enough room for one person to walk along the overgrown verge.

He was closing the car door when a yellow van whizzed round the bend, moving far more quickly than was safe. In fact, it had crossed the middle line into his lane as it hit the bend and passed so close it caught him on the shoulder, sending him sprawling forward onto the road.

He lay there, squinting at the registration plate.

The driver must have seen him fall but didn't stop. He murmured the registration to himself as he lay there, feeling dazed and trying to pull himself together. He was shocked at how suddenly it had happened.

He was vaguely aware of another car coming to a halt in front of his. A woman's voice, low and pleasant in tone, brought him back to the situation.

'Are you hurt?'

He managed to find some words. 'Only bruised, I think. Can you write this down? It's the registration number of the van which hit me.'

'Tell me. I'll remember it.'

She repeated it after him then said, 'We have to get you off the road before another lunatic whizzes round that bend. My granddaughter's keeping watch.'

He tried to get up and found it difficult. She tried to support him, but had difficulty because she was much smaller than him. A teenage girl ran to join them and together the two helped him round to the verge side of his car just before another car whizzed by, luckily on the right side of the road this time.

He leant against his vehicle, feeling shaky, but remembered enough to say, 'Please – can you write that number down?'

She fished in her car and wrote it down, reading it to him and getting his approval of it. 'What exactly happened?'

'My car's engine cut out so I let it roll to the side of the road and had just got out when a speeding van came round the bend in the middle of the road. Yellow, it was, with some sort of logo on the side. In red.'

She wrote on her pad again.

'Something, maybe the wing mirror, clipped my shoulder, sending me flying. The van didn't stop.'

As she scribbled again, he tried to straighten his body and winced. 'Oh hell, it hurts to move my right shoulder.'

'But you can move it?' the girl asked.

'Yes.'

'Then it's probably not broken or dislocated.'

He stared at her, surprised that a teenager would venture to comment so confidently.

She must have realised what he was thinking. 'I did a first-aid course, an advanced one. We should get you to the nearest A&E and let them check you properly, though.'

The woman nodded agreement. 'I'm Cassie, by the way, and this is . . . Lacey.'

'Hal Kennedy.'

She studied him. 'You look pale. I'll call an ambulance.'

'No, wait. I'm already feeling better. And Lacey's right. I can move my shoulder.' He eased it cautiously forward and backward, but though it hurt, it wasn't a major pain and he was quite sure nothing was broken. Relieved, he leant back against the car again, because that felt more comfortable.

Another car drove past and pulled up just beside them. A man stuck his head out of the window.

'Anything wrong?'

So Hal explained what had happened again.

'Have you called for help?'

'I called the breakdown service before I got out of the car. They're on their way but they said it'd take an hour or so. I think my shoulder is only bruised.'

'Well, if I can't do anything, I'll be on my way. Good luck!'

Hal continued to lean against the car, feeling like an idiot. The movers would get to his new house and find no one to let them in. And they wouldn't be likely to use this narrow lane as a shortcut, as he had, because of the size of their vehicle, so he wouldn't be able to flag them down. He'd have to phone Molly Santiago and see if she had a key to his house, and then heaven knew where they'd dump his things.

'I'm going to be late,' he muttered.

'Where were you going?' Cassie asked.

'Penny Lake Leisure Village. It's not far away. Do you know it?' The woman looked vaguely familiar, now he came to think of it, but he couldn't work out where he'd seen her before.

She let out a huff of laughter. 'That's where we're going.'

'Really? Then perhaps you could give me a lift? I have to open my new house and let the removal crew in.'

'What about your car?'

'I'll put my key under the passenger seat and phone the breakdown people, ask them to tow it to the nearest garage and let me know where that is. After all, no one can drive off in it if the motor won't start.'

'If you give me the key, I'll put it in place for you,' the girl said.

'Thanks. I appreciate that.'

The woman opened her rear car door and rearranged some bags. 'You'd better get in, Hal. You can phone the breakdown service again while we drive.'

She was about to close the car door on him when he suddenly remembered something. 'Oh! I've just remembered. I have one of those gadgets to warn people of a hazard ahead in the boot. Can you wait until I've put it near the bend on the other side? I don't want someone smashing into my car.'

'I can do that for you,' Cassie said. 'I know how to set one up.'

Before he could say anything, she'd opened his boot, found the triangle and got it to flash. She placed it round the bend, out of sight from here but giving more warning. As she went back to close the boot, she asked, 'Do you need anything else from your car, Hal? We can't squash much in, I'm afraid.'

'Could we take that small suitcase and the bag of frozen food from the boot? I don't want to leave that out for too long and the suitcase has important documents in it.'

She went to rummage and held them up. 'These?'

'Yes.'

'I'll have to put them in the back with you. Our boot is full up.' She had to put the suitcase on his knee and the food bag on top of that.

By the time he'd phoned up and told a disapproving despatcher what he'd done with the key, they'd reached a wider road.

He switched off the phone. 'The breakdown service will bring the car to my home if it's a simple fix, since it's not far away. I've got my fingers and toes crossed.'

'Good. And we've only five minutes to go now, according to my satnav. It's a real coincidence that we're moving into that leisure village too. Oh, look. We're nearly there.'

They all stared at the hotel as they turned off the road and drove slowly past it, then moved away from the car park and across to the group of houses.

'This development isn't really big enough to be called a village, is it?' Cassie said as she slowed down. 'Which house is yours?'

'That one at the far right.'

'Ah. We're going to be next-door neighbours, it seems.'

'Amazing coincidence you stopping for me, isn't it?'

'Coincidences happen more often than you'd think.'

Once she'd stopped outside his house, the girl came to take Hal's bag of food out of the car and he turned to her grandmother. 'Thanks for your help, Cassie. I owe you a drink for that.'

He tried to pick up his small case, but winced as the weight tugged at his sore shoulder and let the case drop to the ground again.

As he was reaching for it with his other hand, Cassie said, 'I'll get that.' She picked it up and walked him to the front door.

'I really am grateful to you both.'

'Our pleasure. If you open the door, we'll bring your things in.'

When they'd deposited the food on a kitchen surface, Cassie looked round. 'Yours is completely different in configuration to mine.'

'You must come round for a thank you drink one evening.'

'Happy to.' She switched on his new fridge and freezer, then they left.

He waited at the door to wave goodbye, then closed it on the world, leaning against it, feeling as if he were watching an out of focus film. He had to admit to himself that his head was aching and he still felt rather shaken. But as the girl had said, he could still use that shoulder, so surely it must only be badly bruised?

He really didn't want to visit a hospital, not now with the movers due, and not ever again, if he could help it. Which was silly when the medical system had helped him beat cancer, but there you were. That was how he felt.

He moved around the kitchen area, aching for a cup of strong tea, but of course, although the cooktop was fitted and came on when he tried turning a knob, he had no utensils to boil water or brew tea in.

Still, the movers mustn't be far away now. As soon as they arrived, he'd retrieve a kettle or saucepan and boil up some water.

He went to sit on the stairs, *faute de mieux*. At least he had arrived at his permanent home now, and if it wasn't quite the triumphal taking possession he'd imagined, well, he was here. That was the important thing.

Cassie moved her car to the drive of her own house next door and sat for a moment, smiling at it. She had the same feeling of coming home that she'd had on her first visit. Strange how quickly she'd fallen for this place.

She'd remembered it so clearly that she hadn't come back for a second visit, too afraid of someone from the press following her here. With a bit of luck she was safe from them now, and since she wasn't hot news any longer, she doubted they'd go to any great lengths to trace her.

She was getting over her desire to stay hidden in a bunker now, thank goodness. She turned as her granddaughter spoke.

'They're lovely looking houses. The inside of Hal's place was all big spaces. Is yours the same? Mum and I have only ever lived in small houses or flats.'

'Let's go inside and walk round mine, then you can see for yourself. Though it'd make sense to carry a few things in as we go. It's a wonder we fitted Hal into the back of our car, we'd stuffed so many stray bits and pieces into it.'

Evie followed her round, wide-eyed, murmuring, 'Wow!' in a whisper as she walked through the downstairs spaces, then up to the bedrooms.

'This front one is mine,' Cassie said. 'You can have any of the others you like.'

Evie chose the larger of the two that looked towards the back. 'If I lean out of the window, I can just catch a glimpse of the lake. And I have my own en suite bathroom. My very own. I can't believe that.'

'Believe it. But keep it clean, please.'

'I'm very clean and tidy in my ways. I've had to be, because Mum isn't and I hate having to hunt for my school things amongst the piles of dirty washing she leaves for ages. I can do my own washing, don't worry. I'll try not to cause you extra work.'

'Good. But sometimes extra work is worth it.' They exchanged smiles, then she said, 'Now, let's make a cup of coffee or tea. I don't think Hal will have anything to make a drink with, so I think we'd better take him a cup, too.'

But just as they were about to do that, their removal truck arrived and Cassie said sharply, 'Put that wig on, quick! And don't start chatting to them. Stay out of their way as much as possible.'

'Play the moody teenager?' Evie asked with a smile. 'I don't normally do that but I've seen others do it.'

'Perfect.'

Afterwards Cassie was kept busy deciding what went into each room and she noted with approval that Evie took a chair outside and sat there with a book.

She'd have to buy some more furniture quite quickly. Thank goodness she had a studio couch for Evie to use as a bed.

Hal watched enviously as a removal truck arrived next door. Then, to his surprise, a van with the logo of the emergency service on it pulled up outside his house, towing his car. Oh, thank goodness! It must have been something simple that went wrong.

He went out eagerly to find a cheerful woman on her way to his door.

'Mr Kennedy?'

'Yes.'

'Do you have some ID?'

He got out his wallet and showed her his driving licence and she noted the number of it because it didn't have this address on it.

'It was only a blocked fuel line and a loose connection, so I fixed them and brought your car back here. You can move it onto your drive yourself after I've gone.'

'Thanks. I'm so grateful.'

'Well, the despatcher said you were moving into a new home, and I know what that's like. Here you are.' She held out his car key. 'Can you sign this, please?'

He read the form then signed it willingly, writing 'Excellent service' in the comments section.

After the van had pulled away, he got into his car and moved it. Before he even reached his half-open front door, he was further cheered by the sight of a second removal truck arriving in the narrow little street, so turned to wait. It could only be for him.

'Yesss!' he murmured happily.

It edged skilfully backwards into his short drive, stopping in exactly the best position for unloading.

He saw Cassie at her kitchen window and gave her a thumbs up as he went to greet the removal crew.

Within half an hour, he'd retrieved his kettle, found some mugs and made them all cups of tea. He didn't keep coffee, the smell of which seemed horribly strong since his various hospital treatments and made him feel slightly nauseous.

In just under two hours, the crew had unloaded everything and driven their empty vehicle away. He looked round at the chaos and felt happiness bubble up inside him, for all that his shoulder was still aching.

He really was home now and it didn't matter if he had to take the unpacking slowly. All he needed was somewhere to sleep, sit and eat. The rest could be tackled as and when he felt up to it.

He walked to the doors leading out onto the back patio. He'd have to buy some better outdoor furniture than the few shabby pieces he already had. It'd be a great place to sit and chat to friends, or just read a book.

He hoped to spend his final years here. Life was good.

Keith had worried about leaving Fran on her own but he had an important meeting that he couldn't afford to miss.

When he got home from work, his new wife greeted him with tears in her eyes. She hardly gave him time to close the front door before saying in a wobbly voice, 'There's still no sign of Evie and last night was the second without her. Keith, we'll *have* to go to the police now. She may have been murdered!'

He put his briefcase down, hiding his annoyance about that stupid girl. 'Not her. She'll have found someone to stay with, I'm sure. She's a sly one, I'm afraid, darling. You have to face facts about her. We'll only be pandering to her prima donna antics if we go to the police. And she's bound to tell them lies about why she ran away. That's what teenagers do. Then there will be a huge fuss. You don't want them taking her into care, surely?'

'Take her away from me! Surely they wouldn't do that?'

He put his arms round her and kissed her cheek then her lips, something that usually won her over, but though she clung to him, it only calmed her slightly today. He'd never met such a needy female. Or one with such a pretty young daughter. He'd fallen lucky there. If he played his cards right, he'd be getting two for the price of one.

Pity Fran didn't have much money to contribute to the family purse now they were married, but there you were. He'd make sure she continued working and as for having other children, forget it. Babies and small brats were a pain to live with as he had found out the first time round. He'd had the operation years ago to ensure he couldn't have any more.

With a sigh, Fran pushed away from him. 'Well, Amelia will still be there. She's not going to Italy till tomorrow. I'll just give her a quick ring and see if she's heard from Evie.'

He bit back a sharp response as the two women chatted on and on, then he led the way upstairs and made sure Fran had something else to occupy her mind and body before she cooked his tea.

Females! What a pity one couldn't live without them. And he had an especially strong need for what only they could give him.

Fran pretended to be asleep, angry with herself for giving way to his skilful lovemaking yet again.

She couldn't get it out of her mind that Amelia was worried about Evie too, had said in no uncertain terms that she should have gone to the police. But her cousin wouldn't agree to stay in England, was still planning to leave soon. She'd said Fran must sort things out herself.

Fran sighed. She had a key to Amelia's house, after all, so she could check whether Evie came back and took refuge there. But she wished her cousin was going to stay around, just in case Evie needed her.

Somehow Fran didn't dare to go to the police, not now. Keith had been very emphatic about that, had shouted at her when she persisted. Somehow she felt a girl as clever as her daughter would keep herself safe. She had to believe that.

Why had Keith tried to force Evie to come and live with them when she was so set against it? She didn't think

Evie had agreed, but he'd claimed she had because he'd persuaded her to think of her mother.

Why had Evie run away when he'd sent her upstairs to pack, then?

Anyway, Amelia had told a different story, saying Evie had begged to be allowed to stay with her the previous evening. Fran had begun to wonder why the girl was so frightened of him.

If her daughter had persisted in objecting to moving in here, she'd have let her stay with Amelia for that crucial final year at school, even though it wasn't her favourite option.

Fran chewed one of her nails, then stopped herself because she'd promised him to give up nail biting. And she'd managed it. Well, most of the time.

Why, oh why, had she rushed into marriage with Keith? He wasn't always as nice when they were in his house. What if her marriage alienated her from her daughter permanently? She couldn't bear the thought of that.

Lying in the darkness, listening to Keith's steady breathing, Fran admitted to herself that she was – not exactly frightened, but definitely nervous of upsetting him. He'd proved what anger could drive him to do when he hit her.

She ought not to have married him till she knew him a lot better. He might be OK, but . . . he might not.

Only, her house was now rented out and her furniture in storage. If she decided to leave him, it'd be hard to arrange somewhere else to go without him finding out. And, oh hell, what a fool she'd look if she left him after such a short time married!

It occurred to her that he had poked into every aspect of her life and she was only just realising how much he had started controlling her. The only thing she'd held out about was them keeping their bank accounts separate. She wasn't sure yet that she wanted to have a joint account. It was early days and they were both a bit on edge. He could be so nice at times, charming and caring.

But he had hit her. He might think she'd put up with that occasionally, but he was wrong. He'd better not do it again, even. It was her sticking point. She'd seen a TV programme about how battered women got sucked in and persuaded it was their fault for provoking their partner, and had never forgotten its lesson.

She wasn't going down that track. Another show of violence would prove that he wasn't trustworthy and she'd end their relationship, however humiliating that was.

She snuggled down, feeling she'd taken one good decision, at least: separate bank accounts was something she'd not give way on.

The rest had been put on a rather wobbly footing.

If she only knew for certain that Evie was safe, she'd be able to concentrate better on sorting out her own situation.

Chapter Eleven

Cassie strolled up to the hotel, which took only a couple of minutes, and found out that the snack bar did takeaways, so she took a menu home and rang through an order for the two meals they'd chosen.

She and Evie walked up to collect them but she left her granddaughter outside, because that really was a dreadful wig, not only an obvious fake but well past its use-by date.

They walked back quickly and sat in the middle of partially organised chaos, eating. For the first time in ages Cassie was truly hungry and cleared her plate.

Evie pushed her empty plate away with a happy sigh. 'It's lovely here. Could we go for a walk round the lake after we've cleared up, do you think?'

'Why not? As long as you put that wig on again. In fact, let's go now before it gets dark. We can clear up the kitchen later.'

Evie did as she'd been asked and tugged on the stupid wig, rolling her eyes at her reflection in the mirror.

They stopped at the other side of the lake to look across at the group of new houses.

'Do you have any plans yet for what to do about me, Gran?' Evie asked suddenly.

'Not really. I'll have to contact a lawyer before we make any important decisions. I'd better do that as soon as possible, tomorrow if I can find one. I don't want to be charged by the police with abducting you.'

Evie stared at her in dismay. 'I never thought of that! I don't want to get you in trouble, Gran.'

'I wouldn't be helping you if I didn't want to do it, or if I felt it was morally wrong.' She put her arm round the girl's shoulders and gave her a hug. 'Truly. You really are the best thing that's happened to me for years.'

Evie nestled against her. 'Well, that's the nicest thing anyone's said to me in a long time. *He* does nothing but complain about me. It's as if he's trying to come between me and Mum.' After a slight pause, she added in a near whisper, 'I, um, feel the same about you, too, Gran.'

That brought a lump into Cassie's throat.

They finished their walk and as they passed Hal's house, he came to the front door. 'I'm just about to take a break. Do you fancy a cup of tea? I don't have any coffee, I'm afraid.'

'I'd love a cup of tea,' Cassie said at once and they joined him inside.

'Did you enjoy your walk?'

'Loved it.'

'I saw you go past and would have liked to join you, but my shoulder is aching and walking jolts it too much, so I've postponed that pleasure. Look, I feel like celebrating moving into my new home. How about a glass of wine instead of the tea, Cassie? We can drink to your new home as well.'

'Sounds perfect.'

'And I can offer a choice of tea, drinking chocolate or a can of ginger beer for you, Lacey.'

It took a few seconds for Evie to remember her new name and realise he was addressing her. 'Ginger beer would be lovely, thank you, Mr Kennedy.' When he turned to get it for her, she shot a guilty glance for her lapse at her grandmother.

Cassie grinned and winked at her, and she relaxed again.

They sat in Hal's lounge for nearly an hour chatting and toasting their new homes, then the two women headed next door.

Cassie yawned. 'Another early night for us both, I think.'

When they got inside, Evie flung her arms round her grandmother, surprising her. 'What a lovely day it's been! Thank you so much for saving me.'

'My pleasure. Will you be all right on that old couch? We'll go and buy you a proper bed tomorrow.'

'I could sleep on the floor, I'm so tired.'

Cassie didn't spoil the moment by reminding her that staying here was only a temporary fix for her problems. She wished it wasn't, wished Evie could stay with her permanently.

But the law might decree otherwise.

When her granddaughter had gone to bed, she got out her phone and called a friend she hadn't been in contact with for a while, apologising for that.

'I heard about the terrorist incident and called you, but when you didn't answer your phone, I guessed you were being hounded by the press. Are you all right, Cassie?'

'Yes.'

'Really?'

'Well, I'm getting there, Judy, because something good has happened to balance the scales.' She knew Judy well enough to explain about her granddaughter turning up and her need for a lawyer to help her deal with this. 'Don't you have a relative who is a lawyer?'

Her friend laughed. 'Yes. And what's more, my cousin specialises in family law. I'll give Thomas a ring tonight and tell him he absolutely must fit you in tomorrow.'

'Thanks. I'm truly grateful.'

'The trouble is, he's moved down to Chichester. Will you be able to get there?'

'Actually, that's better for me. I've just moved to a new house near Swindon, so I'm not too far away. I shall enjoy a drive there much more than a train ride into London.' She'd decided to say 'near Swindon' instead of 'near Marlbury' and not mention the words 'leisure village' to hide her actual location.

'I'll ring him at home tonight, then, and you can phone him at work just after nine. Here's his number.'

'Thanks, Judy. I'm so grateful.'

When she'd put the phone down, Cassie smiled, feeling as if fate were on their side. She could drive to Chichester easily and it would be safer for both of them not to have to travel on public transport as they would in London.

But the smile soon faded because she doubted from what Evie had told her that things would go easily with the girl's mother and her husband-to-be. And she knew from checking online that a mother's rights usually trumped a grandmother's when it came to making arrangements for the care of children.

Well, it did unless you could prove there was a problem such as Evie had described, which she doubted would be possible in this case. She believed what her granddaughter had told her about that horrible man, oh yes, because the way Evie said he was acting fitted the type. Only, he'd been clever and had managed not to alert anyone else so far to what he was really after, damn him to high hell!

She didn't think she could bear to send Evie back into the lion's den – but would she have any choice?

She'd have to wait and see what the lawyer said.

But if necessary, as a final resort she'd break the law. She even knew one or two people who would shelter the girl temporarily, people she trusted who hated perverts just as much as she did. She wasn't letting Evie join the homeless and have to sleep rough regularly.

Her granddaughter's safety came before anything else.

Evie proved to be an earlier riser than Cassie had expected for a teenager and was up and showered by 8 a.m., hungry and ready to continue helping her sort out the house.

If only that was all they needed to do today, what fun they could have had going shopping together.

After breakfast Cassie couldn't put it off any longer. 'Don't get up from the table yet. I have something to tell you.' She explained about phoning her friend and finding out about her lawyer cousin.

She hated to see the happiness vanish from her granddaughter's face. 'I'm sorry, love, but we have to find out where we stand. I'd prefer not to flout the law. That wouldn't help our case at all.'

'Our case?'

'For you to stay with me. If you want to, that is?'

'You really mean that, don't you?'

'Oh, darling, of course I do!'

'I can't think of anything I'd like more, but they'll make me go back to Mum, I know they will. I'll run away if they do and live rough if necessary. I love her but I'm *not* living with *him*.'

'Let's find out first where we stand before we panic, shall we? Then we'll make plans together – for all eventualities. If the worst comes to the worst, I can help you do better than live on the streets, believe me.'

She rang Thomas Wutherington (why did lawyers so often have weird names?) just after nine o'clock and was put straight through to him by his secretary when she gave her name.

'Judy rang me at home last night, Ms Bennington.'

'Did she explain my problem?'

'Yes. Well, she gave me a broad-brush outline anyway. Why don't you come in and see me today? I have an hour free at eleven. Can you and the girl get here by then?'

'Yes, definitely.'

He checked that she knew his address and told her where best to park, which was very thoughtful of him, before he rang off.

Evie looked at her, just looked, but it hurt to see the fear on that young face.

'We need to leave immediately. And you'd better wear the wig till we're away from here, then you can take it off. We don't want him to see you looking like that. I'm so sorry to have to put you through this, love. And I can lend you a smarter jacket than that red thing.'

'You don't need to keep apologising, Gran. I don't want you to be arrested.' She accepted the jacket, but clearly didn't care about clothes at the moment.

'You can tell the lawyer that you won't live with Keith, but remember, it makes a better impression to speak your piece calmly and not sound hysterical. And always tell the truth. This is not about pleasing me but getting the best outcome for you and what you really, really want.'

Evie frowned, then nodded slowly as she thought about that. 'You're right. I'll do my best to stay calm. I'm pretty good at it usually. I've had to be, because Mum can get a bit, um, excitable.'

Remarks like that made Cassie wonder what sort of woman her daughter had grown into, let alone what sort of mother she'd been. Evie spoke of her fondly, but sometimes she sounded to have played a more adult role than Fran had.

They were on the road within ten minutes. Thank heaven for satnavs.

Thomas Wutherington was about forty, a big teddy bear of a man, which seemed appropriate for someone specialising in family law. His expression however was distinctly shrewd and Cassie liked that. She wanted the best advice she could get, the very best, not waffling and kindness.

She outlined the situation, then he turned to Evie and offered to speak to her privately if she preferred, but she shook her head.

'I can say anything I need to in front of my grandmother. She's not forcing me to do anything; it's my mother who's trying to do that.'

He then asked a few more detailed questions about her wishes, after which he sat frowning for a while before speaking to Cassie. 'If you were the acknowledged grandmother, Ms Bennington, it'd be a lot easier, because she's nearly sixteen and that's usually the age where a child is considered old enough to decide where to live. But in your case you'd never met Evie until she turned up on your doorstep – what? – two or three days ago? So if the mother creates a fuss about parental responsibility, I doubt it'll be straightforward.'

'What should we do, then?'

'First, I'd advise you to take a DNA test, so that you can prove there's a genuine relationship. Ask them to send a copy directly to me. Their clerk will bring it round, it's so close to here and my clients use their services regularly. That way, there will be no doubt that I got the real results if we have to go to court. Secondly you *ought* to return Evie to her mother's care in the interim.'

Evie leant forward. 'I'll run away if anyone tries to force me to go back, Mr Wutherington. It's not Mum so much as *him*. I'd go back to Mum but I daren't live with him.'

'You may just be imagining this problem, you know.'

She immediately shook her head. 'No. I'm not, Mr Wutherington.' Her shudder spoke volumes, as had her quiet sureness when she answered his questions.

Cassie had watched her intently all the time, ready to step in if necessary. But she was pleased that the girl was continuing to speak calmly and sound convincing. The truth often was its own best advocate when people stayed reasonable, she'd found.

He'd been studying her granddaughter openly. 'I must admit, you seem very level-headed to me, Evie, and mature for your age. Of course, if you've been classified as "gifted" educationally, as you say, that might make a difference to the decision. But unfortunately, nothing can hide the fact that you don't know this woman properly yet, even if she is your grandmother.'

'I'm getting to know and love her, and I trust her absolutely. She's straightforward, tells me the truth and doesn't treat me like an idiot, as *he* does. It's my mother who is the idiot, not me. She's been a bit like this before with a couple of men, but never as bad. She does whatever Keith tells her and seems to believe every word he says. She really needs a husband, but not one like him.'

The lawyer's look was meant to be neutral, Cassie thought, but if you asked her, a couple of times his expression had betrayed a flicker of sympathy. She glanced surreptitiously at a big clock on the wall and tried to move the discussion on, knowing they only had an hour. 'So what else do we need to do, Mr Wutherington, besides getting our DNA tested?'

'I think you should make every effort to stay out of the courts and legal system, and try to settle this informally, which will mean contacting them, preferably voluntarily. I can help you with that, if you wish. I'm not at all sure you'd get a Special Guardianship Order if you went via the courts, you see. Hmm. There's another thing that may help: I gather you want to go to university, Evie.'

'I'm going to go there, whatever it takes. I'm planning to become a doctor.'

'Well, then perhaps that might give you another argument in favour of staying with your grandmother. If you want to go to university, you'll need financial support and it doesn't sound as if your mother can afford to help you much with that – especially for such a long and expensive course.'

When he paused and looked questioningly at her, Cassie didn't hesitate. 'I can support Evie, and I'll do that whether she's allowed to live with me or not. Or I'd be happy to go and live near the relevant university so that she can stay with me, if that's a requirement.' A granddaughter was more important than a house – far more important than anything else in her life.

'That sort of offer might help show your commitment, especially if the DNA proves your relationship.' After a pause, he added, 'What about this cousin you were living with, Evie? Could you go back to her in the meantime?'

She didn't even pause to think but shook her head. 'As soon as school ends she's spending the rest of the summer abroad, doing her art thing. I wouldn't go to her anyway because I'd be too vulnerable there. If my mother came to take me away, Amelia would let her. And Mum has already moved in with *him*.' She shuddered. 'So I don't have another home to go to.'

'I see.' The lawyer glanced at his watch. 'Any more questions? No? Well, then I'm afraid that's all the time I can offer you today. I suggest you think it through carefully and come to some conclusions about the path you want to take. Make a few plans, then come back and discuss the legal implications of them with me.'

Cassie nodded. 'We'll certainly do that.'

'Don't forget to ask my clerk for directions to the place nearby where you can get your DNA tested.'

'I won't. We'll call in there straight away. And we'll definitely come back to you for any further legal advice.'

'It'd be an interesting case and your being famous would add another layer to how it played out, assuming the mother kicked up a fuss.'

'He'd make her kick up a fuss,' Evie said bitterly. 'He controls everything she does nowadays. His attitude towards women is antediluvian from what I've seen!'

Cassie lingered to say, 'I've given up the TV work. I'll be more out of the public eye than in it from now on.' She hoped she hadn't shown her brief feeling of panic at the mere thought of returning to her old role in the world.

'But people will still know Cassandra Benn, so we'll have to make allowances for them regarding you as famous. And it could prove an advantage.'

'In the meantime you won't tell anyone about us, will you – where I live, I mean?' Cassie asked. 'Our personal information will be kept confidential?'

'Definitely. I'll not give it to anyone unless a court demands it or you give me permission.'

He smiled so reassuringly, looking at her in a way that made her suspect he'd noticed her sudden near panic.

'That's not likely to happen at the moment, is it, Ms Bennington? How would anyone even know about me being involved in advising you?'

'I suppose you're right. I'm just trying to be hyper-careful. Thank you for your help today.'

She hated these flashes of panic that struck without warning, had never been vulnerable in that way before.

Chapter Twelve

When they got outside, Cassie needed to get her thoughts straight, so suggested they go into a nearby café for refreshments.

When they were sitting at the table after placing their order, Evie looked at her thoughtfully. 'Are you all right, Gran?'

'Yes.'

'You're still reacting to that terrorist attack, aren't you? Just mildly. From what I've read, anyone would, and you seem to be doing better than most.'

'It hits me occasionally out of the blue, I'm afraid. It certainly takes some getting over.'

'That's another reason why you don't want anyone finding out where you're living, isn't it? Because you really do want to change your life. That often happens, by the way, after a traumatic event.'

'Yes. But I think a change was long overdue.'

'Mmm, probably. You must have led a super-stressful life because you tackled some really difficult topics. From what I've read, there's a limit to how long most people can cope with high-stress lifestyles and jobs.'

Cassie felt surprisingly comforted by her granddaughter's words and also by the quick pat on the arm that accompanied them. This was definitely an old soul in a young body. Evie would probably make a brilliant doctor and she was already a decent, caring and mature human being.

Her mother must be very proud of her.

Evie was clearly waiting till she was paying attention again to continue speaking.

'I want to make it clear, Gran, that I'll do my very best not to involve you, if there's any trouble.'

'No! I want you to involve me. Please promise me you won't run away without at least telling me.'

'How can I when it'd put you in the wrong legally?'

'Evie, I am involved now, fully involved, and I intend to continue helping you. In case you're worrying, I'd not try to stop you running away if there were no alternative, only I could give you some money, arrange how we could contact one another, that sort of thing. In fact, I think we should start a bank account straight away, one that you can just dip into without asking me.'

'I already have a bank account.'

'Does your mother know about it?'

'She encouraged me to start one. But it's my own account and she doesn't know the details.'

'Well, it wouldn't hurt to have another account that she doesn't know anything at all about, and if we make it a joint bank account, we can both access it and I can put in more money as necessary, as well as seeing what you're doing. There will be no need for you to become a street kid, believe me. Also, I am not short of money.'

Evie gave her a look that was both tearful and happy. 'You're wonderful, Gran. You make me feel I'm not alone any more, that there's hope.' She sniffed and then fumbled for a tissue, mopped her eyes and blew her nose.

'You're making me feel the same.'

'I promise faithfully that I'll tell you first if I feel I have to go. If I can, that is. If not, I'll be in touch as soon as it's safe.'

'I'll give you my secret email address and phone number. They're very secure and only people like my sister and my very closest friends know about them.'

'Shall I be able to meet your sister? She's my aunt, isn't she? No, great-aunt! Wow, imagine having an aunt as well as a grandmother!'

'I hope you'll meet her. I think you'll get on well with Zoe. She's fifteen years younger than me and will be tickled to know she's a great-aunt, I'm sure.'

Evie beamed at her. 'I've always wanted family.'

'I have a brother as well, but Michael's more like my parents, rather narrow-minded and unforgiving of what he regards as wrong behaviour.' She sighed and got another pat on the hand.

'Sorry about that, Gran.'

'If you've finished, let's go and arrange for our DNA to be tested and then open the bank account. Oh, and we'd better buy you another wig. That one is absolutely scruffy and if I have to look at you wearing it much longer, I'll scream.'

Evie giggled, suddenly looking years younger. 'It is rather tatty, isn't it?'

The DNA test was accomplished without any glitches, and they signed a piece of paper allowing a copy of the results to be sent to Mr Wutherington as well.

As they came out, Cassie stopped and took Evie's hand in hers. 'I want you to know something else: even if the DNA says we aren't related, I'll still help you. But given your appearance and hair colour, I doubt that will prove to be the case. I just wanted to say it because I find it best to work on the principle of covering all possibilities in a situation.'

'You're wonderful.'

And for all her years of experience at dealing with the world, Cassie could feel herself blushing.

Evie chuckled. 'I'm growing very fond of you, Gran, even if you're not my grandma, but I think you are.'

Evie felt warm inside as they got into the car but was glad they didn't speak much as they drove back. She glanced sideways a couple of times but her grandmother was looking so thoughtful, she didn't try to chat. It seemed to her that they both needed some thinking time.

She couldn't help worrying about what the future would bring, but she was sure now that her grandmother really did want to help her and get to know her. Wasn't that wonderful?

Why did her mother keep turning down the opportunity to get to know her birth mother?

'Let's go in there.' Cassie turned off the main road just outside Marlbury into a shopping centre they'd passed earlier. She pulled into the car park and nodded as if pleased. 'It's bigger than I'd remembered, which is going to be useful. Let's go, kid. Shop till we drop, eh?'

Evie stared round as they walked. 'Wow, it is huge. I don't know about shop till we drop, though. I don't usually enjoy shopping for no reason.'

'Me neither.'

'But I do need a few things today, Gran.'

'Well, I need a lot of things, so please bear with me.'

They started by buying a proper bed and a small chest of drawers for Evie, which made her feel guilty again.

'I shall continue to need a spare bed, whether you're with me or not, Evie. I do have a few friends who'll come and visit once things are settled. I'm just buying it sooner, that's all.'

'Oh. Yes, of course.' That made her feel better.

'As the rear car seats fold down, we'll be able to take these with us, so you'll sleep more comfortably tonight.'

Her grandmother gave her an assessing glance. 'I know we need to buy you a few clothes but first of all let's get a wig if there's somewhere that sells them. I can't stand the sight of you in that thing any longer.'

Evie glanced at her own reflection in a shop window and gave one of her rare girlish giggles. 'It does look awful, doesn't it?'

'Ghastly. Plus we'll need all sorts of fresh food. I like to eat healthily, even if I'm not a very good cook. Wig first, furniture second, clothes third and food last, eh?'

They asked an attendant at a help kiosk and were given directions to a shop selling wigs. They had a hilarious time trying on a few, and settled on a mid-brown in a nondescript, jaw-length style, and a darker one similar to the one that was due to be 'filed under R for rubbish' as her grandmother called it.

Evie poked her tongue out at herself in the mirror in the mid-brown one, which wasn't particularly flattering. That might be a good choice strategically, though, because it certainly wouldn't attract attention or be easily remembered, as her own vivid red hair would. And the darker one was a cheapie fun wig, which didn't even attempt to look real, just in case they needed a different look in a hurry.

As they went into the large store to look for clothes, Evie fumbled for her purse.

Her grandmother reached out to stop her opening it. 'This is my treat.'

Guilt shot through her. 'I don't want to keep costing you money.'

'It's nothing, darling. I'm not short of money, but I am short of buying treats for a granddaughter. Where shall we start?'

As they shopped, Evie soon realised how much her grandmother was enjoying doing this and stopped worrying. It occurred to her that for all the fame and fortune she'd achieved, Cassie must have been lonely a lot of the time. Well, look at what she'd said about the terrorist incident. Why, she hadn't even had anyone to call to pick her up from the hospital. If her ex hadn't come round, she'd have been utterly alone. He must be a nice man.

What must it be like to be so close to being blown up? Evie felt a chill run down her spine at the mere thought and couldn't help looking round the shopping centre for the nearest exit.

They had fun trying on clothes and came away with several large bags. They even bought some jeans for her grandmother, not skin-tight ones, which the salesperson tried to persuade them to buy because they were very popular. Evie had watched other girls at school parade around in these, regardless of whether they were flattering or not – which they usually weren't. She was glad her grandmother had good clothes sense.

Then to crown the pleasures of the day, they found a large bookshop in the complex. Her grandmother led the way inside without even asking her, urging Evie to buy several books. She didn't complain when her granddaughter chose mainly non-fiction, as Evie's mother would have done in yet another attempt to stop her 'being such a swot'.

As if you could switch off your brain or stop feeding it with interesting things that broadened your understanding of the world! As if she should want to limit herself in that way!

She had a peep at the books her grandmother had bought, one about the history of Wiltshire and a couple of cosy mysteries.

Cassie grinned at Evie. 'I still prefer paper books to ebooks.'

'So do I. And I'm not the only one in my class to feel like that. You can cuddle a paper book and it doesn't break if you drop it, but it's not much fun cuddling an ebook reader.'

Cassie held the books out for her to see the titles. 'I have to confess to a weakness for this sort of story, Evie love, cosy mysteries. It's all Agatha Christie's fault. I found her books when I was much younger than you and enjoyed them very much.'

'I haven't read any of hers.'

'We'll unpack some of my books when we get back,

then you can borrow any of them you fancy. Christie's stories are a bit dated now but if you read them as being set against a historical background, they're still good reads.'

'You're very generous.'

She watched her grandmother blink rapidly, to clear away tears.

'I'm thoroughly enjoying having someone to buy presents for.'

It was out before Evie could stop herself. 'Don't you buy them for your sister?'

'I shall do now Zoe and I are getting closer, but our parents kept us apart as much as they could and I'd left home well before she even got to high school.'

'All that because of you having my mother after being raped? That's so unfair.'

'It was because I refused to get rid of the baby, I think. They hate to be seen as unconventional in any way. They tried to impose their own view of the world on their children and failed with me and my sister. Only, Zoe smiles and somehow manages to go her own way. She's more tactful than I could ever be. Anyway, that's water under the bridge now that I'm getting to know her.'

Evie didn't ask any more questions because she could hear the lingering pain in her grandmother's voice. Well, although her mother had never put her first when there was a man around, Fran did love her, she was quite sure of that.

'What does your brother do for a living?'

'He's a civil servant, not sure where he's working at the moment. He hasn't made any effort to get to know me even though he left home a good few years ago. But my sister took the initiative to improve our relationship, to my delight. Zoe's lovely, so kind. You'll like her.'

Later, as she snuggled down in her new bed, Evie thought through what she'd learnt about her grandmother today and decided that no one had a perfect life. Well, no one that she knew anyway.

Perhaps that's why there were so many books with happy endings. You could put anything you liked into a story.

She could put a light on and read herself to sleep if she wanted to here, she was sure. But tonight she didn't need that. Tonight everything felt good. Mmm. She closed her eyes and let the world fade away.

Chapter Thirteen

The following day Hal's phone began to ring and he picked it up, sighing as he recognised the number.

The voice was hesitant. 'Dad?'

'Oliver. Nice to hear from you, son.' It probably wouldn't be nice at all. His son usually only phoned when he wanted something.

'How did the move go?'

Hal rolled his eyes at the thought of what he could say about his recent hassles, but didn't get into that, contenting himself with, 'Pretty well on the whole.'

'Good, good.'

'How are you and Mandy?'

'Um – that's what I'm calling about. We haven't been getting on for a while and – well, we're splitting up.'

'Oh dear. Is there no hope of, you know, mediation?'

'She won't even try that. She's met someone else at work.'

Hal whistled softly. 'I'm so sorry.'

'Yeah, me too. I wondered – could I come and stay with

you for a week or two? I know it's a big ask, but I need to get away. I'm moving out of the house and I'm going to transfer to a branch in another town. The company's been very, um, helpful and it's nearly settled.'

'Goodness.' Oliver didn't seem to be seeking advice, only wanting to talk about it, so Hal waited for him to offer further information.

'I've looked at flats to rent near my new job, which is in Swindon, so I'll be quite close to you. But I can't sign up for a place yet in case something goes wrong with the move. I should be a shoo-in with my experience, but you know how chancy it can be when you change your job. And it costs a lot for the deposit and stuff, so I can't afford to waste money.'

'Why can't you stay in your own home till you're sure of where you're going?'

'It's a bit far away, and Mandy's new guy is going to help her buy me out of my share but he'll only do that if he can move into the house straight away. So the sooner I can move out of there and get the money for a new place, the better.'

'But you loved that house! You did so much work on it when you bought it. Can't Mandy move out for a while? Her new guy must already be living somewhere.'

'Yeah, well. We've argued so much that I've stopped feeling good about that house but *she* really wants to stay there. As long as I get a reasonable amount of money for my share – and they're being fair about the finances, I must admit – I'd prefer to start over somewhere else. I should have enough for a deposit on a small place and I'll rent a flat while I look round for a fixer-upper.'

'What does your mother say? Can't you stay with her? I've only just moved in here, haven't even had time to unpack.'

'She's found a new guy as well. You know how she chops and changes. She's too busy with him, so she can't put me up and anyway, she's still friends with Mandy, takes her side against me. They always did get on well.'

'Ah.' Hal didn't really want this complication, had been looking forward to some quiet time.

'Is that OK, Dad? Me coming to stay with you for a couple of weeks, I mean?'

Hal heard his son's voice wobble and when Oliver suddenly blew his nose, it was obvious he was fighting tears. Hal simply couldn't say no. A marriage break-up could be harrowing as Hal knew from experience. Oliver was clearly very upset, however much he was trying to hide it. 'Yes, I suppose you can stay. But there will have to be some ground rules.'

'What? I'm a bit old for rules, don't you think?'

'Not in someone else's house you're not. I don't care what you do when you're away from here, but I'm going to set rules for when you're at home. Frankly, you don't seem to have changed much since you were a teenager and you still tend to make a lot of noise, regardless of other people's needs, not to mention leaving a mess wherever you go.'

'Why do you say that? I'm not a slob.'

'You were last time you stayed with me, never cleared up after yourself. I'm not going to act as your servant. Plus, I've not only got a brand-new house, I desperately need some peace and quiet myself.'

'Yeah, yeah. That'll be fine. I'll just fit in with you.'

'Oliver, did you hear me?'

'Mmm?'

'I'm not sure you did listen properly so I'll say it again to make sure it's absolutely clear what I'll expect. If you don't tidy up after yourself while you're here, I'll throw your stuff out of the house – literally. I won't put up with *any mess whatsoever*.'

'But—'

'No, let me finish. If you clear up as you go, there is never any need to do big clear-ups because it never gets bad, which is how I choose to live.'

His son's voice was sulky. 'That's the sort of thing Mandy used to say. Has the whole world gone tidy-mad?'

'I don't care about the whole world, just my little part of it. So there you are. If you decide to come and stay, you'll know what to expect.'

'I'll do my best, Dad. But I'm still a bit upset, so you'll have to cut me a little slack here.'

'No. I won't cut you any slack whatsoever where cleanliness is concerned.'

He heard a muttered exclamation, but since his cancer, he'd found that keeping control of his surroundings had become important to him and he wasn't giving in about this.

There was dead silence for a few moments then Oliver said, 'Oh, all right. I'll fit in as best I can. Look, I've a few things to do here. I'll phone and let you know when I'm arriving.'

When he put the phone down, Hal stood staring at it for a while before he moved. He couldn't help feeling upset at the confrontations to come. Oliver was in for a few shocks. And he would lose his precious peace for a while.

Hal knew he'd changed a lot in the past couple of years and was equally sure his son hadn't. It'd take a lot of effort to ride shotgun on Oliver about his slovenly habits, but he wasn't going to compromise on this. He looked round. This place was brand new, after all. Oh hell, he really didn't want to share his living space. And much more important, he didn't want to mess up his brand-new chance of life.

One of the worst aspects of this was that his family didn't know about the cancer and now it'd probably come out.

He should have said no to his son coming to stay. Only, he couldn't.

Anyway, he loved Oliver, even if he didn't enjoy living with him. And his son had sounded deep-down upset about his marriage break-up. Well, who wouldn't be, if they were honest? Marriages usually started with such high hopes. Hal remembered how upset he'd been when he split with Oliver's mother after a few years of marriage, even though that had been by mutual agreement and had gone relatively smoothly.

The only thing he and Gillian had disagreed strongly about afterwards had been how to bring up Oliver. He should have interfered more. But would she have let him? He doubted it.

He heard voices and looked outside to see Cassie and her granddaughter get into the car and drive away. Shopping? Or something else?

They both looked worried and it occurred to him again that they had some problem they were trying to hide from others. Though why that girl was wearing such an appalling wig, he had to wonder. It slipped sometimes and showed the red hair underneath.

Was she hiding from something? Or from someone? She must be.

Well, he had enough on his plate without taking on other people's worries, so he didn't want to get involved. His new neighbour seemed a decent sort and he wished her and her granddaughter well.

It was a rare person who didn't have a problem or two to deal with.

Hal went out soon afterwards. He wanted to stock his house with healthy fresh foods and basic supplies. He'd also have to buy a single bed and bedding for Oliver, because he doubted his son would have thought to commandeer any of the marital household goods. But he wasn't buying junk food or even having it in the house. His son could either put up with healthy meals or go out to eat on his own at food outlets.

There was apparently a big shopping centre on the outskirts of Marlbury, so he found it online and set his satnav to take him there. He had no trouble finding a bed, bedding and a wide range of fresh food, then was tempted by the bookshop. Now that he'd stopped working he'd be able to catch up with the latest bestsellers and any new books by his favourite authors. Oh, the bliss of that freedom!

By the time he got home, his shoulder was throbbing, so he carried the bags of food into the house one at a time using his other hand, put the frozen stuff away, then sat down in his recliner chair and switched on the TV.

He'd just have a short break and catch up with the news before he unpacked properly.

He was woken a couple of hours later by someone banging on his front door. He jerked to his feet, nearly knocking his half-empty mug of cold tea off the small table beside his chair and wincing as he moved his shoulder incautiously.

When he opened the door, he found his son standing there, looking truculent.

'All right if I come to stay now? The bitch threw all my things out into the garden because she didn't like the way I was packing up.'

Hal didn't let himself sigh as he held the door open.

'Can you give me a hand with a few things, Dad? They're a bit heavy.'

'I'm afraid I can't. I hurt my shoulder yesterday.'

'How am I going to get them into the house, then?'

'You may have to leave some of them in the car.'

'But I've got my sound system and it's an expensive one.'

'I'm not having it set up in the house anyway, so you might as well leave it where it is. Your car will be safe enough on the drive.'

'But—'

Hal wasn't going to get into an argument. He turned and went back into the house, hearing a muttered curse behind him as he put the kettle on.

Oliver came in and dumped a big backpack on the floor in the living area. 'Which bedroom am I in?'

'None of them till the bed is delivered. I've not worked that out yet. I was tired when I got back from the shops, so I had a nap.'

His son gave him a puzzled look.

'Cup of tea?'

Oliver peered at the kitchen area. 'I'm not much into tea. What sort of coffee-making equipment have you got?'

'Kettle and tea-making ingredients only.'

'I'll bring my coffee maker in from the car. At least she let me take that.'

'I'm not having it set up. I've developed a very acute sense of smell these days.' One of the strange after-effects of his treatment. 'As far as I'm concerned, coffee stinks the place out and fancy coffee is even worse.'

That got him another puzzled look.

'Cup of tea or I think I've got some instant drinking chocolate?' He waited, hand on the cupboard door.

'Tea.' Oliver's voice was sulky. 'Though I don't know why you won't take advantage of my gadgets.'

'Because I don't want them. I've moved here for some peace and quiet.'

'Are you . . . all right? Your health I mean?'

Hal hesitated, then shrugged. Why try to hide it? 'As it happens, I'm recovering from cancer.'

'*What?*'

'You heard me.'

'What sort of cancer, Dad? Why didn't you tell anyone? Are you going to be all right?'

'Colon cancer. They think they got it in time. It's been over a year since it was found and it was early stage, so they've more or less turned me loose now, except for the regular check-ups.'

His son's voice was soft and hushed, as if he were talking to an idiot. 'That's why you've retired early. Are you *sure* they've sorted it out?'

'It's never one hundred per cent certain even with the more treatable cancers but in my case, it's far more likely than not that I'm clear.'

Silence greeted him and when he turned, Oliver was staring at him with what he'd begun to think of as *that look*. You'd think everyone with cancer metamorphosed overnight into infectious and moronic aliens, the way some people treated you, and yet roughly one in two people would get it at some stage of their lives.

He turned away and finished making the tea. 'Come and sit down for a few minutes. Tell me about your new job and what your plans are for the future.'

'It'll be much the same as the old job, except it'll be in Swindon. I was lucky. They wanted someone there so I, um, volunteered to transfer. Things just need finalising.'

'But what will you be doing there?'

'Same boring old stuff, answering queries about our products, doing market research, you know. But it brings in the money for my real life.'

'Which is?'

'Chilling out with my mates, gaming online and now, I suppose, I'll have to start pulling chicks whenever I need their services.' He patted himself complacently.

Hal found that disgusting and had made his feelings plain about such attitudes towards women before but didn't waste his breath saying so again. It'd be water off a duck's back with Oliver in his present mood. He wasn't having stray 'chicks' brought back here, though. No way.

Oliver took another sip of tea and grimaced. 'I'll have to bring in my coffee maker, Dad. I don't usually do tea and it tastes as bad as ever.'

'Didn't I just refuse to live with coffee? If you don't like my tea there's plenty of water in the tap.'

'*Tap water!* Don't you even buy proper spring water? Honestly, Dad. No one drinks out of the tap these days.'

Hal prayed for patience, didn't find it and once again spoke his mind. 'Well, if you bring bottled water inside my house, I'll chuck it out again. All that plastic isn't good for the environment and it's daft to pay so much for water anyway.

Get it through your head, son, that this is *my* home and as I
told you earlier, if you stay here you'll have to live *my* way.'

'But—'

The doorbell rang and it was just as well. Hal couldn't
help scowling as he went to answer it. He wasn't giving in
to his son. He was going to live in his new home the way
he wanted. It was one of the things he'd promised himself.

He found a couple of guys delivering the new bed and
other packages. 'Great. I'll show you the way. It's upstairs.'

When they'd left, he stood at the top of the stairs and
called, 'Oliver! Come up and I'll show you your bedroom.'

There was no answer, which surprised him. He went
downstairs and found Oliver with earbuds in, beating time to
some music that was so loud Hal could hear the tinny sound of
it from across the room even though it wasn't on the speakers.

He went across and stood in front of his son, arms folded.

It took a couple of minutes before Oliver noticed him
and reluctantly pulled out the earbuds.

'Come up and see your bedroom, then you can take your
stuff up and unpack. And please don't play your music so
loudly in future. If you want to damage your hearing, that's
your own business but I need peace and quiet in my home.
How many times do I have to tell you that?'

'I'll take the stuff up later.'

'Now, please. You've already scattered some of your
things in my living area.'

'Aw, stop fussing, Dad. Chill out.'

Some devil had got into Hal, a devil he'd been holding
in rein for years. No wonder they called some of his son's
contemporaries 'the entitled generation'. Oliver clearly
belonged to that group. He quickly gathered together

the mess of objects and mainly dirty clothes that Oliver had dumped out of his backpack when searching for something, and before his son could stop him, he'd thrown them out of the front door.

That got Oliver out of the chair in one leap.

'What the hell did you do that for?'

Hal folded his arms and leant against the wall. 'As I told you earlier on the phone, I keep my home tidy. Any mess you make goes out of the door the minute I set eyes on it.'

He saw Oliver's hands clench into fists and waited, unable to believe that his son would turn on him.

As a stand-off, it was a non-event. The fists unclenched, Oliver took a deep, growling breath and brought his stuff in, then followed Hal upstairs and helped put the bed together and make it up with the brand-new sheets.

Scowling, he went down again and began unloading the car.

Hal followed him, warning, 'Not your sound system and coffee maker, remember.'

Oliver glared at him, but put the box he was holding back into the boot.

After his son had taken up the last load, he came down and said sulkily, 'You've certainly changed, Dad.'

'Cancer does that to you, son, makes you realise what you value in life, gives you the courage to go for it, too. I shall keep saying it till I get through to you: this is *my* house, and you're always welcome to visit, always, but we do things *my* way here. And the tidiness edict covers your bedroom, too, not just the living areas. I'll chuck out anything left lying around.'

Oliver gaped at him, not seeming to know what to say, so Hal left him to sort out his things and went to sit out on the patio, which was a trifle chilly but at least peaceful.

He was shaking with reaction to their spat because his emotions were still rather fragile and he couldn't cope as easily with conflict, even minor conflict. He hated that weakness, absolutely hated it, but couldn't seem to alter how he reacted at times. Not yet, anyway. He was hoping he'd settle down here and gradually achieve some sort of equilibrium and rhythm to his days.

He didn't know Oliver as well as he'd have liked. Well, let's face it, he'd never had the chance. He'd not been allowed much say in how his ex had brought up their son and you couldn't change much on occasional visits. He was sorry to start off Oliver's stay with a row, but he wasn't backing off.

How would he cope with a couple of weeks of this, though?

Then he felt a smile slowly creep across his face and he began to relax a little. How would Oliver cope with living with his neat and tidy father for that long?

Had his son taken on board properly how much Hal had changed? He didn't think so. Not yet.

He wasn't giving in about how he ran his home. Or about anything else. What did they say nowadays? *My way or the highway*.

No, he couldn't throw Oliver out, but his son might leave in a huff.

Could he even afford to set himself up in a flat? From what he'd let drop he was a bit short of cash till the money from his house came in.

Chapter Fourteen

That evening Cassie looked out of the back window of her house, wondering whether to sit outside for a while. Would she be too cold? No, the patio was quite sheltered and she could put her shawl round her shoulders.

Evie was watching some soap on TV that she'd confessed to being addicted to. Good luck to her. For a teenager, she was surprisingly good about keeping the volume low, hadn't even needed telling.

Cassie ran up to get her shawl, opened the rear doors then turned back. She fancied a glass of wine. Why not? Having one glass wasn't setting a bad example.

She poured a glass of dry white from her favourite Australian vineyard, a place where she'd once done a 'behind the scenes' programme on a round-the-world series about wine making.

Taking her glass outside, she sat down with a long sigh of relief and felt herself immediately start to relax. There was the sound of a chair being moved next door and when she looked round, she saw Hal coming towards her across the newly laid lawn between the houses. It was nice not to have fences. Well, unless you were lumbered with a bad neighbour.

'Refugee from the TV?' He rested his hands on the back of the next outdoor chair, smiling down at her.

'Yes.'

'Me, too. My son has come to stay for a couple of weeks. He's just split up with his wife.'

'Oh, that's sad.' She could see his wry smile in the light from the back rooms of her house.

'Actually, I'm surprised she put up with him for so long. He's a slob. Leaves a trail of mess wherever he goes. I need to warn you about one thing: I've threatened to throw anything he leaves lying around out of the house, and I've already done it once. So if you see piles of what looks like rubbish or old clothes in front of or behind my house, ignore them.'

She chuckled, not even trying to hide her amusement. 'I'd like to be a fly on the wall. Will you really keep on doing that, do you think? It takes a lot to change an untidy person's habits, as I found out when I tried to live with one otherwise nice guy.'

His expression grew very determined. 'You've got to believe it. Living in this house is my dream for the rest of my life. What do oldies call it these days? My death nest.'

'What a horrible concept. You're far too young to be thinking of death.'

He hesitated then said quietly, 'I'm a cancer survivor, Cassie. I've grown used to the thought of dying, though they tell me I'm clear now.'

She'd reached out to clasp his hand before she knew it and he didn't pull away. 'That's tough, Hal. I did a programme on surviving cancer once, and I so admired the people I interviewed. Facing a premature death while you make plans for the family you'll be leaving behind is one of the highest forms of bravery, if you ask me, Hal.'

'Is there anything you haven't done an article on?'

'Oh, lots of things, but I've covered many of the big issues of life over the past twenty years.'

'Especially the last five years of *Life with Cassandra* on the first Friday of the month.'

'You've watched my programmes?'

'Quite often, yes. You have an incisive yet tender approach to your topic and show a respect for the people you involve.'

She was touched by the compliment. 'Thank you. I've had enough of other people's problems, though, and even of their achievements. I want to concentrate on my own life from now on.' She glanced at the glass she was holding and waved it towards him. 'Like to join me?'

'I'd love to.'

'I don't know why I've left you standing there as we talk. Do sit down, please.'

While he made himself comfortable, she went into the house, found another glass and took the bottle out with her. Evie was still glued to the TV and the two people whose lips seemed fused together. She didn't even seem to notice her grandmother coming and going.

Hal didn't say a lot nor did she try to force conversation, but it was nice to have someone her own age to chat to and Cassie felt relaxed enough with him to pour them both a second glass. Although the rear patio was nicely sheltered, it was getting a bit chilly, but she didn't want to break up an interesting conversation. She might have a conservatory built on, so that she could use the area whatever the weather.

She didn't even switch on the outside lights. The rising moon added a soft glow to the scene that was more than enough.

Hal was quite good-looking for a man of his age, she decided, after a surreptitious study of him as he talked, eyes alight with interest first in one thing, then in another, and hands waving to emphasise important points. She hoped the moonlight had blurred the wrinkles on her face, as they had on his.

What attracted her to him most of all was his intelligence and the kind yet not wimpy way he seemed to interact with the world. It was as if he were quietly sure of his own place in the universe and didn't need to prove anything to anyone.

Hal broke off in the middle of a discussion as he heard the sound of a phone ringing several times then cutting off inside his house.

A few moments later the back patio door slid open and a figure peered out into the darkness. 'Dad? Are you out here? There's someone on the phone for you.'

He sighed in annoyance. 'Tell them I'm busy.'

'You didn't even ask who it was.'

'I don't care who it is. I'm enjoying the peace and quiet out here.'

'They'll have heard your voice, Dad.'

Hal sighed and put down his glass. 'Don't go in yet, Cassie. I'll be back shortly.'

Once inside his own house, he picked up the phone and glanced at the number, muttering, 'Oh damn!' Taking a deep breath, he said, 'Hello?'

'Hal, it's me, Sabine. Surely you recognise my number? I've been chasing you for a couple of weeks. Where are you?'

'I've retired to the country, as I told you I was going to do.'

'That doesn't mean you don't want to see old friends, surely? How about I come and visit you for a day or two?'

Her voice had gone low and throaty, a device she employed when she wanted to sound sexy. Hearing it after a few weeks, he decided it had the opposite effect on him now that he knew it for a deliberate trick. 'I'm living a very quiet life these days, Sabine. It'd bore you to tears.'

'Try me.'

'Thank you but no. Look, there's no easy way to say this. We had a nice fling but I thought we'd both moved on.'

'I don't agree. I was just giving you time to recover. I saw you in the distance the other week and remembered how good we'd been together.'

Make that, she'd been waiting to see if he did recover. 'Well, there you are. I've certainly moved on. Thanks for calling, Sabine, but I'm not picking up the past again. Have a good life.' He clicked the phone off, then looked up to see Oliver staring at him.

'She sounded a sexy piece. Why did you turn her down?'

'She's a rather predatory woman. I'm not interested in getting together with her again.'

'Mum always said you were a babe magnet.'

'Then your mother was wrong. And please don't answer my phone again. Or listen to my phone conversations.'

Oliver shrugged. 'Whatever. Who were you talking to outside?'

'My neighbour. And I'm going back to continue our conversation, so I'll leave you to your TV watching.'

'I could come and join you for a glass or two.'

'No, you couldn't. Cassie and I are enjoying each other's company in a very peaceful way that will bore you to tears. And you haven't brought any wine with you.'

'You've got plenty. Surely you don't grudge me a glass or two?'

'I buy good wine. You guzzle it as if it's lemonade and I'm not wasting mine on you. I know exactly how many bottles I have, so don't go taking any after you finish that bottle you've pinched without asking me tonight.'

He had the satisfaction of seeing his son's mouth drop open in shock as he moved outside again. He pulled the sliding door firmly shut behind him and sat down again, trying to switch off his annoyance as decisively as he'd switched off the phone. Only, it was still there, humming away inside him.

'Unwanted caller?' Cassie murmured.

'Definitely unwanted. I went out with Sabine a few times, but that was BC – before the cancer. She vanished quickly after I was diagnosed. She must have heard that I'd recovered. She's probably between men and I'd guess she's looking for a husband now that she's getting older, to help maintain her expensive lifestyle. And she'd prefer one who'll die while she's still youngish and leave her a nice chunk of money.'

'Is she really that bad?'

'I'm afraid so. Gorgeous-looking, good conversationalist but no heart behind the façade.'

She was thinking aloud before she knew it. 'The old Cassie would have wondered about doing an article on predatory women who deliberately marry for money.'

'And the new Cassie?'

She shrugged. 'The new Cassie is much more interested

in helping her granddaughter and making a few carefully selected new friends.'

'I'd love to count myself a friend of yours.'

'It's a bargain.' She raised her glass to him and clinked it against his to seal their agreement, and they smiled gently at one another as they each took a sip of wine, then put their glasses down.

'So, Cassie, how's it going with Evie?'

'Really well. She's a great kid.'

'She seems to be. Very capable too, from what you've told me.'

They chatted about the current political news, then Hal couldn't hold back a yawn. He savoured the last mouthful and put his glass down. 'I think I'll call it a day. Nice wine, that one.'

'One of my favourites. And I must say, I was thinking of doing the same thing. I'm not a late night sort of person.'

'Thanks for inviting me across.'

'I've enjoyed your company.'

'I've enjoyed yours, too. My turn to play host next time.'

When Cassie went inside, she found Evie sitting reading a book and the television switched off.

Her granddaughter greeted her with, 'I can see by the expression on his face that he likes you.'

'And I like him. But not in that way.'

'Not yet.'

'That isn't the first thing I think of when I meet someone, Evie. It doesn't matter to me whether they're male or female, what I want to know before I make friends is that they're decent human beings with a well-exercised brain between their ears. Doesn't even matter whether they're particularly intelligent, as long as they keep the brain they were born with active.'

'Those sound like good criteria for judging someone.'

'I reckon so. Now, I'm going to bed and you should too, don't you think?'

'I was just planning to do that. I'll need a glass of water to take with me. Can I get you anything, Gran?'

'No, darling. But a goodnight cuddle wouldn't go amiss.' She held her breath, waiting. Had she gone too far, expecting too much too soon?

But Evie came across to her smiling and they had a nice hug, swaying to and fro for a few moments before drawing apart.

'Sleep well, darling.'

'You sleep well, too, Gran.'

Cassie was still smiling as she got into bed and listened to her granddaughter making similar preparations for sleep. What a lovely evening it had turned out to be.

Things were going so well. Fingers and toes crossed that nothing went wrong and Evie's mother didn't find out where she was. Well, not yet, anyway. They shouldn't postpone a reconciliation for too long.

But first, Cassie wanted so much to get to know Evie. She liked – no, make that loved – what she'd seen so far.

Surely her daughter must have some good qualities to have produced and raised such a delightful girl? Cassie hoped she could meet Fran and get to know her as well.

Chapter Fifteen

Fran didn't have to go to work that day and after waving Keith off, she went to sit down with a cup of tea and have a think, not only about Evie but about . . . well, everything.

Whatever Keith said, she was still worried about her daughter. Surely Evie could have found some way to email her by now?

She was worried about Keith too. She'd promised herself when she split up with her previous guy that she'd never let herself be manipulated again. And now look at her, married in a blind rush and afraid to do openly what she felt to be right.

For a start, she knew for certain that Evie wasn't sly. Why did Keith keep saying that? If anything that girl was too straightforward about how she interacted with people and hadn't yet developed much tact. Wait till Evie got interested in boys. She'd have to learn to deal with them more tactfully or she'd never keep a boyfriend.

Only, perhaps you could be too tactful. Fran had lain

awake worrying each night that Evie had been away. Keith didn't seem to understand a mother's love and just kept brushing her worries aside and distracting her.

And she still hadn't gone against his wishes and contacted the police! What did that say about her? Only, maybe she'd needed this breathing space, this chance to see what Keith was like in an emergency.

Not as good as she'd expected. Let's face it, not good at all. Of course no one was perfect, she knew that. But – she was beginning to add a lot of buts when she thought about him. Why had she let him push her into marriage?

Well, Evie came first at the moment, then she'd deal with her own problems.

She'd racked her brain about where her daughter could possibly have gone. Amelia was no longer around to take her in. She'd just left for Italy even though Fran had asked her to delay her departure in case the poor girl turned up looking for help.

Amelia had always been like that, avoiding trouble at all costs.

So had she, Fran admitted. She began to pace up and down, trying to set her thoughts in order.

She was off work today. Ought she to go and check Amelia's house, in case Evie was hiding there? She didn't think her daughter would break into someone else's home – not unless she was utterly desperate.

What Fran couldn't understand was why Evie would be desperate enough to run away in the first place?

What was it about Keith that upset her so much? What had she missed seeing in him?

Fran remembered introducing him to her daughter,

how kindly he'd spoken to Evie. And afterwards he'd complimented Fran on how pretty her daughter was. He cared more than most men did how people and things looked, fussed over the house, needed everything just so, had even shouted at her for leaving things lying around.

And . . . I have to admit it, I let him shout at me! That was . . . pitiful.

When she'd finished her drink, Fran rinsed out the mug and went up to her daughter's bedroom, or at least what had been intended for Evie to use as a bedroom till the attic was ready. She and Keith had simply dumped all her daughter's things here in piles when Fran moved in. Then, after Evie ran away, they'd brought back what had been left at Amelia's house, which had added another pile or two.

That was something else that was puzzling Fran. She knew exactly what Evie owned. Her daughter had left nearly all her clothes behind when she vanished. How was the girl managing without a proper change of clothing?

As she stood in the doorway of the bedroom the anger faded and tears welled in her eyes. Evie wouldn't like her things to be dumped in untidy heaps like this. She was good around the house, always tidy, giving little trouble.

In fact, she was much easier to live with than Keith!

Evie could be stubborn, though, when she believed in something. Would she ever agree to live with him? That was, if she came back, if she didn't stay away. Fran pressed one hand to her mouth but the sobs would come out and she fumbled for another tissue to wipe her eyes.

Was it worth losing her daughter to marry Keith? The answer surprised her. *No. Nothing is worth losing Evie for.*

She had to believe that things would improve between herself and Keith. They'd built up a nice life as a couple and developed a circle of friends, most of whom were useful to him for business purposes – which didn't stop them being very pleasant people to socialise with.

The only one she didn't like was his best friend, Ryan, who was a bit creepy, if you asked her. Keith changed when Ryan was round, grew more bossy and, yes, scornful towards her.

She had a sudden memory of seeing Evie through a half-open door slapping Ryan's hand away from her. Evie claimed he'd touched her breast. Keith had laughed it off and said Ryan had only been joking and his hand had slipped.

Had Ryan upset Evie more than once? Was that it? And if so, why hadn't Keith seen it as a problem?

Heart sinking at what this might imply, Fran walked across to the window and stared down into the garden. No, no! Keith was nothing like Ryan, wouldn't defend him if he really was harassing Evie.

She shouldn't be wasting time like this. There was so much to do in their new house. Keith had left her with a list of things to be sorted out today. Only, it was more important to her to find her daughter, so the list could damned well wait.

Should she go to the police? What would they say if she reported Evie missing now? *Why didn't you come to us sooner?* That's what they'd say. They might not even take her seriously.

She screwed up Keith's list and left it lying on the floor. She'd take the day off housework – or the morning anyway – give herself time to think more clearly and decide what to do about Evie.

She turned away, then turned back. The mess in her daughter's bedroom annoyed her. It wouldn't take long to clear this lot up then she'd go out for a stroll.

As she put things away tidily, she checked once again for any hint of where Evie might have gone. They must have missed something the first time they'd searched her daughter's things, must have.

Keith had insisted on them searching Evie's room regularly, saying everyone who had teenage children did it and the girl would never know. But she could see by Evie's hurt expression whenever they did it that she did know someone had been through her room.

When Fran had plucked up the courage to ask a colleague at the office if she did that, Carole had been horrified by the idea of doing that to an older child unless there was a very good reason, which there wasn't with Evie. She was nearly sixteen and wasn't troublesome in any way except her antipathy towards Keith.

Fran suddenly felt deeply ashamed. It wasn't right to have kept invading Evie's privacy like that, and letting a man finger all her underwear.

It occurred to her again as she sorted out the clothes that if Evie had been *planning* to leave, she wouldn't have left nearly everything behind. It looked, it really did, as if she'd left in a hurry, grabbing just a few things.

All Amelia had said about that day was that she'd left Keith on his own with the girl, at his request, and when she got home, he'd told her Evie had run away and shown her a makeshift rope ladder.

He'd later told Fran her daughter had run away in a fit of anger at being told to go and live in his house so that her mother wouldn't worry. He hadn't mentioned the rope ladder to her. Amelia was the one who'd told her about it.

Only, Evie didn't usually do fits of anger.

Fran stared out of the window, appalled at herself for being manipulated. Had she made another big mistake in her choice of a man? She wiped away more tears at that thought. She was such a loser.

Evie would be all right, surely she would? She was clever enough to find some way of surviving. Fran had to believe that or she'd go mad with worry.

Thank goodness it was the school holidays now and her daughter wasn't missing school, so no official need know.

Evie was such a brilliant student, a daughter anyone would be proud of. And though there was no way Fran could afford to support her through medical school to avoid those horrible debts, she might just about manage to stretch her money to helping with accommodation.

Except that Keith wanted to take her money into a joint account and use it to pay off the mortgage. He referred to it as 'their mortgage' but it wasn't. She'd never been able to afford to buy a house. She hadn't agreed to a joint account because her first husband had run off with most of their money from one of those, money that had taken a lot of earning.

She was so glad she'd done that because suddenly she wasn't sure she was going to stay with Keith. If she did, he had to understand that she wasn't going to be a doormat. She'd been reading a book about that sort of thing, one a friend at work had given her, saying she sounded as if she needed it.

She'd been offended at the time, but she'd started to read it anyway in her lunch breaks and it talked a lot of sense about equality and respect in life partnerships. One saying had stuck in her mind: *If you want to be treated as a doormat, first you have to lie down and let people wipe their feet all over you.*

She had been a doormat, she admitted that to herself now. Keith had even said last night that running away might actually do the girl good, allow her to get some real-life experience under her belt before she became a student. And Fran to her shame hadn't even contradicted that.

Then he'd surprised her by adding that the girl was being unrealistic about what she wanted to do with her life. There were enough female doctors around and what the country needed was more males enrolling for such courses. Before she could take issue on that he'd begun making love to her and she'd forgotten all else.

What would he be like as a father if they had children? No, not *if* they had children, *when*, she told herself. She loved children and it was one reason why she'd desperately wanted to get married again, to have a couple more kids before she got too old, and to bring them up in a stable home environment.

As soon as they set the date, she'd given up taking the pill, in the hope of surprising Keith with an unexpected wedding present. To her amazement nothing had come of it so far, yet with the baby she'd lost and with Evie too, she'd fallen pregnant very quickly.

Had her fertility decreased badly already? She was forty-one after all. Or was there something wrong with Keith's sperm count? After all, he was even older than her and he'd had only one child with his first wife.

As she was stacking Evie's school things in the bookcase, the large art file fell out again, scattering sheets of paper across the floor before she could catch it. Clicking her tongue in annoyance at her own carelessness, she bent to pick them up.

As she picked up the last sheet of paper, she gasped in shock. It was a letter, stained and torn in two, then sellotaped together. She recognised it instantly, of course she did. It was from an agency hired by her mother asking her to get in contact. This was the second time she'd been contacted and the second time she'd refused to respond. She didn't want to meet the woman who had given her away at birth like an unwanted package, whatever the reason, definitely not.

Yet she distinctly remembered that after tearing the letter in half, she'd tossed it in the kitchen rubbish bin. Yes, and she'd tied up the liner bag for Evie to take out when she cleared up the kitchen. Had the bag burst, or had Evie seen her doing it and wondered what it was all about? Whatever the reason, her daughter must have retrieved it and kept it hidden.

Surely she hadn't contacted this agency?

Fran scowled as she reread the letter, realising that Evie wouldn't have needed to contact them. Her birth mother's address was freely offered at the end of it.

Evie can't have gone to the woman; surely she hasn't done that?

Only, this might be the way she'd managed to disappear without a trace.

Fran's first reaction was to phone Keith at work and share this with him. She'd even picked up the phone when something stopped her. She hadn't told him about the letter. He'd be furious about that. He liked to know everything she did.

Besides, this was something she ought to manage on her own, to show herself *and* him that she could stand on her own two feet. Putting the phone down, she looked round Evie's bedroom. She ought to finish off the tidying up. Only, she couldn't settle to anything, not now.

She was very tempted to throw the letter away again, only if she did, she'd be throwing away what might be an important clue. After some thought she memorised the woman's name and address and put the letter back in the folder. That was as good a hiding place as any.

She looked out of the window and saw patchy grey clouds, but it wasn't raining. She'd go out for a walk. Fresh air and different surroundings often helped you think more clearly.

Chapter Sixteen

The following morning, Evie fiddled with her breakfast then pushed the half-eaten bowl away and looked across the table. 'What are we going to do about it all, Gran? Long term, I mean.'

'I'm not sure. One option for the short term is to send a letter to your mother by recorded delivery. I'll ask for a response to a PO box I have under another name. Do you think she'll reply?'

'Probably. It depends on what Keith tells her to do, though. He seems to control everything about her. I've watched him gradually take over till he's just about telling her how to breathe.'

She frowned in thought; she said slowly, 'I'd like to send a letter to my cousin Amelia without giving her our address, just to say that I'm all right. Would you mind? Only, I'll have to do it quickly because she'll be going to Italy any day now.'

'I think that might be a good thing to do. I've been

worrying about how your mother is feeling, I must admit. You can simply leave the letter at the hotel and they'll put it in the post with their mail, I'm told. They seem very obliging about such things for people in our village.'

Evie heaved a big loud sigh of relief. 'I'll do that straight away then.'

'Perhaps we should see if we can find out more about this Keith person as well.'

'I've tried researching him online already, Gran, but he doesn't seem to have a past.'

'What do you mean?'

'There aren't any mentions of a Keith Burgess of his age, not that I could find, anyway. And I couldn't find that name and his birth date in the census records, either. He never talks about his family background, told Mum he was an orphan brought up by the state.'

'That's . . . not a good sign.'

'No. But I knew better than to say anything about not believing that to Mum. I thought perhaps he'd fallen out with his family.'

'Well, how about I call in a favour from a friend who's very savvy about tracing people online and in other ways? We'll see if Mitch can trace Mr Elusive before we do anything else about contacting your mother directly, shall we?'

Evie nodded, sagging back in her chair as if a load had been removed from her shoulders. Indeed, her whole body language said more about how she was feeling than words could ever have done.

'How about I go and phone Mitch about helping us this very minute while you write the letter?'

'Yes, please.'

Evie soon had a letter written, then could only fidget and wait for her grandmother to return from the still-messy open space she called her 'office'.

When Cassie did rejoin her, she said only, 'I've left it with Mitch. He's a whiz at tracing people. He's just finished a job and is able to give it his immediate attention. He hopes to get back to us by the end of the day, if not earlier.'

'So we'd better hang around the house.'

'Yes, but we could walk up to the hotel to ask them about putting the letter in with their post. I have a stamp.'

'Might it be best to take a photocopy of the letter before we do?' Evie asked.

'Good idea. If it comes to legal troubles, at the very least it'll show I'm not trying to keep you from communicating with your mother.'

'Isn't it awful that we have to do this so sneakily?'

'Yes.'

They walked up to the hotel and handed the letter over to a smiling young man on the reception desk, then strolled back home.

When they got inside, Cassie said, 'I wouldn't mind a quiet day and I have a few business matters to attend to. Have you enough to do to keep yourself busy? I can lend you an old laptop if you like.'

Evie beamed at her. 'That'd be brill! I couldn't bring my own laptop with me because it's old and quite heavy, but I hid it at the back of the wardrobe before I left. I doubt Amelia will have found it. I definitely don't want it getting back to Mum and Keith.'

Cassie set her granddaughter up in one of the smaller

bedrooms, made sure she could get online and left her to it. She had her own office to sort out and would welcome a chance to put things away and also to come to terms with her new role.

She had a feeling that this was just a lull before a storm so she'd better make the most of it to organise her new home.

Oliver spent the morning in the living room playing some sort of computer game, and when this went on for quite a while, Hal was puzzled. It seemed a childish way for a man of twenty-nine to spend his time.

As they ate lunch he asked, 'Don't you have to go to work?'

'No. Compassionate leave.'

'Do you really need it?'

'I'm entitled to it, so why not take it and have a bit of a rest at their expense? This is a nice place. I may go out for a stroll later, or drive into town and get a real coffee somewhere.' He scowled at his father as he said that.

Hal didn't rise to the bait about that. He cleared his crockery and watched his son walk away from the table without doing the same. 'Hoy!'

Oliver turned round.

'You need to clear up after yourself.'

'Oh, for goodness' sake!'

Hal folded his arms and waited.

Muttering under his breath, Oliver dumped his crockery on the draining board and turned again to leave.

Hal put out his arm to stop him. 'They need a quick rinse and then you put them into the dishwasher. *Voilà!* Clearing up all done, house tidy.'

Their glances met for a second time, but Hal was adamant. He corrected Oliver about where to put the dirty dishes in the machine and watched him do it, then made him wipe down the splashes of tea and milk from the surfaces.

After that they separated. Oliver went back to slump down on the sofa in the living area and started fiddling with his mobile phone.

Hal took refuge in his home office, sighing. This visit was obviously going to be very wearing, but he wasn't giving in on the tidiness side of things.

Half an hour later he saw Cassie come out on her back patio and sit there with a mug of something. He gave in to the temptation to ask if he could join her for a while because the atmosphere in the house was upsetting him.

The postal van arrived earlier than usual at the hotel and the driver went inside to pick up the letters.

The woman on reception looked round for the pile of letters and rolled her eyes when she saw them scattered in one corner. The envelopes hadn't even been stamped with the hotel's name and address. The new young man wasn't doing his job properly.

'Won't be a minute.'

She stamped all the envelopes quickly and passed them over, then started to sort out the incoming mail.

Cassie saw the little red van pull away from the hotel and nodded in satisfaction as she finished her lunch. The letter to Evie's cousin would be on its way.

Evie finished her apple. 'I'll clear up. You go and sit out in the sun and enjoy your coffee.'

'Thanks.'

'Afterwards I'll go back online, if that's all right. I've found a really interesting website about black holes.'

Cassie sat down outside, enjoying the sun on her skin. She was enjoying not having to rush around seeing lawyers today and they had enough fresh food to manage for the time being.

When she heard the outer door next door open and close, she turned her head and raised one hand in greeting to Hal. As he walked across to join her, she was surprised at how stressed he looked.

'If I'm not intruding on you, I'd welcome a little sane, adult conversation.'

'Isn't your son an adult?'

'Only physically.'

She gestured to a chair, studying him, head on one side. 'Still not getting on with him?'

'No, I'm not. I made it a condition of him coming here that he keep the place tidy but I have to stand over him even to make him put his dirty dishes in the machine or pick up after himself. He's twenty-nine, dammit, not seventeen. And I'm not giving in. I can't bear to live in a pigsty. So it's making for a very bad atmosphere.'

'Wow.' She waited a minute and he stared blindly into the distance as he continued to talk.

'I hadn't realised how utterly lazy Oliver is. After they were married and bought a house, he worked hard on it for a year or so, and I thought he'd grown up at last. But he's always liked working with his hands so either that kept him going, or else Mandy kept him at it. Since he got here he seems to have nothing constructive planned, only to laze around and play games on his tablet.'

He picked up his mug, stared at it as if it were an alien artefact before putting it down again without taking a drink. 'I know from my ex that he's been told to get some more qualifications but he's made no attempt to do any studying. His former wife has just got her Master of Business degree apparently.'

Hal looked so stressed, her heart went out to him. 'I don't guarantee that my conversation will be fascinating but I think I'm fairly adult and you're welcome to come across and chat any time I'm sitting out here.'

'Thanks. Am I making too much fuss about details, do you think, Cassie?'

She had no hesitation in reassuring him. 'It's your house and up to you to choose the way you want to live in it. I think any guest should automatically respect that. How old is your son, did you say?'

'Twenty-nine.'

She whistled softly.

Hal sat in silence staring at the lake in the distance then looked at her. 'Will you do me a favour?'

'If I can.'

'Will you and Evie come up for an evening meal at the hotel with me and Oliver, as my guests, tonight or tomorrow, whichever you prefer? That ought to make for one pleasant evening, at least.'

'You don't need to pay for us. We intend to go up there occasionally for dinner anyway. I'm not the world's greatest cook.'

'If I'm the one inviting you, I'd prefer to pay.'

'Very well. You can pay this time, I'll pay next. We'd

love to accept, but Evie will have to wear her new brown wig.' She hesitated, wondering whether to explain.

He seemed to read her thoughts. 'You don't have to tell me why you called her Evie if you don't want to.'

'I think perhaps I ought to, in case there's trouble.'

'Trouble?'

She explained the whole story and saw that she'd distracted him.

'That's terrible for the poor girl. If I can help in any way, Cassie, you've only to ask. If you don't mind, I'll mention it to Oliver, so that he doesn't put his foot in it.'

'Yes, we'd better tell him. And thanks for the offer of help. That's kind of you, but we're going to wait and see what my friend finds out about this Keith Burgess fellow before we do anything. In the meantime Evie has sent a message to her cousin Amelia, asking her to tell her mother that she's all right. And then we wait for Mitch to turn something up.'

'What if he doesn't?'

She grinned. 'That's like saying what if the sun doesn't rise tomorrow. Mitch is the best at finding things out about dodgy people, the very best. Keith is a living, breathing human being and must have left some sort of trail through life.'

'You know, it sounds as if the fellow has deliberately taken on a new identity. But why would he do that? What could he be running from?'

'Wow. I hadn't thought of that.' She frowned, thinking it over. 'You may be right.'

'I've met it once or twice in my work as a lawyer.'

'Well, he's not going to hurt my granddaughter and I—'

Just then the back door of Hal's house slid open and his son stuck his head out.

'Oh, there you are, Dad. Look who's turned up to visit. Your friend Sabine.'

As Oliver pushed open the door and gestured to someone inside to come out, Hal gasped in dismay and in anger too. How dare that woman pursue him down here! He leant closer to Cassie and despair made him ask for her help. 'Can I pretend you're my new girlfriend? I can't shake off this woman with words. She's the one I told you about, the one I think is intending to marry me – well, marry my money, anyway.'

For answer, Cassie leant forward and took hold of his hand. 'Of course you can ask for help. Let's have a bit of fun with her. Give me a kiss and pretend you didn't hear what your son said.'

Her eyes were dancing with mischief as he pulled her into his arms and started to kiss her. His anger was suddenly diluted with amusement and as the kiss deepened, that turned into something else that neither of them had expected – a proper kiss, one filled with passion and promise.

Hal really did forget about Sabine for a few moments and was furious when someone broke the spell by tapping him on the shoulder. He pulled away just a little, but kept his arms round Cassie as he glared sideways at his son.

'What do you want?'

'Didn't you hear me?' Oliver asked. 'Honestly, Dad, what a way to behave! Aren't you a bit old for sitting out snogging in full view of the whole world and his wife?'

'No, I'm not too old at all to enjoy the pleasure of that. What the hell do *you* mean by interrupting us?' Only then did he look beyond Oliver and pretend to be surprised. 'Oh.'

Sabine was glaring at them from his own back patio. 'Sorry to have interrupted,' she snapped and swung round. She went back into his house, heels clicking on the paving of the patio and then fading away across his polished wooden floors.

He didn't attempt to follow her but kept hold of Cassie's hand.

There was the sound of a door slamming and a car starting up at the front of his house then the person drove away.

Oliver was still standing there, gaping at them both.

'Go away, damn you!' Hal exclaimed. 'And stay away.'

He watched his son jerk round and vanish into the house, sliding the door shut with a bang. Taking a deep breath Hal turned back to Cassie, who was still leaning into the circle of his arm, making no attempt to move away.

'Do you mind if we try that again?' he asked. 'It's a long time since fireworks have gone off inside me when I kissed someone. I thought . . . I thought the cancer treatment had put paid to such reactions.'

'It's been a long time for me too, Hal, and yes, I'd really like to try it again.'

So he kissed her gently and she responded tentatively. And since no one interrupted them this time, it turned slowly into an enthusiastic kiss.

When they pulled their heads apart, gasping for breath, he traced a line down the soft curve of her cheek, making no attempt to move away.

'I didn't plan that, Cassie, but I'm very glad it happened. It not only reassured me about my masculinity but gave me great pleasure.'

'I'm glad too. For similar reasons. It's been a long time since I've enjoyed being with a man. I'd been worrying that I was past it.'

Reluctantly, he let her pull away and as she leant back in her chair, he did too. But they kept hold of one another's hand.

'I don't think that was a one-off physical reaction to an attractive woman; I think I'm as attracted to your mind and personality as your body, Cassie.'

'I'm attracted to you in that way too.' She gave a soft chuckle. 'Some would say that sharing a few kisses is a rather old-fashioned way to approach a relationship, but I think it's what we both need just now. Softly, softly.'

She looked at him uncertainly before adding, 'After my marriage broke up, I vowed to give up men. And I didn't find that particularly hard. Today, well, it took me by surprise how much I enjoyed it.'

He flourished a mock bow. 'I'd be grateful, then, if you'd give one hapless male a chance to prove himself worthy of your attention.' He waited again.

Slowly, very slowly she smiled and inclined her head. 'Yes, please. Only, could we not rush things, Hal? I'm still recovering from that terrorist incident and there's Evie to think of. Who knows where that will lead me? She has to come first till her mother and I settle what to do about her future.'

'Of course she comes first. And I'm a bit hamstrung at the moment by having Oliver hanging around, as well as by my surprise at being able to react like that to you.'

'What a pair we are! We'd never fit into a romance novel, would we?'

'I've never read one.'

'Some of the modern ones seem to be more about bedding one another than falling in long-lasting love. I've read quite a few. When you're travelling and things go pear-shaped, you pick up any books that are lying around in hotels in desperation.'

He didn't attempt to let go of her hand and she smiled back and continued to hold his just as firmly.

A short time later his hand slackened and she saw that he was frowning again.

'What is it now?'

'Oliver. I don't know why but I get the feeling he hasn't told me everything.'

'Do they ever? Oh damn.' Her phone was ringing from inside the house and she ran to answer it, then poked her head out to say, 'I have to take this. See you later.'

He walked slowly back to his own house, feeling pleased. When he'd thought he'd lost the ability to be roused by a woman, he'd grieved about that. Surely tonight's reaction couldn't be a fluke?

He paused on the threshold, realising abruptly that he was also happy because the one to stir up such feelings was Cassie, a woman he'd admired on the television for years, and who was even more impressive in person.

She seemed to be a good person, too, which was equally important to him. He thought about the way she was looking after her granddaughter and how fond of one another they seemed already. That aspect was particularly important to him, because he'd had to deal officially with some conniving cheats in his working life, people who believed business laws, or indeed any laws, didn't apply to them and that other people were only there to be used.

Some had sickened him with their callous disregard of other people's life savings, like the one he felt pretty sure his recent work had helped to catch at last, who must surely be facing and deserving a jail term.

He forgot about that and smiled again. In his retirement, he'd hoped to enjoy the company of decent people and lead a simple, quiet life. But to have the companionship of a woman like Cassie would be way beyond what he'd aspired to.

Surely it wasn't too late for love to bloom again?

He hoped not. Though like her, he wanted to take things slowly. Just in case.

But oh, he wished Oliver wasn't here to complicate matters!

Chapter Seventeen

As always, Fran felt better in the fresh air. She began walking, striding out along a road she'd driven along only once since she moved here. If she remembered correctly, there had been a small park at the far end. She would give herself the time to explore it today, time to think without being interrupted by the phone.

Ah yes, there was the park. After walking in through its elegant wrought-iron gateway and up the slight slope, she stopped near some flowering bushes to admire them then stayed there to watch the children playing on the swings in the small playground to one side. Some mothers were sitting on a bench nearby chatting while keeping a watchful eye on their offspring.

On the other side of the path an older couple was occupying another bench, chatting animatedly if their hand gestures were anything to go by. As she watched they stood up and strolled away hand in hand.

It all looked so innocent and peaceful. It made her feel

more relaxed, but as she was about to continue her stroll she noticed a man hovering at the far side of the play area. His strange behaviour drew her attention and she began to worry about what he was doing there.

He was half hidden behind some bushes that were similar to those near her, but he'd had to step off the path deliberately to get amongst them, while she was still on the path. His attention was focused on the children and his expression was – well, avid was the only word to describe it – as if he could see something that made him hungry.

He had a beanie pulled down but she still recognised him and to her surprise it was Keith's friend Ryan. He hadn't noticed her, thank goodness. What was he doing here at this time of day, watching children?

Watching them like that! Alarm bells rang in her brain.

A woman jumped to her feet suddenly from one of the park benches near the swings, her phone in her hand. Her voice floated across to Fran.

'That pervert's back again. I've just taken a photo of him and I'm going to report him to the police. Will someone else take a photo too?'

Ryan must have heard her because he immediately swung round, pushing into the bushes, not going back onto the path. As he hurried away, he tugged his collar higher in an attempt to hide his face.

Fran stood there for a few seconds unable to move, so shocked was she. No! Surely he wasn't one of those horrible types you read about who preyed on children?

Only – his expression while watching them hadn't been right somehow.

'I got him too,' another woman said in a satisfied voice,

showing her phone to the one who'd drawn attention to him. 'He's been here a few times now. I'll come with you to contact the police. Maybe they'll be able to find out who he is. You can't be too careful these days.'

Before she realised what she was doing, Fran had moved forward to join the duo of angry young women. 'I saw what happened. I know who that man is and where he lives.'

'Really? That's wonderful.'

She gave them his name, even gave them her own before she realised how that might pull her into the mess if Ryan was proved to be acting wrongly.

Keith was going to be furious, whatever came of it.

But surely her husband wouldn't protect Ryan if he was proved to have those disgusting tendencies?

Only . . . the two of them were very close friends and had been for years.

She'd often wondered why an intelligent man like Keith would be so close to a dull man like Ryan. She clapped one hand to her mouth as one reason occurred to her. Keith had often said, 'Oh, we like the same things, Ryan and I.' Surely he couldn't mean . . .

Before she could pursue that unwelcome line of thought, a sudden heavy shower took everyone by surprise.

The women collected their children and Fran ran for shelter to a nearby rotunda, standing near the entrance staring out in dismay at the rain sheeting down. She hadn't brought an umbrella, had been too eager to get out into the fresh air.

'Who'd have thought it'd rain so soon?'

She turned with a jerk at the sound of a voice behind her. An older woman was there and she gestured outside.

'This morning's weather forecast said showers this evening but clear this afternoon. Who'd have expected it to rain like this when it started off so sunny?'

'I certainly didn't.'

'Haven't seen you in the park before and I know just about everyone who comes here regularly by sight.'

It was only then that Fran realised the woman was wearing overalls with a motto on the front pocket and behind her there was a trolley containing tools and a rubbish bin, also bearing the same motto. She must be a council gardener.

'I've just moved in nearby,' she explained. 'The park is so pretty, I'll probably come here regularly.'

'Good. I hope you enjoy your visits. We pride ourselves on our flowers.'

'They're lovely.' But Fran hadn't really looked at them after she'd seen Ryan. She was about to turn away when the woman grabbed her arm and tugged her to one side.

'Stay quiet. He's back and I don't think he's seen us.'

There was a man peering sideways from behind some bushes at the rear of the rotunda, not looking at them but back at the now-empty play area: Ryan again.

'What's he doing hiding there?' the gardener wondered aloud.

'He's been watching the children. He must be waiting for them to come back. It made me shiver to see the look on his face. Their mothers saw him and two of them took photos. They said they'd seen him round here before and were going to report him to the police.'

The woman became very still. 'They're sure it's the same man?'

Fran nodded. 'Yes. And I was able to tell them who he

is because I know him. He's a friend of my husband's. Not
my friend, though.'

The woman pulled out an ID card which showed she
was a police officer. 'I've been sent to act like a gardener
and watch for suspicious activity because a couple of people
have already reported a man loitering near the children's
playground.'

'Oh dear.'

'Give me your name and address, please. I'm going to
follow him and I'll want to interview you afterwards.'

Fran did this but was beginning to feel afraid. What had
she started? How would Keith react to this?

Only, she didn't like the idea of why Ryan might still
be loitering here. And how could she not help the police to
protect children?

'I can wait for you here, if you like,' she offered.

'I'd rather come and visit you at home later. I don't know
how long it'll take me to follow him and question him.'

Fran watched her stow the tools behind the rotunda
and leave.

Keith would be furious if she'd helped catch his friend,
whether Ryan was guilty or not. She was quite sure of that.
He didn't have a very high opinion of the police, she'd
never understood why.

She was suddenly glad that Evie wasn't living with them.

If she was with Fran's birth mother, would her daughter
be safe? She had to believe that her birth mother was a
decent person because now she knew why Evie wouldn't
live with Keith, she didn't want her daughter coming
anywhere near him. No, there would be less risk with her
birth mother, surely?

What was beginning to worry her was whether she herself would be safe once Keith found out that she'd identified his friend. If he got into one of his rare tempers he might hit out at her again – and really hurt her this time.

Did she want to risk that? No.

How quickly her feelings for him had shrivelled away. What he and Ryan were doing was . . . horrible.

The worry for her own safety sent Fran hurrying home, heedless of the rain which was still pouring down.

When she got home, Fran was soaked through and shivering. She glanced at her watch. It was only two o'clock.

She couldn't face a confrontation with Keith, just couldn't. Seeing Ryan spying on children had pushed her another step towards ending her relationship with Keith. A possible decision to leave him had suddenly turned into an urgent desire to do so.

It wasn't just because he was Ryan's closest friend, but because she was starting to feel frightened of him. He'd hit her once, and hard too. And even though he'd apologised, that had left her nervous of him.

She might have been stupid enough to rush into marriage but she wasn't stupid enough to live the rest of her life in fear – or put her daughter in danger. If she hurried, she'd have time to pack most of her clothes and leave.

Where could she go, though?

She had a key for Amelia's house and had promised to check on it a couple of times, but Keith knew about that so it'd have to be a B&B.

Since she'd married Keith and moved into his house, he'd changed so quickly she couldn't believe it was the same man who had been so charming over the past few months. He'd grown rougher and hadn't hesitated to show his anger and take it out on her. It was as if he now felt sure of being able to control her.

Was what had driven Evie away fear of Ryan hurting her? Or was it worse? Was Keith like his friend Ryan where children were concerned?

She couldn't forget the look on Ryan's face today, kept seeing it again in her mind's eye. She'd done the right thing giving those women and the police his name.

But what was the right thing to do for herself?

That was a no-brainer. She needed to leave.

Why was she such an utter fool about men? Never, ever again!

As Fran was packing her final bag a couple of hours later there was the sound of a car pulling up in the drive. She peered out of the bedroom window and her stomach muscles clenched in fear. Oh no! Keith had come home an hour early, something he rarely did.

He stormed up the stairs and burst into the bedroom. 'You rotten bitch!'

She didn't need telling why he was angry. How had he found out about Ryan so quickly?

He studied her final suitcase and the other two standing ready. 'What's this in aid of?'

'I'm leaving you.' She was upset at how her voice wobbled, but the look on his face terrified her.

'Oh no, you're not. You're married to me now, remember? That gives me rights. But I'm going to make sure you don't tell lies about my friends again. Enjoy your trip to the park, did you?' He gave her a hard shove, sending her staggering backwards.

'No. I got caught in the rain.'

'Was that before or after you'd been maligning a decent man?'

He took another step towards her and she edged back till she bumped into the dressing table.

He smiled, not a nice smile. 'Well, we're going down to the police station in a few minutes and you're going to tell them you've made a mistake in identifying Ryan.'

'I didn't make a mistake.'

'Oh yes, you did. You'll say you were upset because you and I had had a row, and you hadn't been thinking straight. And you'd better make it convincing.'

His fist suddenly shot out and he punched her in the belly. It hurt so much she screamed and backed into the bay window, gasping in pain. He smiled as if he had enjoyed doing that, such an evil smile that she started throwing the items off her dressing table at him, yelling for help all the time.

When the front door opened, he didn't seem to hear it, because he had just punched her again, sending her sprawling on the floor. But she had heard it and yelled for help again, trying to curl up to protect herself. This time he kicked her, making her cry out, then drew back his leg to do it again.

As she cowered in terror, waiting for another blow, he jerked away from her instead.

Then she saw the woman from the park holding him with his right arm shoved up behind him. Only, this time the woman was wearing a police uniform and there was a male officer standing beside her.

'I'll look after him, you see to the lady,' he said.

'Thanks, Ali.'

Keith began to struggle and yell as she shoved him towards her companion, but though the male officer was no bigger than him, he somehow managed to use the arm lock to stop him. After that he held Keith with his face against the wall, jerking on the arm and making him yell when he tried to get away.

'You all right, love?' the woman asked, holding out one hand.

Fran let her help her up and subsided on the bed, clutching her stomach. 'No. He – hurt me.'

'Show me. I'm Janice, by the way.'

Fran looked across at the two men, reluctant to have a strange man see her undressed.

'I presume that man is your husband?'

'Yes.' She moved incautiously and winced.

'It'd be best to show me what he's done to you immediately and in front of my colleague, then your husband won't be able to claim it was done somewhere else,' Janice said.

Feeling deeply ashamed of what had happened, Fran lifted her skirt. She winced as she moved to show her belly and side, both of which already had big bruises showing on them.

'Can I photograph them?'

'She came home with those bruises!' Keith shouted. 'She'd fallen in the park, could hardly walk.'

Janice winked at Fran. 'Good thing you and I had already met in the park, eh? You were showing no signs of being in pain then.'

Sickened by this behaviour from a man who had been pretending to love her for the past few months, Fran allowed Janice to take a couple of photos, then straightened her clothes.

'Can you keep him here while I finish loading my car?'

'I think it'd be best if we take you to a doctor and get you checked.'

Fran almost refused. She just wanted to get away and never, ever see Keith again. Then she saw him glaring at her, mouthing something that looked like, 'I'll get you.'

Something snapped in her and she turned to the woman beside her. 'I'll need to take my possessions away from here, but then I'll go and see your doctor. My husband and his friend have to be stopped.'

A sigh of relief escaped her companion and she said in a low voice, 'Thanks, love. So many women don't carry through on getting their abusers to face justice.'

'I've read about it. But it is frightening. He's only just started treating me roughly. We got married recently and after I moved in with him he changed. Believe me, I'd not have married him if he'd done anything to hurt me sooner. And I'm not staying with him, whatever he says or does.'

Keith cursed her as he again tried to escape from the policeman's hold, but failed.

'Let's get things organised then,' Janice said. 'I'll carry your suitcase out.'

'Don't let her steal my things!' Keith shouted. 'She's loaded up the car with my possessions already. I demand to see my lawyer.'

Janice merely smiled and said politely, 'We'll see that everything is done properly, believe me, *sir*. Ali, I'll help you get him into the car, then I'll take Fran to the station and meet you there.' She took handcuffs from her belt.

It took the two police officers a while to subdue Keith and get him safely downstairs.

'Good thing we came in this car, eh?' Janice said as she shut the rear door on the compartment they'd locked Keith into.

She turned back to Fran and said in a gentler voice, 'Anything else you want to take with you?'

'My books and music stuff. Oh, and there are some things of Evie's too.'

When they'd carried those out, Janice said, 'Come on, love. Let's go and see the doctor.'

Fran turned at the car to look back. How happy and hopeful she'd been when she came here. How quickly dreams could crumble.

Four hours later, Janice came to talk to Fran, who was feeling numb. She'd seen a doctor and the woman had said it was only bruising. They'd taken photos of it, though, which she found utterly humiliating.

Janice came back to join her after that was over. 'Where are you going now, Fran? You'll need to keep in touch.'

'I don't know where to go.'

'Haven't you got any friends who'll take you in?'

Fran stood thinking then stared at her in shock as the truth sank in. 'We only see his friends now. We moved away from where I was living and I've lost touch with most of my old friends and neighbours over the past few months.'

'Family?'

She was about to shake her head when it occurred to her that she did have one family member that Keith wouldn't know about.

'There may be someone I can ask for help. But I'm not sure.'

By the time Janice had escorted her out of the police station and they were standing near her car, she'd changed her mind.

No. She just couldn't do it. She couldn't go and ask her birth mother for help after she'd hated the woman for years, refused to see her twice and vowed never, ever to speak to her.

She didn't know why she was so reluctant to meet her, but she was.

Janice waited patiently. 'Something else wrong?'

'On second thoughts, I can't ask the person I was thinking about. The connection is too distant. And anyway, I need to go somewhere *he* can't find me.' She was on the verge of tears again. How could she have been so weak, let him walk all over her?

'Let me call someone to help you temporarily, then. You're in no state to drive anywhere.'

'Who?'

'Someone from the women's refuge. They have emergency beds there.'

And heaven help her, Fran agreed to it.

Anything to keep her safe from Keith. She was so sore from his punches, it hurt to move her body.

Most of all she needed time to come to terms with this sudden change in her circumstances. And there was Evie. She was still worried sick about her, prayed that her guess about where her daughter had taken refuge was correct. What if Evie came to Keith's house looking for her and he was there?

It didn't bear thinking of.

'I'll drive you there,' Janice said quietly. 'Ali will come and pick me up afterwards. Just let me tell him.'

Fran could only nod acceptance of that offer and get into the passenger seat.

Chapter Eighteen

Zoe phoned Cassie later that evening. 'Doing anything in particular at the weekend, sis?'

'Um, no.'

'I'm in London and I have to be down here for a meeting next Monday as well. I thought rather than going back to the north for such a short time I could come and visit you in Wiltshire.'

Cassie didn't know what to say. Of course she wanted to see her sister. But there was Evie to think about.

Zoe's tone of voice changed, grew stiffer. 'If you're busy, I can come another time.'

'No, no! I do have a guest, but when I think about it, it's someone I'd really like you to meet. It'll be a nice surprise. Do come.'

'You're sure?'

'Very sure. Trust me, you'll be interested.'

'OK. I'll be down tomorrow evening, then.'

Cassie went to find Evie and hurry her out to purchase another single bed.

They walked round the shops arm in arm, happy to be together.

'I never thought I'd need other spare beds so quickly,' Cassie said. 'I'm amazed by how my life is changing.'

'It seems to me you're enjoying having people you care about with you in a quiet place, both friends and family.'

'Yes, I am. But most of all, I'm enjoying having you.' She glanced sideways and added, 'Something's worrying you, though, isn't it, Evie?'

'Yes. I wish Mum could be with us. I'm sure she'd love you if she gave herself a chance. But—'

'But what?'

'If I could only find out how she's getting on, I'd feel a lot better. I don't trust him to look after her. She gets so anxious sometimes.'

'She'll have received word from her cousin that you're safe by now, surely?'

'I hope so. But I'm afraid *he* might get hold of the letter first. If he did, he'd destroy it, I'm sure. And then he'd come after me, which is why I didn't tell her where I was.'

For an intelligent girl like Evie to believe that this man was so threatening to her safety made Cassie sure there was something very wrong with him. She'd never met such a mature youngster. Was he really the sort of pervert his focus on a young girl seemed to indicate?

Surely her daughter couldn't have married a man with such a warped mind? But Evie had said he could be charming when he wanted. What a mess!

Fran let Janice take her to the women's refuge and park her car, then she got out a bag into which she'd slung some

overnight things. Janice escorted her inside and they went
into the matron's office, where she gave a few particulars,
feeling utterly humiliated to be here. She'd never expected
to wind up in a place like this, never.

'I have to go now,' Janice said. 'You'll be all right here, I
promise you. He won't be able to get to you.'

'Thanks for your help.' She watched the police officer
leave then followed the matron upstairs to her bedroom, a
very small space with a shabby duvet on the single bed and
one tiny wardrobe.

'I'll leave you to settle in then you can join the others
downstairs. There's a toiletries pack in the top drawer,
if you need it. The bathrooms are at each end of the
corridor.'

Fran used the bathroom, but couldn't bring herself to
unpack let alone go downstairs, just couldn't do it. She
flopped down on the bed, sitting hunched on the edge, not
wanting to face anyone, thank you very much.

A few minutes later, however, someone knocked on
the door. She didn't answer, but when there was another
knock, she sighed and straightened up. 'Come in. Oh, it's
you, Matron.'

'Call me Tracy. We don't stand on formality here. I
gather you've been hurt. Is it something I can help with?'

Fran shrugged, not wanting to go into details, not really
knowing what she wanted, if truth be told.

'Would you let me look at your bruises before we join
the others? I have a salve that helps bruising get better more
quickly. No need to prolong the pain, eh? You won't be the
first to need it.'

Fran nodded, feeling like bursting into tears at the

kindness in the older woman's tone and expression. She let the matron tend to her sore belly and side, trying not to whimper and not always succeeding.

Afterwards Tracy screwed on the cap and handed the tube to her. 'Keep it. And Fran – you were right to come here. This beating was done to hurt you as much as he could without it showing or creating permanent damage. People like that can go on to do far worse.'

'I figured that out. I'll never forget the look of pleasure on his face as he thumped me.'

'There are some warped people out there. Now, one more thing. The police weren't sure how long you'd be staying when they called in for an emergency bed. Do you have any idea at all? We won't throw you out on the street, I promise, but it helps if we have some understanding of your situation and whether you have someone else who'll be able to help you.'

'I'm not sure. This has all blown up so suddenly. I've only been married to him for a few days, though we've been seeing each other for several months.' She couldn't hold back a sob. 'How could I not have realised what he was like? I must be the stupidest person who ever had to take refuge here.'

'You'll only be stupid if you go back to him. Some women do that, believing the promises of no more violence. One or two have died because of it, sadly.'

Fran gasped then bowed her head. 'That's terrible. I definitely won't be going back to him, though. I'd already decided that. It's the only thing I'm at all sure of. But I shall need to find somewhere to live and . . .'

She hesitated, then told Tracy about her daughter

running away. 'My birth mother is looking for me, you see, and I'm hoping Evie may have taken refuge with her. It's the only thing I can think of, unless my daughter's sleeping on the street. I'm adopted, so don't have any close blood relatives.'

'Then isn't it a good thing your birth mother is looking for you?'

'Not really. She gave me away in the first place. I'll never forgive her for that.'

'How old was she when she had you?'

Silence, then Fran muttered, 'Fifteen.'

'She might not have had any choice.'

'I still don't want to see her.'

'Didn't you say your daughter is fifteen? Can you imagine your Evie keeping a baby with hostile parents refusing to support her in that option, when she's legally too young even to leave school? If your grandparents had done as they threatened and pushed your mother out onto the street, she'd probably have had the baby taken away. It wasn't as easy in the past for underage girls to find help. Not that it's *easy* now. Having a baby with no support never is.'

It was the thought of Evie in that dilemma that hit home hardest of all and that only added to the confusion Fran was experiencing.

Tracy waited a few moments then stood up. 'Let all that go for now. This is no time to make important decisions. You look utterly exhausted. I think what you need most is to rest in peace and quiet. How about I bring you a cup of coffee and a snack, then you take a nap?'

She was back within a few minutes. 'Here you are.

I'll leave you for a while, but do come down if you want company or feel hungry. Just follow the noise of people chatting at the rear of the house.'

'Thanks. I think you're right. I'm way beyond exhausted.'

'Just a word about tomorrow. A cooked breakfast is served from 7 to 9 a.m. If you miss it, you can find something in the kitchen in the fridge and cupboard marked with red tape. Same if you're hungry later. Anyone will show you where to go.'

'I'm not really hungry.'

'Well, just bear it in mind. The women here are very supportive, you'll find. Well, those who have enough emotional energy left to support someone else are. Some of the more recent arrivals are like you, stunned by what's happened to them.'

Fran watched the door close, then ate half the piece of cake and drank some coffee. But she was too tired to be hungry, so visited the bathroom, put on a nightdress then curled up in bed.

She'd expected to cry herself to sleep, but she didn't cry at all. She felt too numb.

It was bright daylight when Fran awoke and she was amazed to find that she'd slept right through the night. She had to rush to find a bathroom, after which, since it was past nine o'clock, she went back to get her towel and took a leisurely shower. She was horrified by the size of her bruises and avoided looking at them as much as she could while she put on more of the salve.

When she was dressed, she took the tray downstairs and found a group of women sitting chatting in a shabby room full of armchairs, sofas and small tables.

As she stood hesitating by the door, one of them got up. 'I'm Polly.' She waited, head on one side.

'Fran. I, um, got here last night.'

'Yeah, we heard another woman had come in. Welcome. This is a good place to find your feet again. Now, I bet you'd like a cup of coffee or tea to start with?'

'I'd kill for one. And I'm hungry, too.'

'I'll show you the kitchen. Here, give me the tray.'

With Polly's help, Fran got herself something to eat, still expecting questions. Only, they didn't come. Indeed, the other woman sat sipping a mug of coffee opposite her at the small table, staring towards the window, clearly giving her the choice of talking or not.

'Are we allowed out?'

Polly chuckled. 'Of course we are. Do you think you're in prison or something?'

'I don't know what to expect. I didn't think I'd end up in a refuge, that's certain. I only got married to him a week or so ago.'

'Known him long, had you?'

'Several months.'

'I bet he was taking the time to separate you from your friends first so that he could get you to depend only on him.'

'How did you know?'

This time Polly's laugh was totally mirthless. 'Because that's how my ex started off with me. Ah, to hell with men like that! Where do you want to go? Not to see him, surely?'

'Heavens, no!'

As the silence lengthened, Polly said, 'You don't have

to tell me anything, but you should know I'm a part-time counsellor here. I understand what it's like, you see. I was training to be a real counsellor until I met my ex. I'm working on my studies and earning my keep here by helping out. Up to you if you want to chat any time. Do you have a car?'

'Yes.'

'Just a warning. He'll know it by sight if you go to any of your former places.'

'I hadn't thought of that.'

'If you pay for the petrol I can drive you where you want to go in mine. It's old, not much to look at but reliable. Besides, you'll be safer if you're not on your own. He's likely to be angry.'

'Oh yes. He was absolutely furious with me for identifying his friend.'

'Then let me take you round.'

'Can it be that easy to get on with things?'

'What's easy about picking up the pieces and trying to start a whole new life? It's hard going, especially when you leave here and face the world.'

'Yes. I suppose it is. I'm not really thinking straight yet.'

'Which only shows you're normal!'

'Normal but stupid.'

'Don't put yourself down.'

'I have to face facts. No one forced me to let him take over my life.' After another moment's thought, she added, 'Look, I can not only afford to pay for the petrol but I'd really welcome some company.'

Polly smiled. 'Good. I like going out for drives – as well as helping other women in the same situation as me. Let's find you some clothes that are nothing like what you'd usually wear and a beanie to pull down over that hair of yours. It's a dead giveaway, red hair is.'

Fran gaped at her. 'Is that necessary?'

'Who knows? But if it is, we'll be prepared, eh?'

Chapter Nineteen

When they arrived at Amelia's house, Polly parked a little way down the street. 'Don't get out yet. We'll watch the house for a few minutes before we even go across to it.'

Her companion sounded as if she'd experienced this situation before and been caught out, so Fran would rather be too careful than sorry. Her bruises reminded her of that at regular intervals.

There were no signs of life so Fran pulled her borrowed beanie right down to hide her hair and they got out of the car. As they were approaching Amelia's gate, Fran was sure she saw a curtain twitch in the front bedroom upstairs. 'Don't go in!' She tugged her companion past the house. 'I saw the curtain move.'

'So did I,' Polly said. 'Let me take over.'

She turned in at another house a few doors along and knocked on the front door, saying brightly, 'I'm very sorry to trouble you, but is there someone called Svenson living in the street?'

'Not that I know of.'

'Oh dear, I must have got the address wrong. Thank you so much for your help.'

'You're welcome.'

The door closed and they returned to Polly's car.

'What is your ex's car like?'

'A red Ford with a slightly dented boot.'

'See if you can spot it.' Polly drove slowly up the next street and down the one after.

'That's it!' Fran exclaimed, shocked because she hadn't really expected to see him near here and had almost persuaded herself that they must have seen the curtains move slightly by a stray current of air. 'It must be him inside the house, looking for me. Who else could it be? Amelia's away.'

'Good thing we were careful. We'll get a police escort to come back to your cousin's later. We're not risking any more physical violence. Look, I don't know anything about your background, but is there absolutely no one else you think your daughter could have gone to for help?'

Fran bent her head, feeling sick that it had to come to this, then admitted in a choked voice, 'There is someone. My birth mother.'

Polly let out a soft whistle of surprise. 'Could you not have gone to take refuge with her last night?'

'I've never met her and I don't want to. I only know her address from when she tried to contact me recently. Evie must have found it when she was clearing up the kitchen because the letter I'd thrown away was hidden amongst her art things. I'm hoping she took refuge with her grandmother. She'd be far safer there than on the street, whatever the woman's like. I suppose we'd better try her house.'

'You're sure you want to go there? From the tone of your voice, you don't sound as if you're ready to face the woman.'

'Since she's been trying to contact me, I'd guess she would have been happy to help Evie.'

'Perhaps you'd better think carefully about it before we go any further.'

'No. I don't have any choice now. It's the best chance I have of finding my daughter, I'm sure, because there's nowhere else Evie *can* have gone.' Nowhere else Fran could go, either, that Keith wouldn't know about. But she didn't like to admit that aloud yet.

'You're sure your ex doesn't know where your birth mother lives?'

'Pretty certain, yes. I doubt he'd have left the letter amongst Evie's things if he'd spotted it. Knowing him, I'm sure he'd have burnt it so that I didn't have anywhere else to turn . . . don't you think?'

'Your guess would fit the behaviour pattern of men like him. Come on, then, tell me where your birth mother lives.'

The address Fran had memorised turned out to be in a very nice suburb, with rows of well-maintained houses, neat gardens but few people around at this time of day.

Fran scowled at it. 'She's not short of money, then.'

'Did you want her to be?'

She didn't even try to answer that, but felt a bit ashamed of being so surly.

They stopped outside the house and studied the façade.

'It looks empty, with all the blinds drawn like that,' Polly said. 'Are you sure this is the place?'

'Yes, I'm sure. Let me do this on my own.' Fran summoned up all her courage and got out of the car, knocking on the front door with an old-fashioned brass knocker in the shape of a cat, for lack of a doorbell. There was no response and the sound seemed to echo inside.

She knocked again, but to no avail.

Polly came to join her. 'She could be at work.'

'But Evie wouldn't be and if she were inside and saw me knocking, she'd have opened the door, I know she would.' Fran went to try and peep in the window, but the blinds were drawn and covered the window completely.

They tried the tall side gate that led to the rear, but it was locked and fitted the gap so closely they couldn't see what lay behind it.

'Whoever lives here really values their privacy,' Polly commented.

As they went back towards the car, a woman walking a dog along the street stopped to call, 'She's moved out.'

'Oh. Do you know where she's gone?'

'Sorry, but I don't. She kept herself to herself. Well, famous people usually do, don't they?'

Fran looked at her in puzzlement. 'Famous people? I'm looking for Cassie Bennington.'

'Yes. But she's Cassandra Benn when she's on TV. Didn't you know?'

'No. I've seen Cassandra Benn on TV, but I didn't know it was her I was looking for. I've been checking my ancestry, you see, and we may be related. You don't know where she's gone?'

'No, sorry. And I don't think anyone round here will, either. She was away a lot and didn't do more than nod when she passed you in the street, even when she was at home.' She raised one hand in farewell, gave the dog's lead a little tug and walked on.

Fran stared at Polly. 'Cassandra Benn can't be my mother, surely!'

'I've seen her on TV. She has your colour of hair.' She studied Fran. 'Could be, you know. There's a resemblance, same shape of face, if I remember correctly, same slender build, too.'

'Let's go back to the refuge. I don't know what to think or what else to do.'

'We could contact the police when we get back and ask if they'll help you visit your cousin's house safely.'

'Not today. I'm just . . . gobsmacked by what that woman said.'

It felt as if not only her present life but her past had been turned upside down, somehow. Could Cassandra Benn really be her mother?

When they got back Fran once again went up to her room, claiming to feel exhausted. All she wanted to do was come to terms with what she'd found out, only her thoughts seemed to be in a worse tangle than ever. How could she be the daughter of the famous journalist? The woman didn't look old enough to have a daughter approaching forty-two.

And as she lay on the bed, a picture of Evie came into her mind. She had the same red hair as her mother and grandmother – same resemblance to them both!

The only thing Fran was sure of was that she should have gone to the police as soon as her daughter went missing. Why had she let Keith persuade her not to?

It was inevitable that she went on to wonder what she would have done if Evie had been assaulted and made pregnant as her own mother had. The answer was a no-brainer: she'd have helped her, that's what. She might be useless at choosing a man worth falling in love with, but she'd never, ever threaten to throw her daughter out on the street, whatever the circumstances.

Her mother's parents had done that and forced her to have the baby adopted. How cruel!

Fran sighed. The more she looked into this, the more uncertain she became about what was the right thing to do next, or even how she now felt.

All she was sure of was that she wasn't going back to Keith. She was utterly certain of that, and her decision was reinforced every time her bruises hurt.

She would probably give up men for ever, and with it the chance to have another child. She couldn't face any more catastrophic relationships and break-ups.

In the middle of the night, she woke with a start and couldn't get back to sleep. She lay thinking for a while, coming to the conclusion that she was being cowardly. It was obvious that she needed to go into Amelia's house because if there was one place Evie would send a message, in order to make sure Keith couldn't intercept it, that was it. Finding her daughter was far more important than anything else in this mess.

The curtain at Amelia's house had definitely moved even though the window hadn't been open to let in a breeze. They'd both seen it. Had Keith already broken into the house? Got hold of any messages?

She shivered. She wouldn't be surprised if he had.

Nothing he did would surprise her now. How was she going to protect her daughter if she couldn't even find Evie?

She rolled over without taking care and whimpered as she hurt her bruised belly. That made another shiver run through her. She didn't want to face her ex again. He was much stronger than she was. She definitely had to ask for a police escort before she went anywhere near Amelia's house, just in case he was waiting for her there.

Even if there was a message from Evie asking for her help, she didn't even have a home to take her daughter to now.

She couldn't think beyond going back to Amelia's house and praying that she'd manage to find her daughter.

It was a long time before she got to sleep again and she woke feeling utterly exhausted.

The next day dawned with heavy grey skies and the damp feel of rain threatening. After she'd showered and dressed, Fran tried in vain to phone Amelia's mobile. There was no answer and no answering service either, which was unusual. Usually when Amelia went overseas she kept in touch with her friends.

She gave up trying in the end and sent an email without much hope of a reply. She made it down to the kitchen by half past eight. Polly waved to her to come across to the table where she and three other women were chatting.

'Dump your handbag and get some food. It's self-serve.'

Fran went to fill a plate, but could only face toast and jam.

When she rejoined the group, Polly introduced her then said, 'You don't look as if you slept well.'

'I didn't.'

'Now why am I not surprised?'

'I didn't sleep all night through for weeks after I got here,' one woman said. 'Give it time. You'll gradually settle down and start thinking more clearly.'

Fran nodded, managed to force a half-smile and tried to eat her toast. Only, it seemed to stick in her throat and eventually she pushed the last half of it aside.

'How about a stroll round the garden before it starts raining?' Polly suggested. 'Daylight's good for you when you're feeling depressed.'

Fran didn't even bother to deny that she was feeling down. The other women seemed nice, but she didn't want to chat to them, so she put her dirty dishes away and contented herself with nodding to them as she left.

When they got outside she breathed deeply, enjoying the freshness of the damp air, in spite of the lack of sunshine. 'I did decide one thing last night, Polly. I want to go to my cousin Amelia's house today in case there's a message. How do I arrange for the police to come there with me?'

'We can get Tracy to phone them. You're sure about that?'

'Yes. It's the only place I can think of where Evie might try to contact me. I tried to phone Amelia this morning but there was no answer.'

'I'll go and sort that out now.'

It seemed a long time till Polly came back. 'The police can meet you there at about eleven. They don't want us to go inside till they arrive, not even into the garden.'

'Not until then?'

'We aren't exactly their first priority.' She smiled sympathetically. 'I know. There's a lot of hanging about to put up with while you sort things out, but we'll gradually work through it all and find a way to help you.' She led the way back into the kitchen. 'How about another cup of tea? And maybe a piece of fruit?'

Feeling guilty about taking up so much of Polly's time, Fran took a banana, peeling it slowly and carefully, not really wanting to eat. 'You must have better things to do than babysit me.'

'Not today, I don't. You really need me.'

'I always seem to be needing someone. You'd think by my age I'd be able to manage my own life.' She took a small bite of the firm, white banana and forced it down.

'You're just going through a bad patch. Just one more thing. Tracy asked me to check whether you've contacted work to let them know you won't be in.'

She gaped at Polly. 'No. What was I thinking of? I have to do that straight away. I don't want to lose my job on top of everything else.' She dropped the banana on the wooden bench and took her phone out of her handbag, then paused with it in her hand. 'What shall I tell them?'

'Say you had an accident and will need a few days off to recover. We'll get you a doctor's note.'

She made the phone call, dissolved in tears when she tried to explain and had to let Polly finish for her.

Only, the call continued and Polly's expression grew grimmer and grimmer. 'No. He doesn't speak for his wife . . . That man is the *cause* of her present problem, for heaven's sake . . . Please tell him nothing in future. No, not even whether she's still off work.'

The person at the other end seemed to be protesting and Polly cut the conversation short. 'Her husband is dangerous. He attacked her yesterday and the police had to get involved to stop him. Do you want to be responsible for him hurting her again?'

The voice started up, louder now, and after a few seconds she interrupted the speaker. 'Is there someone in HR I can speak to? I think they'll have a better idea what to do. As you say, this is not your area of expertise.'

She sighed and waited, rolling her eyes at Fran, then speaking earnestly to someone else, explaining yet again that Keith was the cause of Fran's indisposition and that the assault was now being handled by the police. This time she nodded a lot and the grim expression lightened gradually.

When she put the phone down, she said tartly, 'The human resources person was much more understanding than your section boss, thank goodness.'

'I didn't want them to know.'

'I had to say something. The guy you're working directly with hasn't a clue about this sort of situation and he'd actually agreed to let your husband know if you turned up to work. We needed to stop anyone there giving your ex information about you. The guy in HR was very angry to hear your section head had done that, so I'm pretty sure he'll take care to prevent that from now on.'

Fran nodded. She couldn't see herself going back to work there now that she knew what her boss had done. She'd never really taken to him but now, she'd not trust a single word he said. Besides, she didn't want to go anywhere she might run into Keith and he not only knew where she worked but where she usually had lunch. There wasn't even anyone on duty at the entrance to the building to vet those coming in.

She might have to start all over again, finding a job in

another town and building up a life from nothing. She'd done that a couple of times before, hated the stress and loneliness of it. She'd be even lonelier without her daughter to look after and love. And there had never been such a dire need for secrecy as there was now. She wondered if she'd ever feel safe again – ever *be* safe.

Thank goodness she'd still kept control over her savings and bank accounts. It wasn't only a matter of having the money but of knowing that she hadn't been totally stupid.

And when she'd eventually realised the danger she was in, she'd had the sense to try to get away from him quickly, too. From what the other women here had told her she'd done well there.

Those were signs there was still hope for her – weren't they? That she wasn't totally brain-dead?

She hoped so.

Chapter Twenty

Hal finished his breakfast and cleared his things away, sitting over the remains of his cup of tea to keep an eye on his son, who had got himself a mug of drinking chocolate but hadn't yet eaten any breakfast.

Oliver finished his drink and went to sit in the living area, caught his father's eye and without saying a word, went back to put the mug in the dishwasher. Then he sat down and started fiddling around with his smartphone.

Must be bad news, judging from his son's expression as he glared at his messages. Hal didn't say anything, waiting to see if he would share the news.

Fists clenched, Oliver sat scowling into space for a few moments, then looked round, opened his mouth as if to speak then snapped it shut again.

'Is something wrong?'

Oliver came across to join him at the table, still clutching his phone.

Sometimes, Hal thought, those phones seemed more

like children's toys or even children's security blankets than communication devices.

'They want me to go on a course before I start work at the new place.'

'An interesting one?'

'No. Interpersonal skills.'

'Grooming you for a promotion perhaps?'

Oliver stared down at his phone, then switched it off and scowled at his father. 'No. If you must know, the new job is a demotion and this is an update of a course I did a couple of years ago. I already know all the blah-blah politically correct crap in it by heart.'

Hal waited a moment or two to ask, 'Why a demotion?'

'Some stupid bitch complained that I was sexist and anti-gay.'

'And are you?'

Oliver stared down again. 'I don't think so. Not really. I was just a bit . . . well, a lot angry and spoke without thinking. She took exception to it and we got into a row. You can't open your mouth these days without upsetting someone.'

'You must have done something more serious than that to have got yourself demoted.'

'Yeah, well, I was having a bad day and needed to be on my own, only she kept following me around and talking at me. I apologised afterwards for shoving her out of the way, didn't I? And I didn't *hurt* her. She didn't fall over or anything. What else do the HR people want from me, a pint of blood?'

Hal watched him thump one fist down on the table but couldn't help noticing that his son's eyes were over-bright.

'Sounds to me as if you need counselling and an anger

management course more than interpersonal skills training.'

'Oh, they want me to do that as well. The latest email also gave me details of my first appointment with a counsellor. The new lot who bought out the company last year pride themselves on helping their employees through bad patches in life, you see.'

Hal didn't know what to say to that. No one had helped him through his recent close brush with death. He might have been glad of a little help because it shook you up good and proper to face cancer.

Mind, it was probably his own fault because most of the people he'd worked with hadn't even known what he was going through. Would he have welcomed counselling? Who knew? He'd just got on with things.

He realised Oliver was glaring across at him.

'Well? Not got anything to add to it, Dad? No little lectures from a fond parent?'

'Only that if there's anything I've learnt in this life, it's not to let bad news swamp me. I've had to find ways to stay calm in the past year. You're not the only one who's been facing problems, you know. What'd happen if we all lost our tempers and hit out at others?'

The silence lasted a long time, then Oliver muttered, 'Sorry. I was forgetting. I should have been there for you.'

'That's all right. You didn't know about my problems.'

'No. Nor you about mine. So just to keep you informed now, I definitely don't want to take this job at a lower level. It's far less interesting. And all the people there will know I'm *in remediation*. That's what the people huggers who took over a perfectly good company call it. Hah!'

'Then find yourself another job.'

'I can't.'

'Oh?'

'Not in my area of work and at a decent salary, anyway. Not till I'm able to get a full reinstatement and a good reference. I'm a great salesman, in case you're interested, and they know that or they'd not go to this much trouble.'

'You could take casual work for a time?'

'No way. Anyway, I can't go back to serving in a bar or any of the casual jobs I did when I was a student, because I have a big credit card debt to pay off.'

'I thought you were getting a payout for your share of the house.'

'I won't use the money I'm going to get for that or I'll not have enough left for a deposit on a new place. Besides, I'll need a steady job to get a mortgage. That's important to me. I don't intend to lose owning my own home on top of everything else.'

'Then you'll just have to bite the bullet, go back to work and face the new people.'

A growl was his only answer.

'Why don't you get some breakfast, and after you've cleared it up, go out for a nice, long walk? It always helps me to get out in the fresh air.'

Oliver shrugged, gave him a dirty look and made several pieces of toast, slathering them so thickly he used up the last half-jar of his father's favourite black cherry jam.

This wasn't the time to talk about nutrition, or selfishness. Indeed, Hal couldn't think of anything he could say to help. It was up to his son to make the necessary decisions about his own future. But if Oliver was trying to preserve his house money, even if he wasn't going the best way to lower interest payments, that surely said he hadn't completely lost all common sense?

He stayed at the table, pretending to read an article in yesterday's newspaper and waiting to make sure his son cleared up after himself. He intended to keep reinforcing the lesson about how he wanted his home treated, because control over his surroundings was important to him – ridiculously important perhaps, but hey, this was his beautiful, brand-new home.

From the scowls shot in his direction, Oliver was well aware of why he was lingering, but at least he did what was necessary before slamming out of the house.

There was the sound of a car starting up outside and Hal let out a long, slow breath, then another. Phew! His son's visit was going to be harder than he'd expected.

He wasn't going to offer to lend Oliver the money to pay off the credit card debt, even though he could have easily afforded it. His son had to take charge of his own messed-up life and work his way through it, learning from the experience, hopefully.

Only if absolute disaster threatened would Hal step in.

A little after eleven o'clock, the police turned up to meet Fran and Polly outside Amelia's house. It was a different pair of officers but just as kind, and their mere presence made Fran feel safe.

She had her key ready but when she tried to insert it into the lock, something seemed to be blocking it. When she bent to try to peer into it, she saw only darkness. The officer who did the same thing said something must be obstructing the inner end.

'Let's go round the back and see if we can get you into the house that way,' he suggested. 'I'll go first.'

When he opened the side gate, a box that had been hidden on a nearby shed roof was pulled down by a rope attached to it and fell on him. It must have been heavy because he yelled and jumped aside, kicking it and rubbing his shoulder as if it hurt.

His companion yanked the two women quickly back out of the way. 'Booby trap. Stay there and don't touch anything.'

Fran stared after him open-mouthed. She could guess who was to blame for these problems. But why? Had Keith gone completely mad? Was he so determined to hurt her further that he'd planted a booby trap for her cousin? Or did he know Amelia was away and had meant it for his wife?

Well, if he'd wanted to further stiffen her resolve not even to consider going back to him, he had succeeded.

The officer who had been with them returned. 'You can come round to the back safely but stay on the path.'

They both stopped dead as they saw that the other officer, who looked as if he had the beginnings of a bruise on his cheek, was now standing beside a broken kitchen window, which had a hole in it big enough for an adult to get through. Fran could see shards of glass littering the surfaces inside the room as well as outside the house.

'I'm presuming this wasn't done before?'

'No, of course not. Amelia wouldn't go away and leave a broken window. What's it like in the rest of the interior? Has Keith done anything else?'

'You sound sure it's him.'

'I'm quite sure.'

The officer tried the sliding door and it opened easily.

'The intruder must have come out this way and not been able to lock it again, or not bothered to try. I'll have a quick check of the inside before anyone else goes in.'

He walked round the dining area and vanished into the front of the house. When he came back, he said, 'Well, there's more damage but it seems to be on a smaller scale. You know the place well, so we're hoping you can tell us if anything's been touched apart from the obvious vandalism.'

Fran had been nervous until now, but as she looked round the interior, that feeling began to give way to anger. Most of the big room next to the kitchen hadn't been trashed but one beautiful art glass vase that Amelia had particularly treasured, and had shown with pride to Keith the first time he came here, had been smashed in the centre of the floor, sending multicoloured splinters of glass everywhere. It was as if he'd wanted to make a threat about what he could do to her by destroying a precious possession.

She pointed to the side. 'Amelia's studio is in the conservatory over there and it also contains her office equipment and files.'

The other officer had found a sweeping brush and led the way across to the conservatory, brushing glass aside when necessary, though some smaller pieces still crunched underfoot.

They all stood in the doorway, staring in disgust at more vandalism. A beautiful painting of a meadow of spring flowers on an easel had been daubed with a cross of white gloss paint, then the tin of paint had been upended on the floor nearby. All three drawers in the filing cabinet had been pulled open, with papers and art materials scattered nearby.

'He could have been searching for something specific from the looks of this,' one officer said.

She knew now, oh yes – she might have let love blind her before but now she was utterly certain Evie had been right to fear him. 'Keith wants to find my daughter. She said he made her feel uncomfortable and I didn't realise – didn't listen. Well, you don't expect that sort of thing from someone who has always been charming to you, do you?'

'No.' The officer's voice was gentle. 'People like that can be quite clever in manipulating people.'

'I should think Keith wants to get hold of both me and my daughter now. The police took his friend and business partner Ryan in for questioning yesterday for hovering near little children at the playground in the park. I was the one who gave them Ryan's address and I can give it to you.'

'If you're talking about Ryan Ogle, we have it already, because that wasn't the first time he'd been taken in for suspicious behaviour near children.'

'No!'

'We searched his house yesterday but there was no sign of anyone else living there nor was there any evidence of wrongdoing on his computer. We'll check out your ex's house in more detail after this and see if there's anything untoward there. We'd be grateful if you'd help us by asking us to go in to help collect the rest of your things.'

She nodded. 'Of course. There are some books I wouldn't mind getting, but I put my furniture in storage when I moved in with him.' Thank heavens she'd told Keith she'd sold it. He'd said it was rubbish, but she loved her old pieces, some of them genuine antiques which she'd refurbished with loving care.

'Good. Now, let's have a good look round here and see if there's anything else out of place.'

She sighed as they studied the carefully targeted destruction of items. 'Poor Amelia. It's not fair. It's as if Keith's punishing her for what I've done.'

'No, it isn't at all fair, if it is him and that's what he's doing. Shall we go and look at the front door next to see why you couldn't get the key in the lock?'

It was immediately obvious that glue had been used to block the keyhole.

'I should think he did this to make sure you went round the side.' The injured officer rubbed his shoulder.

'I'll have to get someone in to fix this for Amelia, since it's my fault he did it,' she said.

'Not yet. Keep trying to contact your cousin and in the meantime we'll get a team here to see if we can find any prints or DNA samples. Keep your fingers crossed that he cut himself. We'll take your prints to eliminate you before we let you go back to the refuge, if that's all right.'

She nodded.

They'd just turned to go out through the back when there was the sound of something falling through the letterbox into the hall. One of the officers went to check it and called, 'It wasn't the post, but an envelope must've been stuck in the letterbox.'

He came back holding it by one corner. 'It's marked "Delivered to no. 15 by mistake". It's from some hotel in Wiltshire. Is the hotel somewhere you go to or know?' He held it out.

The envelope caught Fran's attention immediately, not the explanatory scrawl but the handwritten address. 'This letter must have been written by my daughter. I'd recognise her handwriting anywhere. Can we open it? I'm hoping she's asking Amelia to pass on a message to me.'

He handed her the envelope and when she turned it over, she saw that it had indeed been stamped with the name and address of a hotel in Wiltshire. She answered his earlier question. 'And this isn't a hotel I've ever heard mentioned, let alone stayed at.'

She memorised its name and address quickly before opening the envelope and pulling out a letter. 'It *is* from Evie.' Tears of relief came into her eyes as she read it.

Dear Amelia,
Will you please contact my mother and tell her I'm safe?
I won't give you my address because I don't want her letting Keith know where I am. But I'm with someone who cares about me.
Love,
Evie

Fran looked at the envelope in puzzlement. 'She said she wasn't giving her address but there's the hotel information on the back of this.'

'She might be staying there and have handed it to them to post. She'd not have known that they stamped the back of the outgoing letters,' Polly suggested. 'When we go back we'll look up the hotel online.'

'And then I'm going to phone and ask if she's there, so that I can drive down to get her.'

'You shouldn't go there yet,' one of the policemen said hastily. 'Your ex is very determined to cause trouble and you shouldn't go anywhere on your own till we're sure you'll be safe. We'll get in touch with the police down there and ask them to check out the hotel first.'

Fran shook her head. 'No. I've not been the best of mothers but I love my daughter and I've let her down badly recently. I have to see her . . . just have to, and take her somewhere safe.'

'I can come with you, but we'll have to go in your car,' Polly offered. 'Mine's a bit old for long journeys.'

'I can't ask you to do that.'

Polly grinned. 'It's no sacrifice, believe me. I've not been out for a drive in the country for ages.'

'Does your husband have any idea about this hotel, do you think, Mrs Burgess?' the younger officer asked.

She shook her head. 'I can't see how he could, because until now I'd not even heard of it. And could you call me Ms Milner from now on, please? It's my maiden name. I don't want to use his name any more. I'm going to divorce him as soon as it can be arranged.'

'We can't stop you going to look for your daughter, but we'll call the police in that part of Wiltshire and let them know about your situation. That way, if you need to call for help, you'll get it more quickly. You're not going there today, are you? It's too late for that, surely?'

'No, but I'm going to phone them today and see if she's staying there. Maybe I can even speak to her.'

'Why don't you try now?'

She nodded and took out her phone, dialling the number stamped on the back of the envelope and adding it to her phone number list. But the person who answered said there was no one of that name or description staying at the hotel.

'I'd have noticed if a young woman with red hair had visited us recently, madam.'

Fran had a sudden idea. 'Are there any holiday lets nearby?'

'There is a leisure village attached to the hotel, but I don't think any of the houses in it is used as a holiday let. It's not a big place and they're still building. All that have been completed are owner occupied.'

After Fran had ended the call she gave the two police officers a very determined look. 'I'm going there tomorrow. Evie has to be nearby, surely, if this was posted from the hotel?' She shook her head sadly, even more worried about her daughter. It was dusk now but she'd set off at first light. Why was Evie in Wiltshire, for heaven's sake? That wasn't even near to where her birth mother had lived before. Or had the woman moved right out of London?

Cassandra Benn might have taken Evie to Wiltshire, for some reason. Two redheads should be easy for people to remember, surely? She wouldn't phone again, though, she'd turn up at the hotel in person.

After seeing what Keith had done, she was even more certain that she was never getting romantically involved with a man again. She'd made a lot of bad choices in men over the years, but none had proved as terrible as Keith. She was getting worse at it, not better.

She knew men weren't all bad, of course she did. But that was beside the point. The biggest weakness lay in her. She clearly didn't know how to distinguish good males from bad. Her track record had proved that conclusively.

Nope, no more romances for her.

Chapter Twenty-One

It was just after seven when Zoe drew up outside her sister's house. Cassie peered out of the window, then came hurrying out to greet her with a big hug.

That was the first time her sister had been openly affectionate of her own accord, and it made Zoe glad she'd fudged the truth about having a meeting in London on Monday as an excuse to come down here, instead of obeying her parents' command to go home for the weekend.

'For goodness' sake, forget about your older sister,' her mother had ordered. 'She hasn't been a credit to the family and our careful upbringing, so we don't owe her anything. It's about time you showed *us* your loyalty. I don't know what's got into you lately.'

Zoe had had more than enough of being nagged by them, enough too of them trying to keep her away from Cassie.

'I love my sister and intend to see a lot more of her, whatever you say or do.' She'd stormed out, sick of their hypocrisy and cruelty to poor Cassie.

She'd left home decades ago, even though at first she'd lived in the same town, but they'd still tried to control her, so she'd left her friends and reluctantly moved to Manchester. Though she dutifully phoned her parents now and then, and even visited them once or twice a year, when she couldn't put it off any longer, distance had enabled her to see them even more clearly. They were cold and more concerned about appearances than other people's troubles. Especially when it concerned their elder daughter.

They weren't even proud of how successful Cassie had been, always putting her down when people commented, saying the topics she featured in her TV programmes were disgusting and should be kept out of the limelight.

Zoe stared in surprise as Cassie grabbed her arm to prevent her from going into the house.

'I have such a wonderful surprise for you, Zoe. Let me tell you about it before we go in.'

'OK. I'm all ears.'

'I have my granddaughter staying with me at the moment.' She paused and stared challengingly at her younger sister.

'*Your granddaughter?* You have a granddaughter?'

'Yes. The agency found my daughter only once again she turned down seeing me. Her daughter did want to see me, though, and she's here.'

'That's great! I can't wait to meet her.' She turned away to get her suitcase out, but as she closed the car boot, Cassie grabbed her arm again.

'There's more. The guy my daughter married recently upset Evie so much she ran away and came to take refuge with me.'

'That's a bit of an overdramatic reaction, don't you think?'

'No. He sounds like a paedophile to me, from what she's said.'

'Oh no!'

'My daughter wouldn't believe anything was wrong, but since Evie saw the letter from my agency, she knew my address so came to ask for my help. She didn't want to live with him, didn't dare.'

'Dear heaven, what a terrible situation for the poor girl! And for you.'

'It was such a close-run thing, it makes me shiver. Evie turned up seeking my help the day before I moved down here. If she'd arrived two days later, she'd have missed me and would probably be living on the streets now because I didn't leave any information about where I was going with the neighbours.'

She shuddered then gave her sister a watery smile. 'She's a great kid.'

Zoe gave her a hug. 'I couldn't be more pleased for you. Aw, love, don't cry.'

Cassie swiped at her eyes. 'I'm so happy to be able to get to know her and help her. And what am I doing standing out here, blubbing like a big baby? Come and meet our newest family member, Zoe. You'll like her.'

'I'll *love* her, I hope. Hey, just think, I'm an auntie to a girl, no, great-auntie. Michael's only got little boys and they're a subdued pair who never say much when I visit. He's nearly as bad as our parents for being strict.'

'Yes. I pity them. Anyway, here we go.' She flung open the door. 'Evie, darling, this is my little sister, Zoe.'

Evie looked across towards the door apprehensively,

but Zoe simply held open her arms and moved forward. 'You're my very first great-niece.'

They met in the middle, hugging, then separating to stare at one another.

'You've got the family hair,' Zoe commented. 'Do you get called "carrots" at school?'

'Yes.'

'Used to drive me mad.'

'Cup of tea, you two?' Cassie asked. 'Or do you want to do some more hugging?'

They laughed and moved apart.

Zoe beamed first at her sister then at her niece. 'A glass of champagne would be more appropriate, don't you think? This is something to celebrate big time. And I'm sure a half-glass wouldn't hurt our Evie, who's almost grown up. It's such a wonderfully special occasion.'

She saw the girl mouth the words 'Our Evie' and could have wept all over again for the wobbliness of her niece's smile, which said a lot about her hunger for family. It must have been as strong as Cassie's hunger to find her daughter.

What a mess their family was in! Well, if Zoe had any say, she and her sister were going to stay together and help build a real, loving new family. Their parents might be sadly lacking in parenting skills but she'd been lucky to have her father's spinster sister living nearby. Mary had showered her with love, so she hadn't grown up without experiencing genuine affection.

Poor Cassie had left home before Auntie Mary came to live nearby, so she'd missed that affection. Well, when things settled down, Zoe would bring Mary to meet the others. Her aunt would love that. Mary sure gave the lie to the idea of old women sitting around needing to be helped as they tottered towards death. She still helped others, volunteering at a couple of charities, and she had loads of friends.

But that was for another time.

Cassie went to the fridge and took out the bottle of champagne she'd bought on their big shopping trip. It had been chilling there, waiting for a happy occasion, and lo and behold, that had happened sooner than she'd expected.

She poured two full glasses and one half, then put it away again, passing the glasses to the others.

Zoe raised her glass. 'To us! Family for ever.'

They each clinked their glasses against hers and took a sip.

'This is a very nice drop.' Zoe put her glass down and looked from one to the other. 'My goodness, you two are so alike! Why didn't I get that lovely colour of hair instead of this faded mousy brown?'

'Mine's completely white now,' Cassie protested.

'Silver. And it looks as good on you as the red used to. You have a very elegant bone structure. Evie's got it too.'

'Took me a while to stop colouring my hair. The sort of people I worked for weren't openly sexist but they definitely preferred to hire female journalists who didn't look too old on the TV screen. I wonder if the current fashion for grey hair will change that?'

'My mother has the same colour of red as me.' Evie patted her short, wavy hair and stared across the room at her own reflection in the mirror. 'Though she has one or two silver threads now and boy, does she hate that.'

'I'm so looking forward to meeting her,' Zoe said. 'I

hope she'll come round to the idea of extending her family to include us.'

'Evie told me that what her mother desperately wants is to have a husband and more children, even though she's over forty. Only, she shouldn't have them with a creep like him.'

'No more talk about him today, please,' Zoe said firmly. 'This is a time for celebration. Here's to aunts and grandmothers everywhere!' She took another sip and smiled at her sister. 'Can you sit down comfortably now? We all need to chill out.'

'I will and—' Cassie snapped her fingers as something occurred to her. 'I'd better go and cancel our evening out with Hal and his son before I relax, though.'

'Who are they?'

After this had been explained, Zoe shrugged. 'Why not ask them instead if it's OK for me to join you? I'm happy to pay for my own meal.'

'I'll go and see Hal straight away, just to make sure it's OK. He's relying on us to keep the peace between him and his son so I don't think he'll mind another person. Oliver turned up yesterday and seems very unhappy about something. I won't be long.' She got up and left the house by the back door.

Zoe took another sip and smiled across at her niece. 'Tell me about yourself.'

'What do you want to know?' A guarded look replaced the smile.

'Anything and everything. Let's not focus on why you ran away, though. Let's concentrate on good things tonight, like what you want to do with your life and what you want to know about our side of the family.' She lowered her voice dramatically and added, 'I know all their dark secrets and am willing to sell them to you for money.'

Evie was surprised into laughter.

Zoe grimaced. 'I'd better warn you, though. Our parents won't welcome you into the family. They don't have anything to do with your grandmother.'

'I've gathered that. It's cruel. She's such a lovely, kind person.'

'Yes. I agree. But Auntie Mary will want to know you and I'm sure you'll love your great-great-aunt.' She explained about their oldest relative.

Cassie found Hal sitting on his back patio in the sheltered spot he seemed to have made his favourite retreat. He was staring across the garden, his expression so bleak she paused, hesitating to interrupt him.

The minute he noticed her, the unhappiness vanished from his face. Jumping to his feet, he held out one hand, smiling. 'Cassie! Do come and join me. I was in need of cheering up and the mere sight of you lifts my spirits.'

'Just for a minute. I have a visitor.'

'I noticed the car arrive.' He let go of her hand to pull a chair out for her, giving her a quick hug before he allowed her to sit down.

'What brought on your fit of the dismals, Hal?'

'Oliver.'

'Ah.'

'Turns out he's been demoted and has to attend a course on interpersonal skills before he can take up his new lower-level job, as well as undergoing counselling.'

She let out a soft whistle. 'Did he say what he did to upset people?'

'Sounds as if he bad-mouthed women and gays, and shoved a female colleague out of his way.'

'Bad tactics but he must have been upset about his marriage breaking up, so can't they give him a little leeway?'

'It seems not. The new owners of the company are extremely politically correct.'

'It's not a good way for him to behave but I know I was very upset when my last relationship ended, and that was a reasonably amicable split – though Brett initiated it, not me.'

'The guy must be crazy to have dropped you.'

She smiled. 'You say the nicest things. But actually, he was right. At the time, I was too focused on work to make a good life partner. It took the terrorist incident to shake me out of that and point me back towards being a normal human being, not a work-focused automaton.'

'His loss, my gain – I hope.'

'You're good for my morale too, Hal.'

'Well, that's a great start for our relationship, don't you think?'

They sat smiling at one another for a few seconds then she told him about Zoe's arrival. 'So is it all right if my sister joins us for dinner?'

'Of course it is. The more the merrier. Moreover, if she's closer to Oliver's age, perhaps he'll find he has something in common with her and show us all his better side, which I admit I haven't seen much of so far this visit.'

He paused for a moment then asked, 'No word from your daughter?'

'No. But hopefully she's received Evie's message and isn't worrying about *her* daughter's safety. Only, from what Evie has told me, I think it's Fran we need to worry about now. Her new husband sounds to be a wrong 'un, as an old friend of mine used to call unsavoury folk.'

She got to her feet. 'I really have to go, Hal. Zoe's not been here long and we have a lot of catching up and bonding to do. You should have seen Evie's expression at having a great-aunt as well as a grandmother. That girl is hungry for love, someone to give it to as well as someone to receive it from.'

'We all need both of those in our lives.'

The world seemed to stand still for a precious moment and she could have sworn that she could feel his affection for her already, a tangible presence. He was such a nice man, would be so easy to love.

Was she reading too much into their friendship? She thought not.

At seven o'clock they met outside the front of the two houses and Zoe gasped in surprise. 'Oliver Kennedy.' Her exclamation was hidden by the voices of the others.

'Zoe.' He glanced quickly towards his father, then looked back at her apprehensively and lowered his voice. 'Can we please start our acquaintance again? I'm sorry I was so rude to you. I do remember that evening, the beginning of it anyway. My wife had just told me she was leaving me, which is why I drank way too much and acted up.'

She sighed but held her hand out to shake his. 'Here's to second time lucky, then. You certainly didn't make a good impression the first time and I shan't give you a third chance to get the social niceties right, if you mess up again.'

He took her hand. 'I can't remember much, though I do

remember your face and how disgusted you looked. Was I very bad?'

'Yes, very. The things you said about me and all women were . . . horrible.'

He swallowed hard. 'Oh hell.'

His father turned towards them. 'Nice to meet you, Zoe. Did I hear that you and my son have met before?'

'Only once, and it was at a party, so we didn't interact much.'

He waited till his father had turned away to whisper, 'Thanks.'

Oliver watched in admiration as Zoe turned away any other questions about their previous meeting, then she stayed next to him to walk across to the hotel. He must have upset half the world in recent weeks. What a pity he'd picked on her. Her attractiveness didn't come from make-up and expensive clothes, but from her face and personality. She was lovely in a girl-next-door way, all warm and friendly – 'bubbly', people might call her.

What would they call him? The word 'grumpy' sprang into his mind. That's what his father had called him tonight as they were getting ready to come out, anyway.

'What do you do for a living?' he asked.

'I'm a commercial artist.'

'Do you have a speciality?'

She laughed. 'What is this? Practice for Starting up Conversations, Unit 101?'

He could feel himself flushing. He didn't usually have trouble talking to people but it had thrown him to find he'd made such a bad impression on such an attractive woman. Her sister must be much older than her, but she was attractive too, and the niece was going to be good-looking when she grew out of her gawkiness. Only, tonight she looked as if she were worried about something and why on earth was she wearing what was obviously a wig? Who was going to know her here? She was overreacting to the situation if you asked him.

He followed the others into the hotel, pleased that they'd got a round table to sit at. It was always easier to chat on those though he intended to let his father lead the conversation most of the time. He didn't want to stuff up.

The menu wasn't at all bad, he soon decided. 'What do you recommend, Dad?'

'The beef and ale pie. One of the best I've ever tasted. They don't go for fancy stuff here, thank goodness, just good, hearty fare.'

A woman came across to greet them. 'Hi, Cassie and Hal. How are you settling in?'

'We're starting to sort ourselves out. Everyone, this is Molly Santiago, one of the owners. Molly, meet my sister Zoe and my granddaughter – um, Lacey.' She shot a quick warning glance at the others.

Curiouser and curiouser, Oliver thought. An assumed name as well as a wig. Things must be bad. She had lovely red hair, he'd seen her sitting out on the back patio, but whenever she went away from their house, she put on that wig. Why buy one that didn't flatter you, though?

He looked sideways at Zoe.

'Don't ask her anything,' she ordered in a low voice. 'I'll answer your questions another time, those that I can, anyway.'

'OK. I know a rough outline, was just thinking she was overreacting. Um, I've seen your sister on television, but she had red hair then.'

'She got fed up of dyeing it and after she got caught up in that terrorist incident, she didn't want to be recognised. She needs peace and quiet to recover.'

'Oh yes. I remember seeing it on the news. Rotten luck, eh, but at least she survived.'

'Yeah. I'm pretty glad about that, I can tell you.'

She raised her voice and joined in the general conversation and he followed suit, though he didn't contribute as much to it as she did. She was a lively one. He enjoyed just watching her.

What had he got into here, though?

He'd have to ask his father to explain the details more fully when they got back. He didn't want to put his foot in it. And maybe whatever it was would add interest to a rather boring stay. He wasn't going to start the new job until he had to.

But he couldn't avoid the damned counselling session, more's the pity, had to go to the first one tomorrow in Swindon.

They sat chatting till half past nine, then Zoe yawned. 'Sorry. Been a long day. I think I'll stroll back home.'

'We all will,' Cassie said. 'It's not good to be walking about after dark with half-built houses and piles of junk to provide hiding places for troublemakers.'

Zoe looked at her sister in surprise. 'This village doesn't seem the sort of place where you'd be in danger of getting mugged after dark.'

'No.' She took a deep breath and her voice grew sharper. 'Neither did the block of flats where I was interviewing that poor woman seem dangerous, and that incident happened in broad daylight, killing some people.'

Which was when Zoe realised that her sister had been left even more upset than she'd realised by the incident. Minor PTSD at least, but Cassie was trying to hide it. She leant across to give her a hug. 'We'll all stroll down together, then.'

'I might stay up here and have another beer,' Oliver said. To his surprise he caught Zoe giving him a scornful look and to his even greater surprise realised he didn't want to be on the receiving end of that scorn.

He shrugged. 'On the other hand, it's no fun drinking alone, so I'll head home with you, Dad, and borrow one of your books.'

His father had also been scowling at him, but now he nodded as if in approval. And when Oliver followed his father's next glance, he saw that it was focused on Cassie. He suddenly realised there might be something serious going on between the two of them. Hey, who'd have thought?

Chapter Twenty-Two

As they strolled across to the houses, Oliver tripped because he was again staring at Zoe instead of watching where he was going.

He was brought to a sudden halt as he grazed his hand on a concrete bollard at one edge of the storage area for the building works. Wincing, he steadied himself on the stupid object and that was when he caught sight of a guy sitting in a car staring at their group. There was little doubt about what he was doing because there was nothing else to see in this direction except the group of people on the lighted footpath.

Since Oliver had very good distance vision, he could even see that the guy had a very sour expression on his face. Was he Evie's stalker? No, surely not!

Then the man must have suddenly noticed Oliver looking in his direction, because he slid down in his seat as if trying to hide. That made Oliver even more interested in him. He tried to hide that, however, by setting off walking again, using his eyes to glance sideways but trying not to turn his head.

He definitely hadn't imagined it. The guy was still watching them. Oliver walked slowly after the others, letting them get further ahead, and saw that the man was still staring at the women leading the group. He was positioned lower in the car to do it. Must be uncomfortable.

Should he say something to his father about the watcher or not? Oliver wondered. He was watching. Why else would anyone be sitting in a poorly lit car park without trying to start up his engine?

He stopped again, pretending to refasten his shoe, while staring at the stranger. He was pleased to see that the car's number plate showed up clearly from this angle, so memorised it on principle.

Nothing else he could do, so he speeded up to join the others who had almost reached the houses now. He said a general goodbye and went into the house. He'd definitely ask his father what he thought and whether they should mention this to the women.

This looked rather serious, because if he were watching them the fellow would have had to come down from London. You didn't drive for two hours on a whim. And stalking could be a prelude to violence, everyone knew that.

Oliver didn't usually forget details about people, which was why he was such a good salesman, but while he was thinking about it, he scribbled down the car's registration number on a receipt which was the only piece of paper he had on him, and stuffed it back into his pocket. Numbers were too easy to get wrong.

Yawning, he waited for his father to finish saying goodbye and join him in the house.

Hal was beaming happily as he came in. 'Cassie and I are going to sit outside and have a quiet chat on the patio because neither of us is sleepy yet. You get off to bed, son. Don't wait up for me.'

Which meant his father wanted time alone with her. Strange to see the old man so taken by a woman. Oliver didn't raise the matter of what he'd just seen. More important to give his father a chance to spend time with his neighbour. Ah, he was probably just imagining that the guy in the car had been watching them, anyway.

But as he sat there alone, Oliver continued to worry about what he'd seen. Could this be the stepfather? Surely not? How would he have found out where Evie was?

He waited for his father to come in again, but fell asleep in the chair and was woken by someone shaking his shoulder.

'You'd be better sleeping in bed, Oliver.'

'Dad, wait.' But he must have mumbled it too softly and by the time he'd come out of his grogginess, his father had gone up to bed. He could hear him humming happily as he closed the bedroom door.

Never mind. He'd tell him about the watcher in the morning. It couldn't be all that urgent. No one was going to kidnap that girl tonight. They'd have trouble snatching her anyway, because she never strayed far from her grandmother and he'd never seen her even sitting out on the back patio on her own for more than a minute or two. Now that the aunt had turned up as well, Evie was well guarded.

He smiled. Very attractive woman, that aunt. He'd have to find out if she were seeing anyone.

Then he shook his head. No, better not get involved with her or anyone else for the moment. He didn't want to upset his father and lose this place of refuge. He desperately needed a few days to pull himself together and have a think about his future, still missed being married, to his surprise. Though he didn't miss the quarrels with Mandy.

He didn't really know what he wanted to do with his new life as a single chap, if truth be told. But he felt to be calming down a bit already. This evening had helped. Nice group of people.

It suddenly occurred to him that in the past he'd mostly gone out to drink with his so-called mates after work. And rather than chatting, they'd poured down drinks and watched sport on TV. Sometimes when he'd had a bad day he'd gone home drunk. Only, those guys weren't long-time mates, just chance acquaintances and friends of fellow workers.

He definitely hadn't paid enough attention to his wife; he admitted that to himself now and regretted it. He'd been upset big time when Mandy had told him she wanted to split up because she'd met someone else. Even more upset when she'd refused to go for marital counselling because she was in love with the new guy.

It had taken a while before sheer honesty made him admit to himself that he hadn't been a particularly good husband in several ways. You could see things more clearly when you moved out of the picture – and also, when you stopped drinking so much.

He wasn't sure he'd want to try marriage again for a good long time. It was too complicated living with someone and finding out it was different in so many ways from what you'd expected.

And splitting up hurt like hell. He hadn't anticipated things going so very wrong. How could you ever tell for sure that things were going to turn out OK?

With another sigh at how complicated relationships were, he went upstairs, flung off his clothes and crawled into bed. It was a long time before he managed to fall asleep. He kept nearly dropping off then jerking awake and listening for a prowler.

The man sitting in the car park watched them go inside, taking note of which houses the various people went into. He hadn't tried to get a room at the hotel or even buy something to eat there because he wanted to stay anonymous. No one had seen him, unless that fellow who'd been staring had. No, the distance was too great to see anything clearly at the best of times, let alone after dark.

It'd mean a long, hungry drive home again now, but it was worth it. He'd be better prepared for his own needs next time he came here and would bring a snack and a bottle of water.

Pity he'd have to stay home to open the shop the next day, but he had no choice. Ryan was still too upset to deal with certain special customers.

Ah, he'd manage to stay awake. Mind over matter, that was it.

He let out a soft chuckle as he started the car. They'd be sure he hadn't seen that letter at Amelia's. He'd not opened it, too risky, but he'd noted where it came from when the neighbour pushed it through the door while he was at the house, because he'd recognised Evie's handwriting on the front. It was a very showy script, all dark ink and slashing strokes.

And he'd found her quite easily from the hotel stamp he'd seen on the envelope, hadn't he? She might be wearing a wig but he'd recognise her anywhere. And who was the old biddy she was with, someone even older than his stupid and ungrateful wife?

He intended to make Fran sorry she'd not done as he told her, very sorry.

She'd not get away from him. Neither of them would. She belonged to him now and so did her daughter. The stupid bitch would never out-think him. Nor would the police. He'd learnt through a very hard lesson to be extremely careful what he did.

Fran would come down here soon as well, bound to. Then he'd work out how to get her back.

There was no way he was going to act immediately, though. This had to be planned with meticulous care. He would never let his anger rule him again.

Oliver wandered downstairs in the morning to find the house empty and his father's car gone from the front of the house.

Damn! He'd missed another opportunity to tell him about the guy in the car park. And today he had to go to Swindon to see the counsellor.

He found a note from his father, who had gone shopping, glanced at the clock and forgot about last night. He'd have to hurry to get to his appointment on time. Why was he sleeping so badly lately? He should be relaxing now he'd finished sorting out the many bits and pieces of business connected with ending his marriage.

He grabbed a couple of pieces of bread, slathered them with butter and searched in vain for a jar of jam.

Then he remembered that he'd finished one off yesterday. Oops! Must have been the last one. He hoped his father hadn't wanted any for breakfast.

He drove into Swindon, had trouble finding a parking place and arrived for his appointment five minutes late, breathless from running. Hell, he must be way out of condition. Another reason to cut down the drinking.

He was shown straight in and found himself facing a motherly woman, which was not what he'd expected. He'd rather have spoken to a guy. He was still panting. 'Sorry! I hadn't realised – how hard it'd be – to find a parking place. I don't know Swindon very well.'

She gestured to a chair. 'Well, as long as you don't make a habit of being late, I'll let it go this time.'

She waited till he was settled. 'Now, tell me why you think you were sent to chat to me.'

He tried to answer briefly, but she dragged more and more details out of him, piling one intrusive question on another. To his utter horror, it revealed feelings that had him brushing away a few tears, then a few more. He couldn't remember the last time he'd cried in front of anyone.

'Here.' She passed him a box of tissues. 'In case you're interested, I think it's hopeful that you're so upset.'

He gaped at her. 'It is?'

'Yeah. Shows you haven't put up your barriers against emotion too high.'

What did that verbal garbage mean?

By the time he left, he felt wrung out and exhausted, and he wasn't at all sure he could face coming back for his next appointment. The counsellor might look motherly but she was as sharp as a razor – or an axe!

He stopped on the way home at the big shopping centre he'd passed before and bought a few supplies, which included a couple of jars of cherry jam to replace the one he'd eaten. It must still be his father's favourite and was one of his, too. He'd eaten a lot of toast since he'd set up on his own in the flat. He'd better learn to cook or he'd not get fit again, and it was cheaper than buying meals out.

He slapped his midriff. Oops! He really needed to shape up a bit. So he nipped into the bookshop and found a cookery book for guys setting up on their own. Who'd have thought there would be exactly the sort of book he needed? There hadn't been any in the supermarket.

As he got back he saw the three women from next door setting off in their car and waved to them. They looked happy and very much together. He envied them that.

His father still wasn't home yet and the silence inside the house seemed to echo around him. Where had the old man gone?

He had a sudden horrible thought. Surely his father wasn't still facing cancer and going for treatment? He'd said the doctors had cleared it up.

What if they hadn't? He couldn't imagine life without his father to turn to.

He clutched his head in his hands for a moment, trying to calm down again. As if he hadn't got enough to worry about!

The three women had decided to do some sightseeing so went to visit Avebury, which wasn't too far away. The massive grey stones, erected so long ago for who knew what reason, spread out in a half-circle and were also dotted about in the village, singles mostly. And unlike those at Stonehenge, you could go up and touch them.

Cassie watched Evie approach a huge stone, lay her hands on it, palms down, and touch her forehead to the rough surface as if communing with it.

'I wonder how they found the strength and endurance to build them without modern machinery and equipment,' the girl commented as she rejoined the others.

'Driven by faith of some sort, I suppose,' Zoe said. She'd been unusually quiet since they got here and seemed affected by the stones as well.

She fitted in so well with them, Cassie thought. How lucky she was to have a sister who'd taken the initiative of bringing the two of them closer. And such a lovely granddaughter as well.

Evie came to walk next to her, to Cassie's delight. Without thinking about it she gave the girl a quick hug and got a smile in return.

'This place puts our human worries into perspective, doesn't it, Gran?'

'It certainly does.' Not for the first time, Cassie thought that Evie had a wise old head on her shoulders. Had she been born with such common sense about the world, or had her upbringing brought out those qualities in her? Common sense wasn't as common as its name suggested. It sounded sometimes when Evie talked about her life as if she were the mother and Fran the daughter.

Ah well, they could all have done things better with the benefit of hindsight. Cassie had made a mess of her personal life, too, even as recently as in her relationship with Brett.

The important things were firstly to learn from your mistakes and secondly not to hurt people if you could avoid it.

When they got home there was a letter waiting for them.

Cassie picked it up. 'It's the DNA results.' She couldn't wait, tore open the envelope and dragged out the contents as soon as she got inside the house.

When she looked up with tears in her eyes, she realised they were all of them still standing just inside the door and the other two were waiting to find out the results.

'Why are you crying? Is something wrong?' Evie faltered.

'Everything is wonderfully all right. These are happy tears, so very happy, darling! We are definitely closely related, you and I.'

With a shriek of joy, Evie grabbed her and danced her round the spacious, partly furnished room, chanting, 'Grandmother, grandmother, grandmother mine!' in a very loud voice.

Then she let go and grabbed Zoe, doing the same to her, except she changed the chant to, 'Auntie Zoe, Auntie Zoe, *my own* Auntie Zoe!'

After that, they pulled themselves together and made lunch. But none of them stopped smiling.

As they ate, Cassie explained to Zoe the details they'd discussed with the lawyer, and why it might be very important indeed to be able to prove that they were related.

Chapter Twenty-Three

That same morning, Fran and Polly went out to her car which was parked just in front of the building. They were chatting happily, ready to load it for the journey, when they saw it.

'Oh no!' They stopped in dismay. All four tyres had been slashed and were not only flat but clearly beyond repair.

'How did anyone get close enough to do that without being seen on the CCTV?' Polly asked.

'Must have crawled round, I suppose, hiding behind the other cars.'

Fran clutched her companion as this sank in. 'This means he's found me.'

'Looks like it. Let's call the police.'

'What can they do? I need to call for help getting the tyres changed and then move right away from here.' She clapped one hand to her mouth. 'Only, I have to find Evie first. What am I going to *do*?'

'We really do need to call the police first. He may have

left some traces. And you'd be a fool to leave the refuge. He might have got into the car park, but he won't break into the building without getting caught, believe me. Our inside security system is second to none and there are always other people around to help you.'

'I doubt Keith will have left anything to trace him by. He's clever as well as cunning.'

However, Polly insisted on phoning the police so Fran humoured her new friend, who had been so incredibly supportive already, and waited till after their visit to call for help with the tyres.

The police turned up an hour later, checking everything out carefully. There were no fingerprints anywhere on the car around the tyres, but there was a strand of blue fluff, which looked as if it came from a knitted garment, caught on the wheel arch. There was also a half-footprint at the edge of the gravelled area that might have belonged to whoever did this. Someone must have been kneeling there and made the mark when moving away.

When the woman officer shone a blue light slowly over the car, she also found a partial set of fingerprints on the edge of the boot. Beneath them and to one side the paintwork had been wiped clean recently and again there was another tiny piece of blue fluff caught in a crevice. It was amazing that this partial set had been left. The person must have missed it when wiping the area clean.

'Do you have any blue gloves?' the officer asked Fran.

She shook her head. 'Mine are black, but Keith has some that he keeps in his car and yes, they are blue.'

'He must have been fiddling with something delicate

and taken them off, then thought he'd wiped the area clean afterwards. Strange, that, because slashing the tyres doesn't require any particular dexterity. Why would he have to take his gloves off? Hmm. We'll need to check this out properly, so I'm afraid you won't get your car back for a couple of days. There's a new push on stalkers since that woman got murdered by one last month.'

Fran mouthed the word 'murdered', not even wanting to say it aloud! 'Oh no!'

'We're rather wary of stalkers who go to such lengths to upset one particular person, because research has shown them to be possibly on their way to committing much more serious acts. I reckon you're in more danger from this guy than we at first supposed, Ms Milner. If he's nearly fifty, as you say, it's amazing that he's stayed so completely off our radar for this long, though.'

They took Fran's and Polly's fingerprints and waited for a tow truck to take the car to an investigation centre for vehicles involved in crimes to be more thoroughly examined.

Left alone, the two women looked at one another and let out simultaneous sighs.

'That's mucked up our trip.' Polly gave her a sympathetic pat on the back and turned to go inside.

Fran didn't move. 'No, it hasn't. It's only delayed our starting time, that's all. I'm going to see if I can hire a car and we'll drive down as soon as we can get hold of one.'

'But the police want you to stay at the refuge, where you'll be safe.'

'How can I be safe here unless I never poke my nose outside? And that won't help me to find Evie, will it?' After a moment or two's thought she added slowly, 'Keith found out where my car was. How the hell did he do that?'

They looked at one another and Polly asked, 'Is he good with technology?'

'Yes. Very good. He always mocked my mistakes and that made me nervous of doing anything.'

'Didn't want you learning to help yourself.'

'And I let him do it to me.'

'He might have put an electronic tracker in your car. And isn't there a tracking app you can put on people's mobile phones?'

'I'd never have let him put one on mine.'

'He might have done it without you knowing. We'll have to check it. One of the women is good with technology. We'll ask her.'

Dead silence then Fran followed her reluctantly inside. 'I must be the world's biggest fool to have thought myself in love with him.'

'No, you're not. You've been conned by an expert. I hope the police can trace those fingerprints or find a tracking device in the car. It'll all build up against him. I'm going to phone them and suggest they look for one.'

'They're not stupid. They'll have thought of that.'

Polly got a stubborn expression on her face. 'I'm not relying on anything, better to be sure.' She took out her phone and made a call to the woman they'd been given as their first contact.

When she ended the call, she smiled at Fran. 'You were right. They are wondering about that, too. She said we should definitely wait here for further news.'

'Keith can't possibly know where Evie is. That letter with the hotel's address on it wasn't delivered till after we got into the house. I very much doubt that even he can get into the post office depot where the letters are sorted.'

She stiffened her spine. 'I'm determined to find my daughter and make sure she's all right, Polly, or I'll go crazy worrying. I'm going to hire a car and we'll know for certain there won't be a tracker in that. You can come with me to Wiltshire or not. Up to you.'

'I'd better come and keep an eye on you. But I'm telling the police what we're doing, and Tracy.'

Polly could tell the whole world, Fran thought, but she wouldn't stop her going to find her daughter.

But first they went to find Leanne, who did find the tracking app on her mobile phone and was able to delete it.

'Thanks. I owe you for that,' Fran said as she took it back.

'I'm happy to stop these rats treating women like possessions.'

To Fran's disappointment, it took much longer to hire a car than she'd expected because the hire companies wouldn't accept the women's refuge as a suitable place of residence, it being temporary and from the tone of the person's voice on the phone, not approved.

In the end she took a taxi and went in person to a third car hire place, a smaller company. She didn't mention the women's refuge and gave her former address at Keith's house, for which she had IDs with her photo on them.

Even then, this company couldn't find her a car until the next day, but she still had to pay the hire fees into their bank straight away and wait to have the payment confirmed before they would finalise the transaction.

Then she had to fill the long, slow hours of the afternoon

and evening. It seemed to go on for ever, and though she joined a group watching television, she couldn't have said what programmes had been on.

That afternoon Hal was cornered by Oliver. 'I have something to tell you, Dad, something important.'

He listened in increasing dismay as his son told him what he'd seen and what he suspected had been happening.

After Oliver had finished, he said, 'I hope you're wrong. If you're not, that chap is more seriously crazy than we thought.'

'I could be wrong, Dad, but I don't think so. I have very good distance eyesight, as you know, which is why I have to wear glasses for reading and close work. I probably saw more than he realised, more than most other watchers would have done. Do you think we should tell the ladies or not? They all went out earlier but they're back now.'

'I think we should definitely tell them. Come on, then. No time like the present.' He led the way out.

Cassie opened the door to them, looking happy and relaxed.

Hal hated to spoil her mood. 'I'm sorry to disturb you and I know it's nearly teatime, but there's something we need to tell you. It's to do with Evie's problems.'

Her smile faded to be replaced by apprehension. 'Come in.'

When they were all seated, Oliver explained what he'd seen and the three women listened to him, looking more and more horrified.

'What was the car's registration number?' Evie asked when he'd finished.

He fumbled in his pocket and it took a minute or two to find the crumpled receipt and read it out.

'That's Keith's car.' She turned to her grandmother. 'He's found me. I have to get away as quickly as I can.'

'Actually, I think you'll be safer if you stay here,' Hal said. 'You'll have four people to protect you.' He glanced at his son for confirmation that they'd both be up for this and was pleased when Oliver nodded without hesitation.

'What do we do, then?' Cassie asked. 'Just sit and wait like bait in a trap?' She couldn't repress a shiver at the thought of facing more violence and still woke in the middle of the night sometimes feeling panicky after a dream of the bomb incident.

'I'm not sure. Maybe we could set a trap of our own.'

'How would we do that?'

Hal couldn't come up with anything quickly. 'I don't know. It's, um, not something I've ever had to do before. We could have a think then brainstorm it, see what we come up with.'

'He's going to make for this house,' Cassie said. 'He must have seen us come in last night.'

'Maybe . . .' Hal hesitated, then completed his sentence, '. . . you should come and stay with us?'

'He'll have seen you two walk across with us and go into the house next door,' Evie said. 'It'd be the next place he looked for me, I should think. It's what I'd do, anyway.'

'How about we ask Molly to let Evie stay at the hotel? They must have a room there that'd be safer than here?' Cassie suggested. 'And lots more people to call on for help, including a security guard.'

'Molly's the owner of the hotel, right? Do you trust her that much?'

'Yes. She and her husband Euan are both great to deal with. Everyone speaks well of them and they can't do enough for their guests. Talk about service. I'm quite sure they'll help if we decide that's the way to go.'

But Evie was frowning. 'I think I'd prefer to stay here, at least tonight. I don't want to be left in a hotel on my own.'

'I'd come and stay with you,' Zoe said at once.

'There would only be two of us there, but there are three of us with two neighbours within call here.'

'Anyway, there's another problem with the hotel. If he's still watching, he'll see her leaving the house and where she goes,' Cassie said thoughtfully.

'I can stroll up and check out the parking area for a car with that registration,' Oliver offered. 'He might just have moved it.'

'Even if he's not there any longer, he could have parked at the other side of the lake and from there he can easily come back to the leisure village on foot.' Evie shivered at the thought of Keith creeping around.

'I have some night binoculars I used to use for bird watching. I know where they are and can use them to keep a check on the public car park across the lake,' Hal offered. 'There aren't usually many cars left there by the end of the afternoon and it's rare to see any at all after dark.'

'Do that now, please,' Cassie said.

'I will.'

She turned to her granddaughter. 'In the meantime the only thing I'm certain of is that you shouldn't go anywhere on your own till this is over.'

'Definitely don't wander off,' Oliver said firmly.

Hal nodded in approval, pleased that his son was

joining in so wholeheartedly and trying to offer help and advice. He was even sounding more like a younger Oliver had sounded, caring and full of energy. He stood up. 'I'll go and get my binoculars and have a look.'

Welcome back, son, he thought as he walked across to his own house.

Oliver had been watching Evie, and it upset him to see how frightened she was now looking. 'We won't let him hurt you.'

'It's not just him hurting me physically. I don't know where my mother is. She may be in hiding somewhere for all we know. Or he may have fooled her into doing things his way. And he may hurt her if I upset him further. Even if we call the police, what if he persuades them that as my stepfather, he's now a suitable person to act as legal guardian for me and they agree?'

'I don't think the police would do that if we all protested strongly,' Cassie said.

'Who knows? He's cunning. I've watched him manipulate my mother. One of the neighbours saw them at the register office and posted on Facebook that they'd got married. How he persuaded her to marry him so suddenly, I can't imagine. She was trying to take things slowly last time she and I talked.'

'If that happens, I'll spirit you away and take you to a friend's house in another town,' Oliver offered.

'Thanks.' She shrugged a sort of acceptance, but looked unconvinced at its feasibility.

'If I could get her into my car unseen, I could take her up to Manchester, but then I'd have to leave her alone in the daytime while I went to work.' Zoe sighed.

'Every alternative we look at means getting her away

from here without him seeing it happen, and finding somewhere to keep her safe. At the moment we don't know whether he's still around or if not, when he'll return.'

A glum silence followed.

'I shall never read a mystery novel again without feeling cynical about what it takes to outwit villains,' Zoe said bitterly. She stood up and added, 'How about I make us some sandwiches? I'm hungry, even if you guys aren't.'

She and Oliver were the only ones who ate with any enthusiasm because the other three said they weren't hungry and only picked at the sandwiches. Evie took a mere couple of bites and gave up the pretence, leaving the rest of hers on her plate.

'I'll go out and look across at the car park again soon,' Hal said.

'Perhaps we should contact the police?' Cassie suggested.

'I'd rather not unless we absolutely have to. The lawyer said we were on shaky ground about custody,' Evie reminded her.

'We can't afford to drink alcohol, because we have to stay alert, or I'd offer you a glass of wine, but I've got some lemonade if anyone's interested,' Cassie offered.

'Thanks, Gran, but I don't feel at all like eating and I don't fancy anything fizzy, either. I can get myself a glass of water when I'm thirsty.'

The others simply shook their heads to her offer as well.

All they could think of to protect Evie in the short term was to make sure the girl was never left alone. Evie nodded agreement to that. Surely it would be enough to keep her safe?

'We're too tired to think clearly, let alone come up with something innovative that he won't suspect,' Cassie said in the end. 'Let's go to bed and Evie, I think you should bring your bed into my room. I don't want you to be on your own at all.'

Evie nodded. She didn't want to be on her own, either.

When they'd moved the mattress and got ready for the night, she could tell that her grandmother was listening to her, so breathed softly and slowly hoping the rhythm of that breathing would lull Cassie to sleep.

Evie heard the moment when her gran fell asleep and smiled.

She couldn't manage to get to sleep, tossing and turning for a long time. She didn't make the mistake of getting up and wandering round the house, though. She was *not* giving *him* even half a chance of catching her on her own.

Eventually she fell asleep, not waking until dawn started to brighten the world. Things usually looked better by daylight, she'd found.

When she looked across the room, she saw her grandmother still sleeping although the tangled bedcovers said she hadn't spent a peaceful night. But the sight of her made Evie relax and fall asleep again.

Next time she woke, Zoe was lying on the other bed. 'Cassie's gone to have a shower. I'll stand guard outside the en suite if you want to use it. Might be a good time for you to have a shower as well.'

'Thanks. And thanks for caring about me.'

Zoe blew her a kiss and she blew one back.

In the en suite she brushed tears away from her eyes. She

felt so loved when she was with them but she missed her mother and was worried sick about her.

How long was this going to go on for?

What was needed now to make life better than ever before was for her mother to leave that horrible creature and join them. But would she? He seemed to have pulled the wool right over her eyes and hidden his true nature.

He'd tried to charm Evie too when she was first introduced to him but she hadn't trusted him. She didn't know why, but she'd found that it often paid to listen to your instincts about the people you met.

And as his subsequent behaviour showed, Keith had proved to be a sleaze when her mother wasn't around. His slightest touch made Evie shudder with loathing.

If her mother refused to leave him, what was going to happen to her? Would she be able to get away from him permanently? If she couldn't, she'd never feel safe again.

She let the shower water pour down on her, hoping it would wash away the worries about what he might do. Only she felt just as worried afterwards.

Chapter Twenty-Four

That evening, Keith drove home from a tedious day at the shop, detouring via the women's refuge because it made him feel good to see the shabby place where his wife was reduced to living. She liked her comforts, Fran did, so that place would teach her a preliminary lesson on where her best interests lay. And he'd reinforce that lesson in various ways till she learnt to obey him. He'd done it before with other women, knew exactly how to set about it.

Her car wasn't back yet. He frowned and checked the tracking device he'd placed in it. The vehicle wasn't nearby, so he followed the electronic trace to the location where the device indicated it had been taken, stopping just down the road.

All he could see from the outside was a big shed with high walls round a yard at one side topped by barbed wire. There were no signs to indicate who the place belonged to. Was her car in there having new tyres fitted? It didn't look like a tyre dealer's. He didn't like not knowing what lay behind all that secrecy.

But she was too stupid to have discovered his device, he was sure of that, any more than she'd discovered the tracing app on her phone for weeks. The bitches in the refuge must have spotted that though, because it had suddenly stopped working. He had to get her away from there.

Ah, he was seeing problems where there weren't any.

Well, she'd have the car taken back to the refuge once new tyres had been fitted, and even if it were parked in the secure area round the back, he'd find a way to get at it again. He'd enjoy figuring out how to do that.

But first he wanted to make another trip down to Wiltshire to see what that girl was doing. Maybe he could snatch her and use her to get the mother back. That'd make it easier to control Fran.

Unfortunately he had to get Ryan back at work minding their shop before he could go away again, because he was expecting a few important deliveries.

His next visit was to his so-called best friend. He grinned. Most helpful friend, more like. Another simpleton. They came in useful.

Ryan opened the door and for the first time ever didn't look happy to see him. 'Come in.'

Keith followed him back inside and accepted a cup of coffee, watching Ryan mix it with meticulous care and then sipping it appreciatively. 'Delicious. You make the best coffee I've ever had.'

After a little more judicious flattery, his friend had relaxed a little, and he risked saying, 'You need to get back to work, mate, because I have to go to Wiltshire again. It really is time to get my wife back.'

Ryan stiffened. 'Get real. You're pushing your luck if you pursue her now she's brought the police into it. You'd be wise to let all that drop.'

'I'm married to the bitch so she *belongs* to me now. You've never been married so you don't understand how much effort I've put into getting Fran used to doing as I wish. Why should I have to train someone else?'

'Up to you, but don't ask me to help you in that sort of thing. I've had a formal warning from the police about keeping my nose clean, so I'm going to stick to photos and online porn sites from now on.'

'They'll catch you if you put them on your computer.'

'I've got somewhere else set up for that.'

'Well, chicken out if you're such a coward, Ryan, but I still need you back at work tomorrow.'

'Oh, very well.'

And with that Keith had to be satisfied.

Ryan was an idiot – but such a useful idiot, he was worth staying friends with. It was another case of managing people so that they did what you wanted.

During the night Polly started feeling feverish, with a runny nose and watery eyes. By morning she had developed a heavy cold and looked so ill, Tracy insisted she stay in bed so as not to pass it on to the other residents.

'I'm sorry to let you down,' Polly croaked when Fran went up to see her. 'Stay over there by the door and cover your mouth with a handkerchief. You don't want to catch this cold, believe me. It's a real stinker. We'll have to postpone our trip for two or three days till I'm feeling better. It'll probably be safer for you to wait and go then anyway.'

'You're probably right.' She tried to sound casual, but Polly looked at her suspiciously.

'You're taking that too calmly . . . Oh, Fran, you're surely not intending to go on your own?'

She hesitated but couldn't lie to Polly. 'Yes, I am. It's too urgent. I have to find Evie before *he* does.'

'Don't do it. You'll be putting yourself in danger.'

'Keith won't know about that Wiltshire hotel. Also, I won't be driving my own car and we've had that app taken off my phone, so he won't be able to track where I go this time.'

'It's still too risky. That man's dangerous, a real sicko.'

'I know that now. I'll be extremely careful, I promise you. I'll go to pick up the car by taxi, and I won't even try to use public transport.'

'Fran, *please* don't—'

'I'm going!'

She got ready quickly and left before Polly could think of any way to stop her. She rang for a taxi, waiting for it at the front door, with overnight necessities stuffed anyhow into her backpack.

She was outside the car hire place before it opened and was the first customer to go inside as soon as the doors swung back. Even so it seemed to take ages to go through the formalities for taking the hired car and then a young guy had to drive her out to where it was parked to hand it over to her.

She watched him leave and set off at last, groaning aloud in relief that she was on her way to find her daughter.

Even though she was anxious to get to Wiltshire as quickly as possible, she didn't make the mistake of speeding or doing anything that might infringe traffic regulations. No way did she want the police stopping her, didn't intend anything or anyone to prevent her from finding Evie.

And if that meant finding her birth mother too, she'd just have to put up with it. She'd be polite, of course she would, but she'd get Evie away as soon as possible. She'd hated the thought of that woman giving her away like a parcel ever since she found out she was adopted. Having a child of her own had only reinforced that feeling.

Surely someone at the hotel would know what had happened to Evie? She must have been there or they'd not have posted her letter. And red hair was so often a dead giveaway. Fran touched her own neat locks. She'd tried dyeing it various colours when she was a teenager, hating that it was so conspicuous, but had eventually come back to her own shade of red. Dyed hair didn't have all the lovely coloured glints in it that natural hair did. And it was easier when you grew up. Other adults didn't mock it as some mean children had done at school.

'Just let me find my daughter,' she murmured over and over as she drove westwards along the M4 motorway. 'Just let me find my Evie.'

Once she'd done that, she'd be able to work out the next steps. It felt as if everything was suspended until then, even her ability to think clearly.

Polly slipped out of bed and stood shivering by the window, watching Fran's taxi leave the refuge. Should she or shouldn't she report this? She didn't want to cause trouble for Fran, but she decided she'd have to report what her friend was doing because it was so stupid.

She'd seen it before in the refuge, women acting irrationally, fixating on something, anything that would make them feel as if they were doing something to get out of the trap – a few times with sadly brutal or even in one case fatal results.

Suddenly certain that this was the right thing to do, she dialled the number of their police contact with a steady hand and croaked out an explanation of what Fran had done.

'She's gone off on her own?' her contact exclaimed. 'That's utterly insane. Couldn't you have stopped her?'

'No. I'm in bed with a cold, or maybe flu. I'm dizzy if I stand up. And anyway, I have no right to try to control her movements.' She began to cough and it was a few moments before she could continue speaking again. 'The women aren't prisoners here, you know.'

'Yeah. I know. Sorry. I just have a bad feeling about this guy.'

'So do I. I begged her not to go but she's absolutely desperate to find her daughter.'

'What mother wouldn't be? Look, I'll pass the word to the Wiltshire police to keep an eye out for prowlers near that hotel and to answer any calls for help promptly.'

'Thanks.'

'Look after yourself.'

Polly crawled back into bed, shivering uncontrollably. She had no choice but to look after herself. She couldn't even stand up without the room spinning. She'd rather be looking after Fran but it seemed that wasn't going to be possible for several days.

She waited till someone was going past and called out to ask them to send Matron up to see her.

One look at her and Tracy ordered her to stay in bed and not even try to get up till she was truly better.

Evie felt restless that day. She helped Cassie clear up the kitchen then tried to settle down to read a book, but couldn't – which was rare for her. She kept worrying about what her mother was doing.

Even when she got out the laptop her grandmother had given her, she couldn't think of any site she wanted to visit or even any game to play.

'I wish I could go out for a good long walk!' she said.

Cassie looked across at her. 'Feeling restless?'

'Yeah.'

'I have some business stuff I need to clear up, I'm afraid, so we can't go out for a drive. You can't keep the tax people waiting for too long.'

'I know. I'll be all right.'

Cassie grinned. 'Yeah, and cats will take up knitting. Look, how about we ask Oliver to drive you and Zoe somewhere in the country and take you for a good long walk. She's nearly as restless as you are.'

'Where is she? I didn't see her go back upstairs.'

'That's because she went outside at the back, and Oliver came across to chat to her. They're discussing antiques. Seems they're both into restoring antique furniture. Who'd have thought? If they're still out there, it'd be safe for you to join them.'

Evie went to peer out at the back. 'They're laughing together. I don't want to interrupt.'

'Go on with you. They're not a pair of lovers. His divorce isn't even final yet. Oh, leave it to me. I'll call them in and suggest you all go off somewhere. Why waste your time indoors while you're in this beautiful part of the world?'

When she called them, Zoe and Oliver came in, still arguing about the best way to clean dirty old wood carvings.

Cassie waited till they'd agreed to disagree to say, 'How about you three going out and doing some sightseeing? With three of you, you'll be safe enough and poor Evie is bouncing off the walls after being cooped up indoors for so long.'

'I'm a bit twitchy too,' Oliver confessed. 'I'm not used to being so inactive, but I didn't want to risk leaving Evie. Where should we go? Any ideas?'

She considered this. 'You could go back to Avebury – or no, I have it! How about Salisbury? The cathedral there is magnificent.'

He looked from Zoe to Evie. 'I'd be up for that. What do you two think?'

Evie frowned at her grandmother. 'That'll leave you on your own. You might not be safe, either.'

'Easily solved.' Oliver took a step towards the door. 'I'll go and ask Dad to come and join you, Cassie. He's not doing anything special today. He'll sit and read if you've got work to do.'

When he winked at her, she realised he'd guessed that she and Hal were getting more than friendly. 'Only if your father can spare the time.'

'Oh, I think he'll enjoy a bit of company.'

He was out of the back door before she could protest, so she turned to Zoe. 'Let me give you some money and you can be in charge of the finances for today.'

Her sister frowned. 'I don't need subsidising.'

Cassie jerked her head towards Evie and said firmly, 'My treat for you all! I insist.'

Luckily, Zoe took the hint.

Within half an hour, they'd gone and Cassie looked at her visitor. 'Are you sure you had nothing better to do this morning, Hal?'

'What's more important than keeping you safe and maybe getting to know you a little better?'

She was annoyed to feel herself flushing at that. 'I'll be about an hour working on my taxes, then we'll have a nice chat. I feel lazy today.'

'Me too. But being lazy here with you sounds nice.'

She could feel herself flushing again. It was a long time since a man had affected her in this way. She smiled as she sat down at her computer again. It was rather nice, made her feel young again.

It seemed to Fran to take for ever to reach Wiltshire. It was only just over two hours, but she hadn't driven so far on her own for a long time, or even done much driving, now she came to consider it, because Keith had always insisted on taking the wheel.

Why had she let him? She usually enjoyed driving but in the past few months she seemed to lose some of her confidence about handling a car in traffic.

The more she was away from him, the more clearly she could see their relationship and how it had eroded her self-esteem and positive attitude towards life.

Why had she married him? That annoyed her most of all. She must have been utterly crazy. It'd cost her a fortune now, and a load of hassle, to get a divorce. And what would he do to stop her? Something, she was sure. She shivered, shaking her head at her own stupidity.

She saw a signpost for Marlbury and drove straight through the town, following the satnav's instructions to the hotel. When she stopped outside it, she sat in the car for a few moments, glad to have arrived safely.

She studied her surroundings and decided the hotel was a pleasant-looking building, not a huge place but big enough and nicely proportioned. A housing development seemed a strange thing to site so close to a hotel. Or perhaps the owners hadn't had any choice? Who knew with builders and planners what was going to be proposed and approved of next.

She went inside the hotel and was tempted by the wonderful aroma of food in the snack bar area, so ordered coffee and a toasted sandwich before she did anything else. She was suddenly ravenous and realised she'd missed her midday meal completely.

Besides, she was nervous about taking the next step and felt she needed a few moments of peace to gather her thoughts.

However, even though she still felt confused about what exactly would be the best approach to solving her problem once she'd eaten, this couldn't be postponed, so she went across to the reception desk.

The woman stared at her. 'Hello. I thought for a moment you were Ms Bennington. You look so like her.'

'Cassandra Bennington?'

'No, her sister Zoe.'

Was Evie pretending to be the woman's sister? No, she couldn't be. There was too great an age difference between her and her grandmother for it to be at all credible. Where had an aunt come from, then? Was this person really a relative? She realised the woman was waiting for her to continue, so said hastily, 'Well, I'm looking for both of them, actually. Are they staying here?'

'Are they expecting you?'

'No. I wanted to surprise them.' To add to her confusion, the reception clerk was now looking at her rather suspiciously.

'Look, I'll fetch the owner. Ms Santiago knows them better than I do.'

Fran wondered if she'd gone too far and nearly left the hotel, but that would have been stupid. She had to find and face the woman who'd given birth to her, and it'd be best not to delay it any longer than she had to, for Evie's sake. The last thing she wanted was for her daughter to get too attached to the woman.

She took a few deep breaths to calm herself as she waited.

A lively looking woman who seemed to be only a little older than herself came out of a side door and joined them at the reception desk. 'I'm Molly Santiago, one of the owners. I gather you want to see Cassie. Shall we discuss this in my office, Ms . . . ?'

'Milner.'

When they were seated in her office Ms Santiago studied her. 'You look very like the people you're seeking. How are you related to them?'

'I'm not quite sure. I've been, um, trying to trace my birth mother.' She hadn't intended to reveal this but it had just popped out.

'Hmm. How about I phone Cassie and let her know you're here? I'll do it from another room, if you don't mind.'

Fran nodded and watched the woman walk out into the lobby again.

Why was this woman acting as if she were suspicious of someone asking for these people? Had something happened here? Surely Keith couldn't have found them? No, of course he couldn't.

The minutes passed very slowly as she waited and worried.

What had she got herself into? What if they refused to see her?

Chapter Twenty-Five

Cassie picked up the phone. 'Hello? Oh, Molly. Hi, there. How can I help you?'

'You have a visitor asking for you at the hotel. She looks so like your sister and Evie, it's clear she's a relative, but she doesn't seem sure of anything except that she's looking for her birth mother.'

Dear heaven! This must be Evie's mother. How had she found them?

'Cassie? Are you still there? Do you want me to send her down?'

She took a deep breath. 'Yes. But thanks for checking, Molly. As I've explained, we have to be very careful what we do.'

'If my opinion is of any interest, your visitor looks extremely nervous and not in the least threatening.'

'Thank you.'

'I'll send her down to you, then.'

After she'd put down the phone Cassie quickly

brought Hal up to date on what was about to happen.

'Do you want me to stay or leave?'

'I think this is one thing I need to face on my own.' Only, she wished she'd had more notice or felt more confident about the likely outcome of this meeting.

'I'll sit out on my back patio, then you have only to call out if you want me to join you, or if there's trouble.'

'Thanks, Hal.'

He cradled her cheek in his hand for a moment and said in his quiet way, 'You're not on your own now, Cassie, unless you want to be. Anything I can do, you have only to ask.'

She clasped his hand and pulled it to her lips, pressing a kiss on it. 'Thanks, Hal. That means a lot to me.'

When he'd gone out the back way she hurried to stare at her reflection in the hall mirror and grimaced at how untidy the hairpiece was before going to peer through the living-room window.

A car was turning out of the hotel parking area. It made its way across to the leisure village, moving slowly as if the driver were uncertain where exactly to turn.

She waited till it had drawn up outside her house, then braced herself and opened the front door without waiting for her visitor to knock.

The woman who got out of the car did indeed resemble Evie and Zoe: same colour of hair, similar features and slim build. But she didn't have their basically cheerful expressions. In fact, she was scowling and looked as if she hated being here, which didn't bode well.

Evie had said her mother didn't want to meet the woman who'd borne her and Cassie's hopes about the potential for their relationship shrivelled to practically zero as she watched her daughter stare coldly back at her. Well, they neither of them had any choice today.

'I'm Cassie.'

Fran stared at the older woman, feeling emotion well up inside her. This was her mother. But she didn't want it to be. Did she? All she could think of to say was, 'Your hair was red on the TV.'

Cassie looked surprised. 'Is that important now?'

Fran shrugged.

'I've stopped dyeing my hair now that I've retired from public life. Um, do come in.'

Reluctantly Fran followed her into the house. 'Is Evie here?'

'No, but she will be later. She's gone out sightseeing with her aunt and a neighbour of ours. You might as well wait for her here.'

That was another thing that puzzled Fran. 'The receptionist mentioned an aunt. Who would that be?'

'My younger sister.'

'Ah. I see. Well, I'm Fran – Fran Milner.'

'Yes, I realised that. Evie has told us a lot about you. She'll be delighted to see you again. She's been so worried about you.'

Fran's emotions were still in turmoil and she couldn't think straight. 'Perhaps I should wait at the hotel till she gets back.'

'I think you'd be safer waiting here.'

Fran gaped at that. '*Safer?*'

'Yes. We think your husband is stalking her. A man

was seen in the car park here in a car with his registration number.'

'How could he have found this place?'

'We don't know, and we can't be one hundred per cent certain it was him, though it's highly likely.'

'It's me he's stalking.'

'I think he's been stalking your daughter as well and his behaviour even before she ran away upset her greatly. Had you no idea?'

'I knew he had been a bit of a nuisance.' Guilt shot through her. She'd not paid the attention she should have to the situation.

'More than a bit, surely?'

'Yes. I can see that now. It took me a long time to admit to myself how uneasy he made her feel. I only started to realise how bad it was when she ran away at the thought of having to live in his house.'

'Yes. She told us why she'd left.'

'But I still don't understand how he could have found her. There was a letter from her posted from this hotel here and sent to my cousin's. It asked Amelia to pass a message on to me, but it only arrived after Keith had been there and it hadn't been opened, I'm sure of that.'

'How did you know he'd been to your cousin's?'

'He'd trashed Amelia's house, I suppose in revenge for me leaving him. Oh, there's no proof it was him, not that satisfies the police, anyway, but who else could it have been?'

'Evie will be upset about that happening to her cousin. The more I find out about this Keith, the more dreadful he sounds. Please – whatever you think of me, do come inside properly and let me close the door. It's better not to stand here in the doorway in full view of anyone who passes.'

She led the way into the living area and to her relief, her daughter closed the door and followed.

Cassie had a sudden thought. 'Will your husband recognise your car if he comes back? If so, you should perhaps leave it up at the hotel.'

'He won't recognise this one because it's a hired car.'

'Oh, good.'

'And I'd rather we referred to him as my ex, not my husband. It may have taken me a long time to realise what he was really like, but I'm not stupid enough to stay with him after he bashed me.'

Fran looked round. 'What about the back door? Is that locked?'

'No. My neighbour is keeping watch and needs to be able to reach us. He'll see if anyone tries to get into my house by the back way.'

Cassie gave her a searching gaze. Fran still looked as if she felt awkward. And Cassie felt she wasn't doing her best at handling her daughter. She was too anxious about the whole situation, too involved. Had she really been a vibrant TV presenter, followed by many? She didn't feel at all like that now, just an anxious older woman worried about her family.

Fran took another couple of steps into the living area, then seemed to give in mentally and accept the seat Cassie had indicated, sitting down on it with a sigh.

'You're sure Evie is all right?'

'Yes. There are three of them and Oliver is a strapping young fellow. Even I don't know where exactly they've gone sightseeing.'

'That's the most important thing to me, Evie being safe.'

'I agree. But it's also important to keep you safe from him.'

'And you. I think he'll lash out at anyone who gets in his way. He doesn't often get angry, but when he does, he's – terrifying.'

Silence fell again and Cassie asked, 'Would you like a cup of tea or coffee?'

'No, thank you. I grabbed a quick snack at the hotel before I came to see you because I'd missed lunch.'

'Then we'll stay here in the front living area, so that we can watch the approaches. There's only the one road from the hotel to the leisure village. We'll not only see the others when they get back, we'll also be able to see anyone else if you've been followed into the hotel grounds.'

Fran frowned across at her. 'I still don't see how Keith can have found out where Evie is.'

'You may have let something drop without realising it.'

'No. I left him a couple of days ago. He hit me a second time and I won't put up with being treated like that. Luckily the police had come to see me about giving a witness statement on an incident at the park and I screamed for help. They stopped Keith and took me to a women's refuge.'

'That still doesn't explain how he found his way here.'

Fran was still trying to work out how that had happened and went through it aloud. 'A letter from my daughter dropped through the letterbox at my cousin Amelia's house while I was there with the police, looking for Evie. It had the hotel address stamped on the back of the envelope. It wasn't the postman but a neighbour who pushed it through, so we thought it'd been delivered next door by mistake.'

She looked at Cassie, feeling swamped by anguish at how he was out-thinking them at every turn. 'Keith must have intercepted it, mustn't he, and seen the back of the envelope? He'd trashed Amelia's house before we got there but the police couldn't prove it was him though he's still in the picture as a suspect. I knew it was him, though. I was quite sure.'

She couldn't understand why she was volunteering all this information. It was the last thing she'd expected to do. She studied her birth mother, who was still looking drawn and anxious. 'Did Evie run away to you?'

'Yes.'

'But why did you bring her here? The address on the letter you sent me was in a London suburb.' She hadn't memorised it intentionally, but it seemed to have stuck in her mind.

'I was about to move house when she turned up. She caught me just in time so came with me. We didn't know whether you were still with Keith, you see, so she didn't come back to you straight away. My neighbour and I have been keeping a very careful eye on her, I promise you. And my sister has too, of course. Evie's a wonderful girl. You've done a brilliant job of raising her.'

'Have I? I wonder sometimes.'

'I don't. I'm sure you did your best and if there's one lesson I've learnt over the years, it's that no one can do more than their best. No one. She loves you dearly. I so envy you that.'

Fran sagged in relief. At least this woman didn't sound as if she'd been trying to come between her and her daughter. And her last words had been poignant. She didn't want to feel sorry for her birth mother, but that feeling was sneaking into her mind.

'We all love Evie,' Cassie went on, 'but she's fretting about whether you're all right, Fran. When she gets back, she'll be over the moon to see you here. And if you've left that fellow, well, maybe you can both settle down again somewhere else.'

'If he'll let me go.'

The silence was fraught with tension.

'I've done programmes about violence against women and men stalking their former partners. Not all men go to that length. Is your ex that bad?' Cassie asked.

'I think he is. I didn't realise for a long time because he was so nice to me – most of the time anyway. Except occasionally when I behaved stupidly, which he teased me about but in a way that emphasised it. Only, I wasn't behaving stupidly, I can see that now. Except by letting him brainwash me.'

'That sort of person can be very clever how they set about their campaigns to control people.'

'Tell me about it. I think he could have persuaded me that black was white – until recently. He certainly persuaded me to marry him when I'd not wanted to do that until we'd tried living together.' She flushed and added painfully, 'I've not got a good track record at choosing men.'

Cassie moved instinctively to comfort her, arm outstretched, but Fran held out her hand in a stop sign.

'Don't touch me! I can't bear you to touch me.' She watched her birth mother flinch but didn't move from her 'keep off me' stance. She'd already said too much, given too much ground.

What was there about this woman that made you feel you could confide in her? Whatever it was, it must be a very integral part of her and had probably helped make her such a well-known interviewer. Did she mean what she'd said? Was she really concerned for Fran as well as Evie? How did you tell what was true and what was false? She'd believed Keith's lies for months.

Cassie stood up. 'Do you mind if I get myself a cup of tea?'

Fran waved one hand permissively but didn't let herself speak. Only, she couldn't help noticing that Cassie surreptitiously wiped tears from her eyes once she'd turned away.

'I'd better let my neighbour know about you.'

She watched her open the back patio door and beckon to someone, then an older guy came across to join them.

'This is my, um, daughter, Fran. This is Hal, my neighbour and friend. As I told you, he and his son have been helping me watch over Evie.'

Fran liked the look of him. He had a kind expression and it was obvious that he cared for Cassie from the way he looked at her.

'I'm pleased to meet you,' he said in a low, pleasant voice. 'And I'm sure Oliver and Zoe will keep your daughter safe today. If you like, I could phone him and suggest they come home straight away? Though it won't make much difference because they were planning to be back in an hour or so's time.' He looked at her questioningly.

'I don't want to upset her. Just . . . leave it be, if you really think they'll soon be on their way back, that is.'

'If all goes according to plan, they will. So OK, we'll wait for them.'

'Would you like a cup of tea?' Cassie asked him.

'Thanks but I just had one.'

She saw him to the back door and hesitated.

'Everything all right? You look – upset.'

'It's difficult with my daughter, Hal. I think I'd be better talking to her on my own. It's – awkward, worse than I'd expected. Can you carry on watching the back of the house?'

'Of course.'

A vehicle drew up at the front just then and they both peered down the gap between their houses to see a big delivery van. A man got out and went towards Hal's front door. Hal called out to him.

'I'm here. Can I help you?'

'Got some paving to deliver. Where do you want it?'

'Round the side.'

'OK, mate.'

Hal shook his head. 'I'd completely forgotten about the paving coming today. Everything happens at once, doesn't it? Look, you go back inside. I'll stay on watch at the back and let them bring the paving round.'

When Cassie came back from speaking to her neighbour and sat down again, Fran said, 'He seems nice. Are you and he – you know, seeing one another?' She was surprised to see Cassie flush slightly. Was her birth mother always so nervous when she wasn't facing a camera? Then she suddenly remembered the terrorist incident and wondered how it had affected her and made her jumpy.

Oh hell, she didn't know what to think about

anything. She realised her birth mother was struggling to find suitable words.

'Hal and I are getting to know one another. It's early days. I haven't been with anyone for a while, so I'm treading carefully.'

When they were both seated again, Fran sought for something else to talk about. 'I was surprised to find a housing development so close to the hotel.'

'This is a leisure village, not a normal housing development, with strict rules to govern living here in peace and quiet. It'd be a lovely place to live normally.'

Silence fell again and Fran couldn't think of anything else to say. She didn't usually struggle to chat to people, but casual small talk was impossible, given how anxious they both were about Evie.

Chapter Twenty-Six

In the end Cassie broke the silence. 'Evie looks very like you.'

'Except she's slim and I'm overweight.'

Cassie gaped at her. 'Overweight? You're not too heavy by any standards I know.'

Tears filled her daughter's eyes and she clapped one hand to her mouth. 'Oh! That's another thing Keith has made me think. I keep realising how he's been sapping my confidence.' She got up and went to stare in a full-length mirror near the front door as if she'd never seen her own body before.

'Some men are horrible towards women. What does he want you to be, a walking skeleton?'

'A slave, unable to think for myself. And he nearly succeeded in brainwashing me.'

'Yes. That happens with some men who have bad attitudes towards women.'

'You sound as if you've experienced it.'

'Not in the same way as you have, but my father

seemed to hate me after I got pregnant, even though it was because I was raped. He never lost a chance to put me down. I only stayed with them for a few years, just till I'd got a qualification. For the whole time they were – ridiculously strict.'

She took a gamble and added a piece of information. 'I was quite ill after I'd had you and they persuaded me to give you up for adoption, made me feel I could never cope with being a single mother. And in one sense they were right, I suppose. I was too young even to leave school, let alone find and hold down a job.' After a pause she added without thinking, 'Though I could have coped if they'd helped me.'

But her daughter's frown didn't change and she didn't say anything, so Cassie gave up trying to break down the barriers between them and let herself fall silent again.

Was it really going to be impossible for the two of them to get to know one another? She could weep at the mere thought of that.

And surely Fran wouldn't keep Evie away from her now?

The thought made Cassie sag against the back of her chair. She wanted to cover her face with her hands and sob her heart out. But what good would that do? She'd done it many times in the early days after she'd had her child and nothing had changed.

When the phone rang both women nearly jumped out of their skins.

'I'd better take it.' Cassie picked up the phone and heard a voice speaking quickly at the other end: 'We've broken down. Well, run out of petrol . . . then there was a power cut because of the storm and the next place couldn't access the petrol pumps. We thought we had enough to get back . . . Don't know where we are . . . called for help. Poor connection . . . get back to . . . soon and—'

The connection cut off abruptly and she was left staring at the device then looking across at her guest.

'That was my sister Zoe. They've run out of petrol and they're waiting for help. There were power cuts, then even that poor connection was cut off completely. How infuriating!'

'Oh dear. I'd better book a room at the hotel for tonight then.'

'You'll be safer here. I've got a spare bedroom.' She saw her guest's expression turn stubborn, then dubious.

'I can't impose.'

'You can't *not* stay, now. We don't have any idea where they are or when they'll come back, and we don't want you or Evie wandering round the hotel grounds after dark.'

There was a long silence, then, 'Very well. Thank you.'

'I'll get something out of the freezer for tea, but I'd better warn you that I'm not the world's best cook. Evie's been doing most of the cooking. She said you taught her.'

'We both enjoy finding new recipes – or we did till I met Keith. He has a set range of meals and doesn't like foreign foods.' Short silence, then, 'I can do the cooking, if you like. I'm pretty capable, I've had to be.'

'Thanks. Let's explore the freezer. I won't offer to feed Hal. I want him to stay in his own home and keep an eye on the rear approaches to these dwellings. Anyone can walk round Penny Lake to get here and you must have noticed the piles of building materials which would provide cover for a person trying to approach from this side without being seen. I prefer to keep the front curtains open and all the exterior lights on so that I can see anyone coming towards the house. Hal prefers to sit in the dark and stare out, says it gives him good thinking time and his eyes get used to it.'

Fran got up and went across to peer out of the rear sliding door and nodded. 'I can see what you mean.'

'I often sit outside at the back because it's quite sheltered, but it looks as if it'll rain again and hopefully that'll help deter intruders.'

A few minutes later it did indeed start to rain, at first a few large drops pattering against the windows, then a steady downpour.

These sounds punctuated the awkward silences and stray remarks that never seemed to lead to any real conversations, or to reveal much personal information about Fran.

In the end Cassie accepted defeat in breaking that icy barrier and offered her daughter a choice of books to read or switching on the TV. Fran picked a book out, but though she held it open on the arm of her chair, she didn't seem to do much turning of pages.

Neither did Cassie and eventually she put her book down again.

They both glanced out of the window quite often.

The weather cleared up for a time then, as it grew dark, it started to rain again, more heavily than before.

'Looks like it's setting in for the night,' Fran commented at one stage.

When it grew late, they investigated the food choices, then Fran put a simple meal together and they sat down at the table.

Cassie tried to force herself to eat, but couldn't do it, so pushed her plate aside. 'I'm sorry. I'm a bit anxious about Evie. I can put the food in the fridge and heat it up again later.'

'I'll do the same if you don't mind. I'm – rather anxious too.'

It was as near as they'd come to complete agreement about anything.

When the car faltered to a halt Oliver called for help and the trio had to stay in it to shelter from the heavy rain. They managed to call Cassie and let her know they'd be delayed, but it was a very poor connection and then it cut out completely.

Oliver stared at his phone. 'Oh hell. Good thing we phoned for help first. Everything's gone dead now. This must be a bit of a black spot.'

A full hour passed and still, the rescue service didn't turn up. And they still couldn't get any of their phones to work at all.

'Well, at least we managed to get through to my sister earlier,' Zoe said. 'So she won't be worrying about us.'

'I think Gran might be worrying now, though,' Evie said. 'She's more fragile than people realise since that terrorist incident. I do wish we could get through to her again. Could you just try it again?'

But there was still no signal.

'I think there must have been a big local breakdown for all our phones not to work,' Oliver said grimly. 'It's been thundering in the distance for a while now. Perhaps something got struck by lightning. Let me try the car radio again.'

But they could only get static.

Zoe sighed. 'We shouldn't have taken this country road, only it was so beautiful as the sun was going down. Didn't the rain come on quickly? And it's turned into a real storm.'

When headlights appeared coming towards them, they all sat up expectantly. And cheered loudly as it proved to be the rescue service.

The poor driver was soaked but he remained incredibly cheerful as he had a quick look under the bonnet. 'You need some petrol. I've just given my last can to someone else. I'll turn round and tow you to the nearest garage. Good thing you called me before the power outage, eh?'

The garage was also without lights.

The owner said, 'I can give you a couple of litres but that's all I have to hand. I can't get at the pumps till the power comes on again.'

'Just do whatever you can,' Oliver said. 'We'll pray we can get home on that.'

Just after dusk a car slipped into the hotel entrance, hidden behind a large van and with its lights switched off. It turned in to the car park and moved slowly across it to the side farthest away from the hotel, stopping in the deeper shadows beneath a huge tree.

The man driving it didn't get out at first but sat watching the houses through some night goggles, smiling grimly at how clearly he could see everything. His determination to get his wife back had built up as the day passed. He'd set off far too early, so had been forced to wait for a couple of hours in a motorway service station. No use getting here before dusk.

But that had only made him angrier. Still, he'd learnt to control his rages, so it didn't really matter if he was simmering a little with anger. He always thought more clearly when he felt strongly about something.

He wasn't going away again without Fran and, if he was lucky, her daughter too. His stubbornness sometimes got him into trouble, but more often than not, it got him what he wanted. And at the moment he very much wanted to tame his wife and her daughter, whatever it took.

He noted that one of yesterday's cars was missing from the parking area in front of those two houses, but another car was parked there today instead. There was no one walking around in such heavy rain and few houses had lights showing so were presumably unoccupied at present.

He walked round the further edges of the car park, checking everything. At one stage he wiped away the rain from his eyes, but mostly ignored the moisture plastering his clothes to his body.

When he was sure he was the only person out, he crossed the car park but stopped again to check all round him, making utterly certain there was still no one nearby. Satisfied, he left it and moved closer to the houses, staying away from the only road into the group of dwellings.

This time he went past the house he was heading for at a distance, approaching it obliquely from the side furthest away from the lake. They'd expect an intruder to come via the lake or from the hotel, he was sure, not from the part that was still like a building site.

He found himself a good vantage point behind a pile

of timber near a new building that was only built to waist height, and stayed there to check out his surroundings again and make sure he was still alone.

Oh yes, he knew how to be careful.

Inside the lighted windows of the house were two women and surely one of them was – he blinked. Yes, it was her: Fran. His wife.

The other was much older, grey-haired. Who was she? And where was Evie? There was another woman who'd been there last time he watched and she was missing too.

There was no sign of the two men from next door, either, and their house was dark. Good. If they weren't at home that was one potential problem solved.

Fran had said she had no close relatives. It had been one of the useful things about her. No one to interfere. But this old biddy seemed to be very at home here, so she must be involved in this somehow. He continued to watch carefully, but she and his wife seemed to be the only ones in the house.

One or the other of them kept coming to peer out of the front window. That probably meant the others were away and due back soon. Well, he could modify his plans and take only his wife home today, but he'd better do it straight away. He smiled. The courts would give her custody of her daughter if she asked for their help – and he'd see that she did.

He still had to cross an open piece of ground, but had a bit of luck when a large combi van pulled up at one of the half-built houses and two men began unloading window frames in the beam of their headlights and a nearby street light. The van gave him the chance to cross the road and hide behind some piles of bricks, which were much closer to the house where Fran was skulking.

From his new vantage point he could see into it much more clearly and he could also walk partway round the row of houses, to peer along the rear gardens. There were no lights, not even a table lamp, inside the house next door.

Really, things couldn't have worked out better.

He was glad now that Ryan had delayed him by a day. Fate seemed to be on his side in all sorts of ways, and about time too. He was due a bit of luck. Triumph swelled within him, waiting to be let loose as his careful planning came to fruition.

She was going to learn not to trifle with him!

Chapter Twenty-Seven

Keith waited for the van driver to leave then moved quickly forward, crouching down as he managed to reach the rear door of the house.

He waited a moment but clearly he hadn't been seen. Reaching out, he tried the sliding door and nearly laughed out loud. It wasn't locked. Pitiful security, ladies! Well, the older woman could be left tied up. He had no use for women who were past their best. She would no doubt regret her carelessness over the long, uncomfortable hours of the night.

He could see how it would all work out, like a brightly lit movie playing in his mind.

He still had his balaclava tugged down to cover his face from the security cameras and he tugged it off quickly because it was annoying him and he couldn't see a camera here. Taking a deep breath, he edged the rear sliding door back and it moved along silently. He had to work quickly now because the sound of rain and cooler air would warn them of an open door.

The two women swung round suddenly and he stood up and started to move steadily forward across the open-plan space. 'You're coming with me, Fran. You're *married* to me, and we're staying married.'

As he'd expected she froze and took a step backwards, cringing. His training was showing nicely and paying off.

He stepped forward more confidently but to his intense annoyance the other woman stepped between them, barring the way.

'Leave her alone. She's not coming with you. She's left you.'

He grabbed her and took hold of her shoulders, trying to shove her aside, but someone must have taught her a few tricks, because she ran one foot down the front of his shin, her shoe connecting painfully with the bony part.

He shouted in pain but his anger about that seemed to lend him extra strength. He tugged her slightly forward and hurled her to one side, in a move he'd learnt at a self-defence class. She stumbled helplessly across into the kitchen area and then fell. He heard the thump as she banged her head on something, after which she lay still.

Stupid cow! Deserved what she got, didn't she? Very useful to have her knocked out.

He turned back to his wife. 'Come here, Fran. *Now!*'

She backed away from him. 'No. I've left you. I'm getting a divorce. I'm *never* coming back to you.'

He moved forward step by step as she backed away. She'd not even moved towards the front door, but had let herself be trapped against the front window. He couldn't help laughing. What was she going to do against him? She couldn't even think straight when he threatened her.

Suddenly she screamed for help at the top of her voice

and continued to yell. Annoying. But who was to hear in the group of deserted or half-built houses? Still, he'd better stop her.

But as he reached her, she half turned and brought something out from behind her back, thumping it down on his head, smashing it.

The room whirled about him for a few moments and her shrill screaming seemed to set his head spinning even worse.

He tried to struggle to his feet. Time to get away and take her with him.

The trouble was, he felt dizzy and had to grab the windowsill to stay more or less upright.

As Fran jumped away from Keith, who was swaying, she noticed the headlights shining into the house from the parking area. Had the others come back? Or had Keith brought someone to help him? For a moment or two she didn't know what to do.

Then the neighbour she'd already met rushed in through the back door and a few seconds later the front door burst open as well. They must have seen through the window that there had been trouble.

A younger man stood by the front door as if trying to work out what to do.

'Phone the police and ambulance, Oliver,' Hal yelled to him. 'And then help me stop that fellow getting away. He's hurt Cassie.'

Fran sagged in relief. The newcomer was on their side. Then she knelt down by Cassie.

Hal knelt beside her.

She was terrified by the cut on Cassie's forehead which

was pouring blood. Her birth mother groaned and didn't seem fully conscious.

She was also terrified when Keith straightened up and looked round for a way to escape.

The younger man had his phone out and passed it to the person behind him. 'Call the police and an ambulance.'

Then he moved towards Keith, as did his father and there was a brief moment of confrontation as he tried to push his way past them. Then they both grabbed hold of him.

For a moment there was silence in the room except for the sounds of the men scuffling, then Fran gasped, 'Quick, we need to tie him up somehow or he'll get away.'

Evie had been standing in the doorway but now she moved forward. 'There's some duct tape in the bottom drawer. That's what they use in movies, isn't it?'

She found the grey roll of tape and though it was a struggle, they managed to fasten the intruder's hands behind him.

Keith cursed and struggled but he was outnumbered. When they got his arms taped together behind his back, the younger man managed to stick more tape round his ankles, not without difficulty.

Only then did Fran smile across at her daughter. Evie was safe. She'd needed to see that with her own eyes.

But she was worried about Cassie and went across, bending down and then grabbing some tissues to staunch the blood. 'She needs medical help. It'll probably need stitching. I hope she's not got concussion. How long will the ambulance be?'

The other woman, who must be the aunt, spoke. 'The police said they'd be here quickly. They'd been alerted to the fact that there might be trouble here by the police in London apparently. And an ambulance is on its way, shouldn't be long either.'

'This is my aunt Zoe. My mother, Fran.'

The two women nodded at one another.

'How did Gran get hurt?'

'She stepped in between Keith and me.' Fran knelt beside Cassie and held her hand. 'She was protecting me. I didn't expect that.'

'She's always cared about you. It was her parents who caused the trouble.'

'But why did Pop and Nanna tell me she didn't want me?'

'My mother and father must have told them that,' Zoe said sadly. 'Cassie said after she got pregnant they seemed to start hating her. No wonder she left home as soon as she could. I was too young to remember much but over the years they've said some dreadful things about her to me. Which even my older brother admitted weren't true.'

Cassie opened her eyes just then and stared dopily up at them both, giving them a particularly sweet smile and saying, 'You are so alike, my darlings,' before closing her eyes again.

Evie turned to her mother. 'Are you all right?'

'Keith probably bruised my arm but that's nothing. It was Cassie who got the worst of it. I did manage to smash a heavy ornament over his head, though, and that slowed him right down,' Fran added with great satisfaction. 'He came after me because I ran away from him. He was determined to take me back.'

Evie brightened. 'You hit him?'

'Yes. Took me long enough to figure out what he was doing to us both, didn't it? Can you ever forgive me?'

Evie gave her a lop-sided hug. 'Of course I can. Especially now you've come to your senses.'

She looked down at Cassie then sideways at her mother. 'You were wrong about her. She didn't give you away willingly. My aunt told me how she kept your first bootees and used to cry over them.'

'Giving away – all my secrets – Evie?' Cassie whispered.

She leant forward to kiss her grandmother's cheek. 'Only the ones that Mum needs to know about. She thought you gave her away willingly.'

'No. Never willingly.'

A couple of minutes later the police car turned up and the officers came inside.

One officer checked Cassie. 'You'll need to go to hospital to get that properly stitched or it'll leave a bad scar. The ambulance won't be long.'

'Well worth it,' she said, still smiling and holding Fran's and Evie's hands.

'Keith threw her across the room,' Fran said. 'That's how she hit her head.'

'Did he now?'

As she was explaining exactly what had happened, and how her ex had been stalking her, the male officer kept looking at Keith and frowning.

'They're telling lies,' Keith called out. 'It's all lies! I love that woman and they're keeping me from reconciling with her after a row. Everyone has rows and they have no right to do this to me.'

The officer snapped his fingers as if something had occurred to him and went right up to where Keith was lying on the floor propped against the wall. 'Now I know why you seem familiar. I never forget a voice. Ricky Bottrell, by all that's wonderful! I wondered what had happened to you.'

Keith stared up at him in horror. 'I don't know what you mean. My name's Burgess.'

'Easily checked. You have a small tattoo on your left shoulder blade if I remember correctly, a whirling comet.' He began to pull Keith's clothing open and though the man squirmed, he was still securely taped and couldn't prevent the officer from uncovering the mark.

He laughed out loud. 'Told you! You're nicked, Bottrell, on top of whatever you've done today and recently.'

'He not only attacked my grandmother,' Evie said, 'but he's been stalking my mother, who is his wife but left him recently.'

The officer grinned even more broadly and looked down at Keith. 'Another wife? Last I heard, your first wife was still living in Bury and hadn't divorced you because she doesn't believe in it. And you can't have divorced her because you vanished off the face of the earth and I've kept an eye on divorces and you've definitely not been amongst them. Seen Hazel lately, have you, Ricky?'

Fran took a quick step forward. '*He's got another wife?*'

The officer nodded. 'Hazel. She phones the local police station regularly to ask if he's turned up. I still have a friend up in the north who lets me know. He'll be delighted to pass the news on to her.'

'Well, he married me recently but when he thumped me, I left him.'

He hadn't stopped grinning since he recognised who Keith really was and now he clapped him on the shoulder. 'Oh dear, that means we'll have to add a charge of bigamy to the list of whatever other charges are brought against you.'

'I was going to divorce him.'

'No need to do that. Your marriage isn't valid. I'd get a lawyer to sort out any details as necessary, though.'

She ignored Keith's scowl and beamed at the officer. 'That's wonderful, absolutely wonderful.'

Evie came to throw her arms round her mother, then they both knelt and kissed Cassie's cheeks from either side.

'All forgiven?' Cassie whispered to her daughter.

'Nothing to forgive, just errors to be corrected. As far as I'm concerned, new page, new life.'

Happy tears were running down Cassie's cheeks and mingling with the reducing trickles of blood. 'That's the best news *I've* ever had in my whole life.'

There was the sound of a siren and more headlights raked across the window.

The first responders came hurrying in and knelt by Cassie, then one ran out again to bring in the wheeled stretcher and they soon had her installed on it.

'I'm coming with you,' Evie said at once.

'So am I.' Fran moved forward to stand beside them.

'You should follow us in a car, so that you can get back home afterwards. Don't worry. We'll look after her, but that's a bad cut and it definitely needs medical attention.'

So Fran got into the car and drove off after the ambulance.

She didn't think she'd ever felt so happy in her whole life. She wasn't married to Keith! And now she had a mother, an aunt and her daughter back – a real family.

She glanced sideways at Evie and her daughter gave her a smile.

'Life is going to be wonderful.'

'You won't stop Gran seeing me.'

'On the contrary, I'm going to move to live nearby and we'll see a lot of one another.'

Evie's voice was choked. 'That's – just – absolutely wonderful.'

'Yes. It is. And I'm never getting involved with a man again.'

Evie hid a smile. She didn't believe that, but surely with her gran's help they'd manage to stop Fran making any more big mistakes?

The hospital came into sight and they parked the car.

'It's like walking into a new life,' Fran said softly, taking her daughter's hand and moving to find where Cassie was.

Epilogue

They planned it carefully and made the necessary phone calls. Two days later Hal went to bring Cassie home from hospital while the others got everything ready that they could.

He made a shooing gesture when he brought Cassie back. 'Go inside. This is a family time for you.'

'Thanks, Hal. But you'll come round for a drink tonight, eh? And bring Oliver.'

'Good idea. I'd like that.'

Evie ran to greet her at the door and after a slight hesitation, Fran followed and even gave her mother a hug. Their welcome brought tears of joy to Cassie's eyes.

'Everything all right?' she asked.

'Brilliant!' Evie handed her a tissue. 'No crying. This is a happy time!'

'I'll do my best. I'll have a rest after lunch because I've invited Hal round for a drink tonight.' As Evie opened her mouth, Cassie held up one hand. 'I'm not an invalid, so I insist on having a little celebration.'

'All right, Gran. If you're sure. We could even put out a few nibblies.'

'Good idea. Get a selection delivered from the hotel. We can make it a bit of a buffet meal. Go and tell them while I'm asleep. I don't want you slaving over the stove. I want us three to talk. I've photos to show you, all sorts of things to ask.'

'That'll be fun.' She watched them smile at one another and exchange glances. There would be a lot of smiling from now on if she had her way.

'How about they come at about six o'clock?' Evie suggested.

'Yes. Nice time to start a celebration.' Cassie stretched. 'I must say I wouldn't mind something tasty to eat then a little nap. Hospital food is awful and you can never sleep well there. They're always waking you up to take your pulse or check your dressing.'

'We'll go up to the hotel and order the food while you rest,' Fran said.

Luckily, the food was delivered while Cassie was changing into more flattering clothes.

'That's another hurdle got over,' Evie said. 'She'd have been asking why we ordered so much.'

Fran nodded. 'It's as if fate is on our side.'

'You all right?'

'Yes. I'm still getting used to my new status, that's all, and getting angry at myself for being such a fool.'

'Well, you'll know better with the next man.'

'There isn't going to be one.'

Evie hid her smile. Of course there would be, eventually. Especially after she'd gone off to university.

When the food delivery was complete, they quickly set the food out on the table and covered it with a tablecloth just as Cassie came down.

'You look great, Gran,' Evie said, leading her into the sitting area. 'Very elegant.'

'And that top suits you better than it ever did me.' She held out one hand to her daughter and Fran joined them. 'That dress suits you too.'

'You have a lot of clothes. It was fun choosing.'

She shrugged. 'They were working clothes as far as I was concerned. I mostly lived in kaftans that I'd picked up overseas when I was at home in the evenings.'

There was a knock on the back door and Evie went to let Hal and Oliver in.

Hal leant close to whisper, 'They're waiting at the hotel, coming down in five minutes. Does she suspect anything?'

'I don't think so.' She led the way in and poured them both a glass of wine, taking a lemonade for herself.

'How lovely to have neighbours who are also friends,' Cassie said.

There was a knock on the front door and she frowned. 'Who can that be?'

'You'll only find out if you let me answer it,' her granddaughter said.

Six people were waiting outside and as Evie showed them in Cassie gaped. 'Brett! What are you doing here?'

'Celebrating your new life and the fact that you're safe. I've been worried sick about you.' He gave her a hug.

His partner smiled at Cassie and did air kisses. 'We both have. Am I allowed in, too?'

'Of course you are. Life's too short to hold grudges and

you kindly lent Brett to me after that incident.' She turned to Molly and Euan.

'We've been invited to celebrate with you as well,' Molly said. 'We like to make friends here as well as build houses, and we hated that you were attacked on our property.'

Cassie hugged them both. She felt like hugging the whole world tonight.

She didn't recognise the other two women, but Fran moved to join them. 'May I introduce Tracy and Polly from the women's refuge. I couldn't leave them out of this celebration, since they helped me so much at a very bad time.'

Polly flapped one hand. 'I'm just recovering from a cold, so I'm not doing kissy-kissy, but I hope you'll let me join you.'

'I'm delighted to meet you. Fran mentioned how helpful you two were.'

With a grin Hal and Oliver brought in the garden chairs they'd sneaked across and left outside ready for the extra guests, and Zoe whipped the tablecloth off the refreshments, shouting, 'Ta-da!'

Cassie pretended to be angry. 'You sneaky creatures!'

'Did you want to cook?' Evie asked with an expression of fake innocence.

She had to chuckle. 'Of course not. I never get the desire to cook.'

'Then you sit down at the head of the table and we'll all enjoy that delicious food.'

When they'd finished eating, Hal poured everyone a glass of champagne. 'As self-appointed toast master, I'd like you all to raise your glasses to our hostess. Cassie!'

They all echoed her name.

Fran surprised herself by calling out, 'And I'd like to add another toast. To my birth mother and Evie's grandmother, Cassie. I'm so very glad we found her.'

They all echoed that as well and as they did so happy tears welled in Cassie's eyes and she thrust her glass at Hal. Standing up, she put one arm round each woman. 'Can someone take a photo, please? Lots of photos. This is the best night of my life.'

'I'll do it,' Oliver said. 'First family photographs of many for you, I hope.'

She could only nod and smile blissfully at the camera. First of many indeed.

Thank goodness Evie had found her that day.

ANNA JACOBS is the author of over ninety novels and is addicted to storytelling. She grew up in Lancashire, emigrated to Australia in the 1970s and writes stories set in both countries. She loves to return to England regularly to visit her family and soak up the history. She has two grown-up daughters and a grandson, and lives with her husband in a spacious home near the Swan Valley, the earliest wine-growing area in Western Australia. Her house is crammed with thousands of books.

annajacobs.com